HEARTS DIVIDED
THE EXCITING CONCLUSION TO
CHERYL BIGGS'S
BRAGGETTE FAMILY SERIES

Brett smiled.

Physical attraction, Teresa repeated silently. That's all her reactions were. All they meant. Nothing more. "I'm not fighting myself," she retorted finally, purposely instilling an icy chill to the words that slipped from her lips as barely more than a ragged whisper of sound. "Only you." Teresa pushed against his shoulder with the heel of her hand. "Now, if you have even an ounce of gentlemanly honor in you, let me go."

Instead of releasing her, Brett wrenched her closer. "I'm not a gentleman, remember?" he goaded. "I'm a Yankee." His arms wrapped around her waist and held her so tightly that she could hardly breathe.

Teresa glared up at him. His face was so close. All she had to do was lean forward, just a bit, and her lips would touch his. She stiffened against the traitorous thought. "I don't want this."

"No?" He smiled, a taunting curve of his lips that piqued her anger yet stirred her excitement. "Your eyes tell me different."

He was going to kiss her. She knew it. Felt it. And God help her, she wanted it . . .

HEARTS DIVIDED

Cheryl Biggs

Zebra Books
Kensington Publishing Corp.
http://www.zebrabooks.com

This book is dedicated to all the men, women
and children who struggled, fought, cried,
and died during the Civil War.

And to all of my readers—thank you for falling as much in love with the Braggettes as I did. I will miss them, but who knows, someday Tyler and Tanner might just tap me on the shoulder and say, hey, it's time to tell *our* story now.

ZEBRA BOOKS are published by

Kensington Publishing Corp.
850 Third Avenue
New York, NY 10022

First Printing: November, 1996
10 9 8 7 6 5 4 3 2 1

Printed in the United States of America

One

Early Spring, 1865
New Orleans, Louisiana

Teresa stared at the letter from her husband. Once it would have brought tears of joy and relief. Now it brought only anger. Knotting, burning, twisting anger. Finally she had proof that he was alive. But it no longer really mattered.

She hadn't heard from Jay in over three and one half years, but she'd heard many rumors of his whereabouts and his activities. One rumor had him killed at Gettysburg while leading a charge against the enemy.

Teresa had cried the night she'd received that news, some small remnant of feeling for the man she'd married still lingering within her heart. Later she'd realized how absurd the rumor and her momentary belief in it had been. Jay was a follower. A schemer. Not a leader. And he was definitely not a soldier. He would never have led a charge. He would never have even considered serving in the army.

Another rumor had him in England attempting to procure funds for the Confederacy. She'd found herself wondering if he would actually turn the money over to the Confederacy if he procured it. Or would he keep it for himself and simply disappear from the world as he had from her life?

And yet another report claimed he had been seen upriver in Natchez, talking with the Union's General Grant while his Federal forces occupied the town.

A traitor. At first she hadn't even been able to consider that rumor. But later, when she thought about it, she had to reconsider, and she had found it in herself to believe that it was possible. After all, she had never expected the man she married to walk, or rather sneak, out of her life on their wedding night, so how well had she really known Jay Proschaud to begin with?

Her gaze scanned his letter again. A lock of black hair tumbled from her shoulder to lay upon her breast, glistening like strands of ebony silk beneath the glow of the oil lamp on a nearby table. Fury burned within Teresa and turned her blood hot as she read his words again. Three and one half years and not an utterance of any kind from him. Not a letter, wire, message, or visit. Not even when their son had been born.

He hadn't even bothered to let her know that he was alive until now. Tears burned her eyes, but they were tears of rage, not sorrow. She wanted to strike out at something, at someone. Teresa blinked back the tears and forced her hands not to curl into fists.

Three and one half years of nothing and now when he finally did contact her he had the audacity, the unmitigated gall, to demand her help. She looked up, her eyes clear and shining. What she wouldn't give to be able to deny his request.

She glanced at the courier who'd brought the letter: a tall man with rangy features and gangly limbs. He stood in the foyer waiting for her response. Teresa wanted to shout at him, to order him to tell Jay Proschaud that she wouldn't lift a finger to help him even if he were the last man on earth, would not shed one tear if he swung from the gallows.

Jay Proschaud could rot in hell for all she cared.

But even as her body trembled from the rage that filled her, even as she ached to send back a scathing message, she forced herself to remain silent and think.

She had to think about what she truly wanted to do . . . what she *could* do. The urge to disregard Jay's summons, to deny him her aid was strong. Almost overpowering. Her fingers closed around the crumpled paper, folding it further in upon itself. She wanted to toss it into the fire that crackled merrily in the fireplace and provided the only light in the spacious parlor. She wanted to see the thin, delicate scrap of linen ignite into flame, see it consumed and turned to a black film of ash. She wanted to pretend she had never read the words Jay had written.

Instead, she sat still, staring neither into the flames nor about the dimly lit room, but rather into herself. Denial was strong in her mind but absent from her heart. She had assumed she would never hear from him again. After all this time, she had accepted the fact that he was gone. That he had abandoned her. That she would make her own way in life. And now . . . Teresa sighed. Did she have the strength to do what he asked?

Her thoughts jumbled about, crowding in on one

another, arguing against responding, yet reasoning that she must. She sighed again. It really didn't matter if she had the strength or not. Nor did it matter whether she wanted to deny or grant him his request. She didn't have a choice.

Stifling a sigh that would have disclosed more than she wanted to her family, Teresa looked up and focused on the room she knew so well, the house that hadn't changed since long before she'd been born. Shadows filled the outer corners of the room, hovered about the ceiling and crouched low behind each piece of furniture.

Her sisters-in-law, Belle and Lin, and her mother, Eugenia, stood only a few feet away. Anxious. Curious. She saw in their eyes that they were also frightened. War did that to people—made them frightened of everything, especially messages and strangers.

They didn't know what was in the message she'd just received, or who it was from, and Teresa had no doubt they'd be indignant once she told them. Particularly when she explained Jay's request for her help. But she couldn't tell them everything that was in the note. She couldn't, and she wouldn't. There was no need to upset them further.

Teresa turned toward the marble-faced fireplace and stared into the flames that danced upon the pile of logs that had been neatly arranged within the grate. A conflict of emotion tore at her heart. Anger. Sorrow. Fear. Even regret. But not love. That was the one emotion she knew with a definite certainty she no longer felt toward Jay Proschaud. He was the father of her child, but he was no longer her husband. She had risked scandal and divorced him, but because he had not kept in touch with her, or even with his father, she wasn't sure if he knew they were no longer married, nor did she care.

In retrospect, asking the courts for the divorce hadn't really been much of a risk. Everyone was too preoccupied with the war effort to worry about a little thing like a wife dissolving her marriage. There'd been no scandal. And both Belle and Lin insisted there had been no gossip either. At least not that they'd heard. And between the two of them, Teresa felt certain they heard it all.

But it didn't matter. If people wanted to talk, now or later, then they could talk and she'd ignore them. She had done what had to be done.

Teresa's fingers curled around Jay's letter. Her crumpling of the paper was the only sound in the room, except for the soft crackling of the flames in the fireplace. Her gaze strayed to her son Tyler, who sat on the floor beside her chair.

As if he felt his mother's eyes on him, the three-year-old looked up, momentarily ignoring the colorfully painted blocks he held in his hands and the small tower of squares he'd built on the floor before him. A wide smile, full of innocence and happiness, spread across his face and his gray-blue eyes lit with joy.

Braggette eyes, Teresa thought with a momentary swell of pride and satisfaction. Reflection from the fire lent pinpoints of light to his curly black hair. It was good that he looked like her side of the family rather than Jay's because he was going to grow up a Braggette. She would see to that.

Her gaze dropped back to her lap and the letter

she still held in her hand. She eased her grip on the fragile linen and the wrinkled paper unfolded somewhat, but she didn't really need to see the words Jay had written to remember them. They'd already been etched upon her memory.

> *"I can give you no details at this time, Tess, other than to state that your help is urgently needed. The situation involves one of your brothers and is quite serious, if not a matter of life or death. You must come immediately to Richmond via Petersburg."*

Fear settled like an icy cloak about her heart as fury burned hot in her mind. She could curse Jay Proschaud and wish him a prolonged stay in hell but she couldn't ignore what he'd written. Not when it involved one of her brothers.

Teresa rose and met the gazes of Belle, Lin, and her mother, and made another decision: they couldn't know that one of her brothers was in trouble. Belle's arm still wasn't quite back to normal since she'd nearly gotten herself killed trying to save Traxton from a Yankee hangman's noose. And Teresa didn't even want to think of what could happen to Lin, Belle's identical twin sister, if she thought it was Trace who was in trouble and tried to go to him.

Lin was the perfect lady, but that might not matter to a bunch of war-weary, Reb-hating Yankees.

Teresa's gaze moved to her mother. The war and worry over Teresa's four brothers had put quite a few more gray hairs on Eugenia Braggette's head, but rather than detracting from her still-pretty face, they glittered among the ebony strands like threads of silver.

Belle took a step toward Teresa. "Tess, what's happened?"

Teresa looked back at her brother Traxton's wife. "I have to go." To keep them from seeing the letter, and the truth of the situation, Teresa tossed it into the fire.

Belle brushed a long platinum curl over her shoulder. She glanced at the letter which was now little more than a wisp of ash, then back at Teresa. Anxiety shone in the brilliance of her blue eyes. "What do you mean *go?* Go where? What's happened?"

Lin stepped forward. "Is it . . . ?" She looked suddenly stricken and about to faint.

"No," Teresa said hurriedly, knowing Lin was terrified that something would happen to Trace before the war's end. "It's Jay."

"Jay?" the trio said in unison, each voice not only surprised but indignant, each face registering both shock and disdain.

Teresa took a deep breath, suddenly feeling as if she were facing a firing squad, not her family. "He needs my help."

"So let him need it," Eugenia said, her tone suddenly as hard and cold as a winter wind. "The mere thought of you helping that blackguard is ridiculous. The man is both a coward and a . . ." She suddenly waved her hand in the air in disgust, as if she either didn't want to finish what she'd been about to say in front of her grandson or couldn't think of a word despicable enough to describe her ex-son-in-law.

Teresa knew exactly how her mother felt about Jay

and agreed with her, but at the moment it didn't make any difference. "Mother, please, I . . ."

"Teresa, for heaven's sake," Eugenia snapped. "The man left you on your wedding night without a word. Snuck out of the house like a thief in the middle of the night. And he knew you were already carrying his child. He is a coward of the worst kind. A blackguard beyond description and you owe him nothing, Teresa. Absolutely nothing."

Teresa glanced back down at Tyler, who'd returned his attentions to his blocks. "I know you don't understand, but I have to go, Mother," she said quietly. Let them think it was because of Tyler, that she couldn't say no to Jay merely because he was her son's father. Or let them think that she was a complete and utter fool and still in love with the man, which was so far from the truth it was almost laughable. But it was better than letting them know that one of her brothers might be in trouble. Life-threatening trouble, if Jay was to be believed.

"You *don't* have to go," Eugenia said.

Teresa turned and swept Tyler up into her arms. She looked back at her mother. "Yes, I do." She tried to smile while at the same time she damned Jay for making it necessary to lie to her family. Why couldn't he have just told her what the problem was?

Because he knew you wouldn't come if there was any way around it. The little voice that whispered to her from the back of her mind was right, and she knew it. If there was any other way, she wouldn't go. But there wasn't.

She handed Tyler to Eugenia. "Will you take care of Tyler while I'm gone, Mama?"

Eugenia gathered her grandson into her arms and kissed his cheek, then grasped one of Teresa's hands. "Teresa, please, reconsider this. It's not safe to travel about the countryside now. Lord knows what's out there."

"I know exactly what's out there," Belle said, drawing their attention. Her eyes blazed with anger. "Yankees."

"Oh, Tess," Lin moaned softly, her eyes full of worry and fear. "Eugenia's right—it's dangerous to travel now. Can't you just send him a note?"

"No." Teresa pulled her hand gently from her mother's, quickly pressed her lips to Tyler's chubby cheek, and walked into the foyer. She paused before the courier who'd brought Jay's letter. "I'm sorry to have kept you waiting so long, but there were some things I had to . . . think about. I'll pack a bag and be with you in a few minutes."

He tipped his hat. "Sorry, ma'am, but uh, I won't be escorting you to Mr. Proschaud. I have orders to go on downriver from here."

"Downriver?" Teresa echoed, shocked. The resolution she'd felt only moments ago when she'd made the decision to meet Jay was suddenly overshadowed by the return of her anger. "Are you telling me I am expected to travel alone? That you won't be escorting me?"

"No, ma'am, uh, I mean yes, ma'am. Sorry. I was told to just wait for you to read the message and get your reply. I'll be telegraphing Mr. Proschaud that you're coming."

"Telegraph?" Teresa frowned. "But the lines are down. It's impossible to send a message from here to . . ." She nearly bit off her tongue to keep from saying Richmond. If the others knew she was headed toward the Confederacy's capital they'd pummel her with a new onslaught of questions. Worse, they might want to accompany her. Especially considering the fact that Trace was stationed in Richmond. And last they'd heard Traxton was somewhere up there, too. But since Traxton was always on the move with the cavalry he could also very well be at the North Pole at the moment, for all they knew. Every letter he managed to send home mentioned a different place, a different battle—some won, some lost.

But that wouldn't matter. Belle and Lin would insist on accompanying her, and she couldn't have that.

As for her other brothers, Travis was still in Nevada as far as she knew, and Traynor was most likely maneuvering his blockade runner somewhere at sea between Carolina and Bermuda. There weren't too many ports open to the runners anymore but if she knew Traynor he wouldn't stop until the last one was closed down. Maybe not even then.

Teresa was well aware, however, that where her brothers were supposed to be was not necessarily where they were. Any or all of them could show up anywhere, at any time, without a moment's notice.

"We got ways to get our messages through," the courier said, interrupting Teresa's thoughts. He smiled slyly at her blank look. "Don't you worry none about that."

Teresa shivered, suddenly glad she didn't have to travel with him. There was a shifty, rather sly look in his eyes she hadn't noticed before.

He tipped his hat again, opened the entry door,

and slipped out into the night. The blackness of his coat and trousers allowed him to disappear into the darkness almost instantly, as if he'd never been there.

Teresa turned away from the door and met the hard stares of the other women.

"Well, I guess that settles that," Eugenia said. "You don't have an escort and you can't very well travel alone."

Teresa didn't answer. Whether she traveled alone or had an escort didn't matter. She had to go.

Two

Teresa stepped into the dark hallway and pulled the door to Traynor's bedchamber closed behind her. The lock clicked into place. It was only a soft sound but Teresa flinched, imagining it bouncing off each and every wall in the house like a snap of lightning and rousing everyone from their sleep.

She flattened herself against the doorjamb. Her heart pounded furiously as she waited for someone to pull their door open, thrust a light into the darkness, and demand to know who was in the hallway. But nothing happened. The house remained quiet.

Finally, her body still tense, her nerves taut, she tiptoed back to her own bedchamber. Not until she had entered her room and closed the door behind herself, turning the key in the lock to ensure that no one could follow or disturb her, did she release her breath and sigh in relief.

But there was no time to dawdle. She hurried across the room and laid the handgun she'd taken from Traynor's room next to her satchel on the bed. Thank heavens he hadn't taken *everything* with him when he'd left home all those years before, though if she'd had to she could have taken one of the guns her father had kept downstairs in the study.

Teresa shuddered just remembering her father, then pushed the unpleasant thoughts aside. It wasn't good to think ill of the dead, but sometimes, most times, when it came to Thomas Braggette she didn't have anything but ill thoughts.

Moving to the mirrored dressing table, Teresa gathered her long, black hair, which she normally wore loose down her back, and quickly pinned it up. She checked her image in the mirror and with a satisfied nod turned back to the satchel.

She had dressed completely in black, having borrowed one of the mourning gowns her mother had been forced, by tradition, to wear after Thomas Braggette's death, even though she hadn't really been in mourning. None of them had. Teresa had refused to wear black for a father whose death meant only relief. Anyway, her wedding had been only a few weeks after Thomas's murder, and she certainly hadn't wanted to get married in a black gown.

Teresa knew she should feel a little guilty at not being sorry her father was dead, but she didn't. And she never would. He was gone, finally, and no one missed him. No one even really cared about catching his murderer, especially since the accused was Henri Sorbonte, Belle and Lin's father.

Teresa snapped the satchel closed and slipped Traynor's gun into the deep pocket of her riding habit. It felt like a cannon and pulled at the delicate fabric, but there was no help for that. There was no telling who or what she might meet on the road and she wasn't going to take any chances.

She took the note that she'd written to Eugenia and

propped it up against a bottle of perfume on her dressing table.

"Forgive me, Mama," she whispered softly and turned away before she could change her mind. Teresa grabbed a heavy black cape from the foot of the bed, slipped it around her shoulders, and fastened the frog closure at her neck. She glanced into the mirror again and hurriedly pulled the hood over her head, then fastened it with a hatpin.

Grasping her small satchel in one hand, Teresa stepped quietly back into the hallway. Magnolia, Belle's cat, lay curled in a ball in the center of the hall just a few feet away. The cat's eyes opened and it raised its head as it noticed Teresa.

She smiled but remained silent and prayed that the cat was the only one aware of her movements. At the landing she glanced back over her shoulder. The cat had gone back to sleep and all the bedchamber doors were still shut.

Teresa made her way hastily down the stairs, then tiptoed across the marble foyer toward the entry door.

Teresa led StarDancer from his stall and hurriedly slipped on his bridle and saddled him, using one of her brother's western-style outfits. If she was going to ride several hundred miles and make good time there was no way she could do it sidesaddle.

The huge black gelding pawed the ground impatiently as if to tell her to hurry even more. She could hardly blame him. The few riding horses left on Shadows Noir didn't get much exercise anymore, what with her brothers gone. She and Belle tried to ride as often as possible, but it wasn't easy, with so many Yankee troops out patrolling and so much to do just to keep themselves in food and necessaries.

And there were always Rebs foraging. There were even a few guerrillas prowling about, and though she hated to admit it she knew they could be just as dangerous as the Yankees.

StarDancer nickered softly and threw his head about. Long strands of thick, shiny black mane swished across Teresa's arm. The animal turned and looked at her. Only the small white star in the center of his forehead would distinguish him from the night, which was exactly why she'd chosen him over her own chestnut mare, Moonbeam.

"Shhh," she admonished gently, patting a hand to the gelding's sleek neck. "If you wake someone up it'll spoil everything, and I can't afford that."

The gelding snorted again, softly, as if in answer.

Leading StarDancer out of the stables, Teresa rechecked the tapestry-covered satchel she'd tied to the back of the saddle. Satisfied that it was secure, she pulled up both her riding habit and the folds of her cloak, shoved a booted foot into one stirrup, and mounted.

She would do whatever Jay wanted of her, *if* it would keep one of her brothers from harm. Otherwise he could just rot in hell and good riddance.

Not wanting anyone to spot them on the moonlit drive, Teresa kept StarDancer to the side of the road. They moved amid the deep shadows cast by the giant oaks that grew tall along the winding entry, draped in curtains of Spanish moss.

She shivered as the icy fingers of night touched the softness of her cheeks and stung the end of her nose.

Each step the giant horse took was almost soundless upon the thick, dew-covered grass, but Teresa held her breath nevertheless. Taking the drive would have been faster, a more direct route to the entry gate, but she couldn't chance the noise StarDancer's hooves would have made upon the crushed oyster shells. Not if they were to get away undetected, which was imperative.

If Belle knew what Teresa planned to do, where she was going, she would have insisted on accompanying her. And Eugenia would have insisted that Teresa wait until a proper escort could be found.

Halfway down the drive she reined in and looked back over her shoulder, as much to say goodbye as to make certain no one was following. Fear of what she was about to do niggled at her breast, threatening to sweep over her in a rush, but she fought it back. There was no room in this situation for second thoughts or jittery nerves. She knew what had to be done and there was nothing else but to just do it. If she stayed off the roads, traveled through the forests and heavily grown fields, and remained alert and cautious, she would be all right. She just had to keep out of sight as much as possible.

Pale moonlight shone down on Shadows Noir and softly illuminated the elegant white pillars that graced the front of the house. It reflected off the second-story windows and their adorning green shutters, yet the main floor galleries remained mostly steeped in shadow. Teresa felt a catch of emotion in her throat. The ravages and hardships of war were not so evident now, muted by distance and the softness of the night's light. Cracked stair mortar and peeling paint, dead rosebushes and chipped plaster had disappeared along with the stark harshness of the daytime sun.

Beneath the soft moonlight even the Spanish moss that draped the gnarled and twisted branches of the sprawling live oaks and swept the ground, badly in need of trimming, looked more like delicate sheets of lace curtain.

Teresa thought of Tyler, so small and innocent, lying asleep in her mother's room. Eugenia was a good grandmother. Belle and Lin were wonderful aunts. But her son deserved a father, a man who would laugh with him, play with him, and teach him how to grow up to be strong and honorable. He needed a man who would love him and proudly call him son. But that wasn't Jay Proschaud.

Resentment burned deep within Teresa's breast but she pushed it away. This wasn't the time to dwell on the past. Or even dream of the future. She pulled the hood of her cloak forward, attempting to further shield her face from the chill of the night air. This was the time to take care of the present, and the danger it posed to her family.

Three

Teresa quietly released the thin branch she'd been holding and let it slip back into place. The leaves rustled softly but the sound was too faint to draw the attention of the men she watched. She frowned. What in heaven's name was she going to do now?

Frustration fueled her anger and overrode her fear. She had to get past them. But how? She reached out to move one of the thin branches again, just enough so she could once again peer past it and catch a glimpse of the men camped only a few hundred yards away.

They obviously hadn't heard her approach, and for that she could only offer up a sincere prayer of thanks. She'd been galloping through the dense copse, going for speed rather than caution. Only the soft glimmer of their campfire and StarDancer's start of surprise had alerted her to the danger. And she'd managed to stop just in time.

Now she had to figure out what to do. Somehow she had to get past them, that was obvious. She stared at the vast sea of white tents beyond the soldiers' campfire and nearly groaned aloud. Petersburg, Virginia, was on the opposite side of their encampment and Lee was struggling to defend it. Past that small town was Richmond, her destination. It would be a delay of hours, maybe days, if she had to make her way around the Yankee encampment. She wasn't that certain of the terrain, and she wasn't about to turn around and go home. She had to get to Richmond, which meant staying on the road. It was her only chance.

Teresa sighed, her mind working frantically and coming up with nothing. Her hands balled into fists. There had to be a way.

Teresa stared at the soldiers, willing her mind to work, her imagination to take hold. Then it hit her. Pushing to her feet she hurried back to StarDancer.

"Sorry, boy," she said softly as she quickly untied his reins and mounted. "We've got to backtrack a couple of miles." It wasn't exactly in her plan but then neither was venturing into a Yankee encampment. Yet that's exactly what she was going to have to do if she wanted to get past them and on to Richmond.

Teresa slouched low in the saddle and hugged StarDancer's neck as she guided him back in the direction they'd come. But this time she made certain to be much more cautious.

It took only fifteen minutes to reach her destination, even traveling slowly. The sight was just as grisly as the first time she'd seen it, only an hour ago.

Teresa slid from the gelding's back and hurried to stand over the dead soldier half-buried in a pile of dried leaves. The fabric of his jacket and trousers had long ago faded; it was impossible to distinguish whether they'd been blue or gray, Yankee or Confederate, and for that Teresa was thankful. She didn't want to know.

The Lord only knew how long the man had been lying there. His skin was dried and taut. One side of his face was missing and what was left of his features were half-sunken into his head. She shuddered at the thought of what she was about to do. He's dead, she told herself again. He's dead and he won't be needing his clothes anymore. But she would.

Wrinkling her nose in disgust and saying a small prayer to be forgiven for what she was about to do, Teresa quickly relieved the man of his trousers, shirt, and jacket.

Thank heavens she wasn't squeamish—having four older brothers had relieved her of that trait, if she'd ever had it. Nevertheless she kept her gaze averted from his face, or what was left of it.

She retrieved one of her petticoats from her saddlebag and covered his body with it, then hurriedly stripped herself of her outer garments and struggled into the man's filthy, tattered rag of an outfit.

Teresa shuddered. She'd never done anything so repugnant in her life. But it was the only way.

A minute later she donned the dead man's shoes, along with his soiled and frayed hat. She stuffed her own clothes into her saddlebag and pushed them down beneath some of the food rations she'd brought, just in case one of those Yankees took a peek into the bag. She rolled up the cape to resemble a blanket and tied it behind the saddle.

Teresa remounted and, taking no precaution now against making any noise, nudged StarDancer's flanks. The gelding broke into an immediate lope.

She touched her heels to his ribs again, urging him into a full gallop. They moved through the densely forested landscape, past the small bush she'd hidden behind earlier, across the dry gully, and directly toward the large Yankee encampment.

"Oh, Lord, if this doesn't work please take me quick," she murmured under her breath, and pulled the brim of the hat down lower.

As she approached the edge of the camp a soldier stepped from the inky shadows that hovered around the trunk of a tree.

His sudden appearance startled Teresa and she jerked on StarDancer's reins. The big horse's muscles strained as he forced himself to obey her command. But he didn't stand still. Instead he snorted and pounded a hoof on the hard ground in protest.

"What's your business?" the sentry demanded curtly. He stood with his rifle held before his chest, the index finger of his right hand steady on the trigger. Only a pointed chin and a mouth lost beneath a scraggly mustache were visible. The upper portion of his face was lost within the black shadow created by the brim of his hat.

Teresa cringed at the loudly spoken question. Good Lord, he'd probably just awakened every damned Yankee in the camp.

StarDancer pawed at the ground again, then threw his head about to further indicate his extreme displeasure at having been forced to stop.

The soldier ignored the large gelding and stared up at Teresa. "State your business, boy," he demanded again.

"I came . . ." Teresa clamped her mouth shut as

the words came out in what she felt was too soft and feminine a tone for a boy. She cleared her throat and, in an exaggeratedly deeper voice said, "I came to bring your commander a message."

"Your papers?" The sentry looked up, revealing a face still young but hardened against the world. He thrust a hand toward her.

She stared at it. Papers? "I . . . I don't have . . . I mean, I can't show them to anyone but your commander."

The sentry's dark eyes narrowed. "Your name?" he demanded.

Name? What was her name? Boy's name. "Uh, Tom."

"Tom what?"

Oh, why hadn't she thought to see if the dead soldier had been carrying any papers? "Uh, Smith. Tom Smith."

"Kind of young for a courier, aren't you, Smith?"

Teresa bristled and stiffened. "I'm old enough," she snapped, growling the words out in what she hoped was a masculine sounding voice.

"Yeah, kid, right." The sentry chuckled, then turned abruptly on his heels. "Follow me."

Follow him? Teresa fought back her panic. She'd thought he would just direct her in the direction of the commander's tent. She didn't want to follow him. She didn't even want to be in this camp. All she wanted was to pass through, as quietly and inconspicuously as she could.

"Taggert, take over the watch," the sentry threw over one shoulder. "I'll be back in a few minutes."

Another man emerged from the shadows beneath

the tree. Teresa's spirit plummeted further. She looked back at the sentry who'd ordered her to follow him. This was not good at all. Her eyes darted here and there, looking for a means of escape.

What was she going to do? She couldn't talk to a Yankee commander. She'd tried that once in New Orleans, just after General Butler's troops had marched in and occupied the city, and she'd nearly gotten herself thrown into jail.

This time she could get herself shot as a spy!

Her tongue suddenly felt like a piece of wet shoe leather.

Teresa swallowed hard and a surge of panic washed over her. What would happen to one of her brothers if she didn't get to Jay? What would happen to Tyler if she never returned home? Her fingers tightened about the thin reins until she could almost feel her knuckles turning white beneath the taut, dark kid gloves that protected her hands against the chill. She had to get out of here. Make a run for it. Most of the soldiers were sleeping. If she took the sentry by surprise and urged StarDancer into an immediate full gallop maybe she could get past the rest of them.

She stiffened, began to lean forward, and started to nudge StarDancer's ribs with her heels.

The sentry turned and slipped a hand around the gelding's bridle. "I'll have your horse taken care of, kid. Just dismount and follow me."

Teresa felt the icy fingers of fear close around her. Her panic threatened to swell out of control but she knew there was no other recourse but to go along with the sentry. If she tried to run for it now they'd fire on her and she'd most likely be shot in the back.

That wouldn't do anyone any good . . . especially her.

Trying to swallow the lump of fear that had lodged itself soundly in her throat, she slid from the saddle. Handing StarDancer's reins over to the man, she waited as he called another soldier forward and told him to take care of "the kid's" horse. Teresa docilely followed the sentry past several more tents. Three soldiers, sitting around a smoldering campfire, stopped talking and looked up at her as they passed.

She hung her head, trying to conceal her features as much as possible.

The sentry led her around a small grove of trees, across a gully, through a maze of bushes, around another campfire, and past several more tents.

Teresa nearly groaned in frustration. Great. They had weaved back and forth so much that if she had to make a break for it she'd never find her way back to StarDancer.

They began to walk past another tent. Its entry flap was thrown back, which allowed light from a lantern to flow out into the night.

"Private Simms."

The sentry stopped and turned toward the light.

Teresa stopped and looked in at the man who'd called out. He was heavy-set and balding. A thick mustache covered his lips and spectacles perched on the end of his nose. He sat behind a table that was obviously substituting for a desk.

Private Simms poked his head into the tent. "Yes, sir, Captain Barnes?"

"Get me some coffee."

The sentry stiffened to attention. "But, sir, I was escorting this . . ."

"I don't care what you were doing, Private," the man thundered. "I want coffee, and I want you to get it. Now! Understand?"

The sentry paled and saluted smartly. "Yes, sir. Right away, Captain Barnes." He turned to Teresa. "The commander's not here," he said softly, almost whispering. "He went out with Noble's outfit this afternoon and they ain't back yet. I was taking you to see Lieutenant Colonel Forsythe." He glanced over his shoulder. "He's in the sixth tent down from here. Just past that campfire. You go on."

Teresa felt a thrill of hope. He wasn't going to escort her. She was on her own. That meant she could get away . . . if she could double back and find Star-Dancer.

"Go on, now," the sentry said. "I'll watch for a few minutes to make sure you got your bearings right."

Hope fizzled as she nodded and mumbled, "Yes, sir," then shuffled away from him. Maybe if she walked toward where she was supposed to go he'd turn away after a few minutes and she could dash off between a couple of the tents and turn back.

Keeping her head bent low, Teresa moved on past one, two, three tents. She walked past another campfire where four more soldiers sat huddled close to the low-burning flames. Teresa glanced over her shoulder and saw that the sentry was still watching her.

"Drat." The word slipped from her mouth as no more than a whisper. She walked on, past another tent, and yet another. Only one more and she'd be past the tent the sentry had indicated. Maybe she could veer off then and if he was still watching her he'd think she'd entered the Lieutenant's tent, as he'd ordered.

She held her breath, afraid to turn around and look again to see if he was still watching her. A few more feet. She only had to go a few more feet, take a few more steps, and then she could make a break for it.

Lamplight filled the tent and filtered out onto the night through the open entry flap. Teresa held her breath. There was no way she could skirt around the light, not without looking obvious about it. She would just have to hurry past and pray that the Lieutenant was asleep. Or gone. She hunched her shoulders and quickened her pace.

A man suddenly stepped from the tent, his tall form nearly filling the entry. The tent's light flowed past him, touching his dark uniform and dissipating into the night.

Teresa's breath caught in her throat.

He stood in profile to her, his jacket unbuttoned. Leather suspenders hung from beneath the garment to dangle loosely over his thighs. He was dressed in the dark blue uniform of a Yankee officer, confirmed by the gold insignia cords embroidered on his sleeves and the epaulets that edged his shoulders

His coat, though hanging open, gave evidence of broad shoulders, while the snug-fitting trousers, tucked into knee-high boots, displayed the long length of his sinewy legs in an almost indecent fashion. He was tall, towering a good foot or more over her own 5′2″, with an air of cool indifference about him that caused her to shiver. This was the man the sentry had been bringing her to see. She was certain of it.

Moonlight touched softly upon his hair and transformed the wavy blond strands to platinum. Despite the light tones, Teresa was left with an almost instant impression of darkness that instilled within her a new thread of fear that had nothing at all to do with being in a Yankee encampment.

He turned toward her then, and though Teresa knew she should look away, she found she couldn't.

Although the moonlight illuminated his hair, it left his face in a conflict of light and shadow. Dusky blackness hung almost ominously over deepset eyes and snuggled comfortably within the hollow of his cheeks; midnight blue darkness followed the strong, hard plane of his jaw, and silver touched the ridged curve of his high cheekbones, the straight line of his nose, and settled softly upon a full-lipped mouth that promised a mastery of both passion and cruelty.

It was a handsome face, perhaps one of the most alluring Teresa had ever seen, yet there was a hardness about it, a coldness that was both indescribable and unmistakable.

Teresa shivered, suddenly more frightened than she had been since starting her journey to Richmond. Yet she had no idea why. All she had to do was keep her head bowed and walk past him. But that simple task no longer seemed so simple. No man had ever looked at her in quite this way. It was as if his eyes, lost to her in those dark shadows, were stripping the clothes from her body. But that was ridiculous. She was dressed like a man, in tattered, soiled clothes that hung on her. She'd rubbed dirt on her face and her hair was pinned beneath a soiled and frayed hat that sat low on her forehead because it was several sizes too big.

Nevertheless, she felt a blush warm her cheeks at what seemed a deliberate appraisal of her carefully disguised female assets.

Teresa nearly jumped out of her skin when his hand moved, then quickly sighed in relief as she saw that he was only raising a cheroot to his lips. He turned away and inhaled deeply, the thin cigar's burning tip glowing brilliantly against the night.

The faint scent of brandy-soaked tobacco momentarily filled the air.

Teresa dropped her head forward and forced herself to keep walking. She would not look at him again. He didn't know she was supposed to report to him, that the sentry had directed her to his tent. For all he knew, she was just another soldier in the camp, maybe on the way back to his own tent after doing some chore. There was nothing to fear.

In spite of her resolve not to, she chanced a glance as she neared him, then cursed her foolishness when he suddenly met her gaze. She felt a start of surprise, then quickly squashed it before it could show on her face.

There was something vaguely familiar about him. She didn't know what it was, but it was there, and it scared her. Maybe it was something within the depths of his eyes, the way one brow arched upward questioningly as he looked at her. Or maybe it was something she saw in his face, something lurking about the corners of a mouth whose lips were now taut and hard, almost expressionless, yet hinted that once, perhaps long ago, they had smiled easily and readily.

She wasn't sure that was it, but there was something . . . and whatever it was it was warning her to remain quiet, to keep her head down . . . and to get out of there and away from him as quickly as she could.

Her body tense, her chin pressed against her chest, she walked past him, forced herself to mumble a "good evening" and touched a hand to the brim of her hat. He was an officer. Every soldier was supposed to acknowledge an officer.

She held her back stiff while keeping her head lowered.

Hopefully he wouldn't get upset because she hadn't snapped to attention and presented him with a formal salute. Or did they even do that out here in the field? Had the hardship of war, the tediousness of it all, and the horror, made everyone too weary to worry about the formalities?

"Private!"

Teresa stopped and her heart plummeted to her toes. Instinct, and the fact that no one else was nearby, told her loud and clear that he was calling to her. An almost mind-numbing terror gripped her. She'd been caught.

Four

Teresa stood still, frozen to the spot. Her mind screamed at her to run, but her legs refused to move, as if they'd suddenly taken root in the ground. Her gaze darted about, taking in the dark landscape beyond the dozens of dingy white tents that stood staked upon the gently rolling terrain. Several yards away another campfire glowed and another trio of soldiers huddled around it.

She could hear the pounding of her heart in her ears. Loud. Harsh. Her stomach somersaulted, then seemed to fall to her feet. She felt a wave of dizziness as her pulse accelerated and her entire body trembled. How far could she get if she ran?

Not far enough, a little voice in the back of her mind answered.

"Private."

Teresa nearly groaned aloud, but stifled the sound while it was still in her throat. She glanced down. Her breasts made a slight bulge against the front of the baggy shirt. She jerked at the lapels of the soiled jacket and pulled it closed. The musty odor of dirt and sweat rose from the rotting fabric of the dead soldier's clothes. Teresa wrinkled her nose in disgust. Would he be able to tell she was a woman?

Anxiety mounted within her breast, clutched at her heart, seized her breath, and threatened to turn into all-out hysteria. She struggled to stop the sensation. Calm. She had to remain calm or everything would be ruined. She just had to keep her jacket front closed and her head lowered so the hat's brim hid her face.

Taking a deep breath, as if to pull night air into her lungs and gather a badly needed dose of courage, she peeked back at the Lieutenant. Maybe he only wanted a cup of coffee like the other officer had. "Yes, sir?" she said, in as low a voice as she could muster.

"Come here."

Come here. She stared at him as the words echoed in her brain.

Teresa swallowed. He wouldn't order her to "come here" or use that gruff tone if all he wanted was a cup of coffee. Her heart sank. She wanted to run but took several hesitant steps forward instead.

He looked down at her, cold amusement gleaming from eyes that were the darkest blue she'd ever seen. And the coldest. Like sapphires of ice, and just as hard. "I need your help."

Whatever emotion hovered behind those thick-lashed eyes, Teresa was convinced it held no warmth.

His voice was deep and somewhat rough, and tinged with just the slightest of drawls. That surprised her. He was southern. And he was a Yankee. Indignation burned within her. Blackguard. The man was a traitor.

Curiosity urged her to look up at him. Logic ordered her not to. She couldn't take the chance that he'd recognize her as a woman.

He spun on his heel and re-entered the tent.

Teresa brightened as hope sparked anew. She could run. He was in the tent. He wouldn't even see in which direction she'd gone—but the three men huddled around the campfire would. They might even stop her.

She looked at the Lieutenant's tent and swallowed hard as butterflies fluttered about in her stomach. Her knees felt as if they'd turned to mush and threatened to buckle at her first step forward. Her hands trembled and she hurriedly folded her arms and tucked her hands beneath them. Is this what it felt like to face the hangman's noose?

"Private?"

The officer's voice startled her and Teresa jumped.

He returned to stand before her.

She wanted to faint.

Not giving her a chance to resist him, he reached for her and deftly propelled her into the tent.

Taken by surprise, she could do little more than scurry around him and smash her free hand onto her head to keep the hat from flying off.

He didn't release her and she found herself extremely aware of the warm hand on her arm. It held her tightly, giving her no chance of escape.

She wished she could jerk away, or reach up and slap him, but she could do neither, not unless she wanted to risk discovery, which she didn't.

A faint odor of brandy and tobacco emanated from him and drew her attention. It was a redolence she'd smelled often when her brothers had been home, and it was one she normally liked. Now it only reminded her of the hand that held her so tightly, of the man who had so effortlessly propelled her into his tent. Most of all, it reminded her that she was in a very precarious, and very dangerous, situation.

"Are you used to ignoring an officer when he speaks to you, Private?" he demanded harshly.

Teresa cringed inwardly, then, remembering to keep her head bent, shoulders slumped forward, and eyes downcast, she shook her head. "No sir."

"Good." He released her and walked toward the rear of the tent. "Because it's a good way to get yourself shot."

Teresa gritted her teeth and remained silent, remembering another time, not so long ago in New Orleans, when she'd stood before another Yankee officer and he'd said much the same thing. Only he'd been about to carry it out.

Brett Forsythe moved around his desk and sat down, a soft sigh escaping his lips as the tension of the past several hours released its grip on his weary muscles and bones. Teresa wasn't the little girl he remembered, or even the proper lady he supposed she'd grown up to be. Instead, dressed in a dead soldier's clothes and with dirt smudged on her cheeks, she reminded him of one of the old rag dolls his hounds used to chew on while lazing on the rear gallery of Twin Oaks. Brett ran a weary hand through his hair. But she wasn't a little girl and she wasn't a rag doll. She was most likely spying for her husband. Or she might even be a member of the Knights of the Golden Circle. He'd heard women had joined the KGC and knew that some of the most successful espionage efforts had been accomplished by them. If her description hadn't been given to Brett he might never have recognized her and she probably would have slipped right past him.

"Come here," he said coolly. Anger toward her burned hotter than he'd expected. It surprised him, and yet it didn't. She was his best friend's sister, and she was about to betray everything they were fighting to preserve, if she hadn't already.

Teresa hesitated.

"I said come here," he barked when she didn't move.

Teresa jumped and scurried across the sparsely furnished tent.

He raised a leg and thrust it toward her. "Help me off with my boots."

Teresa stared down at him as if he were crazy but made no attempt to move. Help him off with his boots?

Brett looked up when she failed to move again. "Private, are you hard of hearing, or just anxious to get shot?"

There was no patience in his tone.

Teresa dropped to one knee while she fought to keep from saying aloud the sharp words tripping through her mind. Help him off with his boots! She'd like to help him off with his head.

"Afterward scrape the mud off them and give them a cleaning."

Indignation swept through her as she grabbed hold of one boot. Scrape the mud off them! Just who in tarnation did he think he was? A stinging rebuke burned her tongue and was just about to slip past her lips when she remembered where *she* was . . . and who she was supposed to be.

With a parade of unspeakable curses marching through her head, Teresa yanked at the boot. Her effort managed to crack his knee, but the boot remained solidly in place.

She looked up at him.

He smiled down at her, but it was anything but a pleasant smile. There was no congeniality in the curve of his lips. No warmth in the fathomless depths of those cold, hard, blue eyes.

She quickly looked away and yanked on the boot again. Several tugs later it finally slipped from his foot. She threw it down and immediately set to pulling off the other one.

"Thanks, Private." Brett stood up, stretched, and resettled himself behind the desk. "You'll find a kettle of hot water on the fire outside. You can use it to clean them off."

"Yes, sir," Teresa mumbled politely. Inwardly she fumed. She'd clean them off all right—when Hell froze over.

Once outside she threw the boots down and took a split second's delight at seeing that they landed in a puddle of mud. She smiled. It was just what he deserved. And he could clean them off himself. The cur!

The three men sitting around the campfire looked up as she stalked toward them.

Teresa kept her head bent low. The nerve of the man . . . demanding that she take his boots off and clean them. What was he—helpless? Her hands knotted into fists. He was probably some rich dandy who did little more than order men into battles they had little chance of surviving while he sat in his tent smoking cheroots, swigging down brandy, and having his boots cleaned.

Oh, and being a traitor to his own kind. She couldn't forget that.

"Just where in the hell do you think you're going?"

No sooner had the words penetrated her eardrums than a hand clamped down on her shoulder. An image of a firing squad, with her as their target, flitted through her mind. Strong fingers grasped her shoulder blade and bit into her flesh. Teresa winced and nearly crumpled beneath the pressure, but had no time to think before she was forcefully swung around.

Her arms flew out automatically in an effort to keep herself from losing her balance.

"Answer me!"

Dumbfounded, Teresa stared up at Brett. Fear had a solid grip on her heart, and had seized her brain.

He held his boots up. Mud covered the high tops and dripped from the heels and soles.

Teresa looked at them and then back up at the man who stood before her, obviously in a total rage.

Her hands clenched into fists. Oh, what she wouldn't give to be able to slap his handsome face!

Yeah, and land in the hoosegow, her conscience said.

Her fingers immediately uncurled and she dropped her head quickly, showing him the topside of her hat's brim and hiding her face. "Sorry, sir. I . . . I . . . I just . . . uh . . ." Anger merged with fear and left her brain totally useless.

"I don't care what you were 'just' doing, Private." He transferred his grip to her arm. "I told you to clean my boots, and that's damned well what I expect you to do—now!" He turned abruptly.

Teresa was nearly jerked from her feet as he stomped back toward his tent, hauling her after him. She grabbed at her hat to keep it from flying off. This was definitely not the time for an unveiling.

Slashing his other hand at the tent flap, Brett threw back the canvas. Mud from the boots he still held flew everywhere. Snarling softly, he pushed Teresa inside and tossed the muddied boots down on the ground before her. "You can clean them in here, Private," the Lieutenant grumbled, "where I can keep an eye on you. And when you're done with those you can clean the ones I'm wearing, which are now also covered with mud, thanks to you."

Teresa stared at the boots lying on the ground. She had never in her life been treated so . . . so harshly. Her gaze rose to meet his. What she'd really like to do was . . . Clamping a lid on her mounting temper, she picked up the mud-covered boots and grabbed the cleaning rag he tossed at her.

"You can sit on that stool."

She looked to where he pointed. A small wooden stool sat in one corner of the tent, next to the foot of his cot. Was that what he made everyone who came to see him sit on so he could look down his nose at the person and feel more important. *Beast,* she thought hatefully. The soft yellow glow of an oil lantern lit the cramped interior of the tent. Teresa glanced quickly at its sparse furnishings: a cot, wooden traveling trunk, stool, a small cabinet, desk, and chair.

She flopped herself down on the stool and began to rub at the mud on one of his boots. The sooner she finished the task, the sooner she could get out of there. She tugged at the brim of her hat. Obnoxious brute. Hating herself for doing it yet unable to resist the urge, Teresa peeked past the frayed brim of her hat. The feeling that she'd seen or met him somewhere before assailed her again.

He was seated at his desk, writing. A small frown pulled at his brow and a wayward lock of hair had fallen forward to dangle roguishly over his forehead.

She watched him push at it several times and felt a spurt of smug delight as the curl rebelled and dropped forward again, resisting his efforts to force it back into place.

Teresa frowned. She knew him. She felt certain she did. But from where? How? Familiarity teased her mercilessly and danced about the edges of her memory but eluded her grasp. It was maddening. And frightening.

What if they *had* met? And what if he remembered before she did? What if he recognized her? A sense of frantic urgency gripped her.

Teresa's gaze raked over him, scrutinizing each and every curve of his face, each line and feature, trying to find something to spark her memory.

There was an aristocratic grace to his features, as if mute testimony to a strain of royalty somewhere in his ancestry. Yet at the same time, she saw a ruggedness there, too. His face was square, his jaw hard and well defined, like the high cheekbones that were prominent yet curved.

He wasn't one of her old beaus—she felt certain she'd remember if he'd ever called on her. Could she have met him at a soirée? She hadn't done much traveling north, but northerners had often come to New Orleans. In fact, several of her friends had married northerners. Then she remembered the drawl she'd heard in his voice and her immediate first impression that he was southern.

He'd taken off his jacket and she saw that beneath the thin fabric of his white shirt his shoulders were wide and muscular, as, she suspected, were the ropey length of his arms encased within the loose sleeves of his shirt. Strength seemed to emanate from him.

Perhaps under different circumstances . . . Teresa jerked herself upright, startled at the direction her thoughts had taken. Different circumstances? Hah! Her hand slid off the toe of the boot and hit her other hand. Mud from the rag smeared onto her knuckles. What was she thinking? Under different circumstances she'd be tempted to have one of her brothers challenge the Mr. High and Mighty Lieutenant Forsythe to a duel and run him through. She wiped her knuckles against the filthy trousers. A little more dirt wasn't going to hurt them.

She dipped one end of the rag into the bucket of water next to the stool, then stared down at it. If she threw the bucket of water at him would he be able to duck? And if not, if she managed to give him a good drenching, would she have enough time to get away?

A sigh slipped from her lips. Probably not, and

when he caught her he'd probably throw her in the stockade. Or have her shot as he'd already threatened. Then everything would be lost, possibly even the life of one of her brothers. She couldn't chance that.

"I have an important meeting in the morning," Brett said, interrupting her thoughts. "Make sure you get those boots clean."

Teresa screwed her face into a scowl and silently mocked him. Twenty minutes later she was finished with both pairs of boots. "I'm finished, sir, so if there's nothing else I'll be going now. Maybe get me a little coffee and a bit of hardtack." She edged toward the flap. "Good night."

"Hold on there, Private." Brett rose from behind his desk and walked toward her. "I'd like you to oil my bridle before you go."

"Your bridle," Teresa repeated, unable to believe her ears.

He pushed open the tent flap and looked out. "Rollins, bring me a couple of cups of coffee, would you?" Brett turned back to Teresa. "Oil's in the trunk at the foot of the cot and my bridle's hanging from the tent post." He pointed to the post just behind her. "There."

"Yes, sir, Lieutenant," Teresa said through clenched teeth. "So it is."

Three hours later Teresa was ready to run Lieutenant Forsythe through with his own sabre. She'd oiled his bridle and then his saddlebags. She had cleaned his sidearm, scraped mud from his greatcoat, polished his sabre and scabbard, and brought him a second cup of coffee.

Now he wanted her to shave him!

Five

Brett settled back in the chair as Teresa dabbed soap foam over the lower portion of his face. He'd kept her busy for the past several hours, giving her one chore after another, and now he almost felt sorry for her. But the key word was *almost.* And it wasn't enough to soothe the resentment he felt toward her or make him stop goading her.

When he'd been informed that Teresa Braggette was the wife of the man he'd been after for the past two years he'd scoffed with disbelief. But that hadn't lasted very long. Brett's sources were impeccable. They had to be. He literally trusted them with his life on numerous occasions and couldn't take the chance that their information was anything but accurate. It had just been so hard to believe that Teresa, Traynor's little sister, was married to a lowlife like Jay Proschaud.

Brett thought back to the past. He'd known Jay Proschaud when they'd been younger and lived in New Orleans before the war, but they hadn't been friends in spite of the fact that their parents, as well as the Braggettes, all moved in the same social circle.

He looked up at Teresa. It was still difficult to believe that she was the same young girl he remembered as his best friend's little sister. But then it had been a good number of years since he'd last seen her.

It was even more difficult to believe that she was married to Jay Proschaud and had a child by him. Brett sighed. He'd always said there was no telling what a woman saw in a man, or what made her love him, but he sure would like to know what Teresa saw in Jay Proschaud. That was a mystery that piqued his curiosity . . . and his anger.

"Make sure you give me a *close* shave," he growled from beneath the white foam.

From the expression he saw in the gray-blue eyes that jerked to meet his he knew instantly what was swirling behind them. A murderous shave was what she obviously would prefer to give him.

He closed his eyes and let his head fall back slightly. Traynor would have said that letting a suspected member of the rebellious and out-of-control faction of the KGC headed by Jay Proschaud get near him with a straight razor was a foolhardy thing to do, and maybe it was. Proschaud's unit was fanatical about defending the South, so much so that their efforts were too extreme and bloodthirsty for most and they'd alienated the very people and government they were fighting to save.

Brett peeked up at Teresa through half-closed lids. He certainly had no death wish, but he needed to keep her close—and he needed a shave. More important, he needed to know how far she'd go. The gun he had nestled in his lap beneath the towel gave him a sense of assurance.

Anyway, he didn't really believe Teresa would attempt to slit his throat. She might be a traitor, as the

Confederate government had pronounced Proschaud's followers to be, but she wasn't a murderer. He hoped.

Brett heard the soap dish and brush being set down on the desk behind him. A second later the unmistakable sound of his straight razor being slapped against its length of accompanying leather broke the silence in the tent.

One swipe of that long, straight, glistening silver blade and his throat could be cut from ear to ear. Brett's shoulders stiffened instinctively and a shiver of trepidation rippled through him. He opened his eyes and looked up at her. It would be a damned shame to shoot her. And he doubted Traynor or any of the other Braggettes would understand. But Brett wasn't about to meet his Maker ahead of schedule if he didn't have to. He eyed her warily and slipped his finger over the trigger of his gun. One wrong move . . .

Teresa slapped the razor against the leather strap. If anybody deserved murdering it was this horrid Yankee. He was insufferable, treating her like a slave. She glanced at him. Even with the soapy foam covering half his face he was still one of the handsomest men she'd ever seen.

The thought fueled her anger, at him and at herself. He might be handsome, but he was a Yankee, and he was causing her a great deal of trouble!

Feeling her gaze on him, Brett opened his eyes and looked up at Teresa. "You have used one of those before, haven't you, Private?" He watched the razor slide up and down the length of leather. Maybe sitting here like a lamb waiting to be slaughtered wasn't too smart after all.

"Yes, sir, many times."

Brett forced himself to remain still and closed his eyes again. He didn't like the way she'd said that. Nor was he particularly pleased at the fury he saw glimmering in her eyes.

Teresa dropped the strap and moved closer. She touched his chin with her index finger and raised the razor to his cheek.

In spite of his resolve, which had slipped drastically in the last few seconds, Brett cringed at her touch. His finger tightened on the trigger. Fat lot of good it would do him if he was wrong. One quick draw of the razor across his throat and he'd be gurgling blood before he even had a chance to point his gun at her.

Teresa saw her hand tremble and fought to steady it, and herself. What if she accidentally cut him? She held the blade poised above his cheek. The blade caught the light of the nearby lantern as it wavered in her hand. Would he automatically strike out if . . . ?

She tightened her grip on the razor. Lord, if she didn't get control of herself she'd end up slicing off his nose. Then she really would be in trouble. He'd most likely have her flogged. No. He'd probably strangle her with his own two hands.

Teresa swallowed hard. Everything was going to be fine. She just had to be careful and stay calm. She could give him his blasted shave. She'd given them to her brothers numerous times and she'd never even nicked one of them. She would shave this low-down, rotten traitor and then leave.

"Private, before you start, hand me the tin of tobacco on my desk, would you?"

Teresa glanced over her shoulder. A small, round tin, red with black lettering decorating its lid, sat on one corner of the desk. She nearly breathed a sigh of relief at the brief reprieve and handed the tin to him.

"Thanks." Brett pulled off the lid, took a pinch of tobacco, and tucked it into his mouth between lip and gum. He looked up and saw Teresa watching him. He thrust the tin toward her. "Here, Private, be my guest and have some."

It was a horrid thing to do and he knew it, but then he didn't have a whole lot of sympathy for a person who would betray her country.

Teresa stared, horrified, at the shredded tobacco. Have some? Was he crazy? She didn't want to put that awful stuff in her mouth.

"Come on, Private," Brett urged. He lifted the tin higher until it was almost directly under her nose. The strong smell of brandy-soaked tobacco filled the tent. "Don't be shy. It's good. Some of the best, actually. Come on, have some. On me."

Teresa forced herself to pinch several shreds of tobacco between her fingers, and with her stomach fairly turning over in disgust, stuffed it into her mouth. Maybe she would kill him, after all.

The acrid taste stung her tongue and nearly made her gag. Nausea closed her throat. She fought it back, swallowing hard and breathing deeply.

"Never had a chew before, hey, Private?" Brett said. He chuckled softly, but there was no real amusement in the cold sound.

Teresa looked up at him and saw that there was none in his hard blue eyes either. She shook her head. Tears filled her eyes and she blinked rapidly, trying to hold them back. What would they really do to her if she killed him? Especially when they discovered she was a woman? She turned to run the razor along the strap again, more to hide her face from him than because the razor needed any further sharpening.

Brett felt a stab of guilt. Maybe he'd gone too far.

Teresa turned back to him. "Ready, sir," she said, her voice sounding like a frog's croak.

Brett settled back in the chair. No. She had chosen the charade. He was just going along with it, at least for the moment. The good thing was that he knew who she was but she hadn't recognized him. He probably wouldn't have recognized her either if it hadn't been for two things: he'd known she was coming his way because of the agent he'd had watching her for the past several weeks; and he'd never met another living soul who possessed eyes that same unique blend of gray-blue as the Braggettes.

In her brothers it was merely interesting. In her it was like seeing the impossible melding of a winter evening's fog and the crystal clear blueness of a spring morning.

She touched the razor to his throat, drawing the blade upward, and Brett's thoughts were instantly pulled back to the present. She was his best friend's sister but she was also the wife of a traitor, and he'd just put himself in a very vulnerable position.

Brett's hand tightened its grip on the gun in his lap.

Teresa pulled the blade down across his cheek.

Whiskers and soap clung to the blade but fortunately no skin. She released the breath she'd been unaware she'd been holding. Turning slightly, she held the razor above the bowl of water and flicked her wrist. The blob of soap dropped into the water. Teresa dipped the blade into the bowl, swished it about, then raised it to his face again.

He opened his eyes. Teresa nearly bit her bottom lip as her gaze met his, something she had been struggling to avoid. It was like the blending of night and day, a fusing that was at once both comfortable and soothing, fiery and explosive. But one thing it definitely was not was the kind of look exchanged between a *male* Private and a *male* Lieutenant. Teresa tore her gaze from his and stared intently at the soapy foam still covering the lower portion of his face.

Her insides were a quivering mess, her thoughts a confused jumble, and in spite of the coolness of the air she was hot. Lord, but she was hot. She raised the razor to his face.

Brett caught her wrist in a steel-tight grasp. His eyes bore into hers. "Be careful, Private," he said softly. The threat in his eyes was clearly evident in his raspy whisper.

Teresa stared down at him, fear overriding any sense of caution, excitement blotting out all thought of the masquerade she had so hurriedly devised for herself. Why did she have the feeling she'd looked into those eyes before? They were so dark. So blue. They seemed to call to her, beckon her.

His strong fingers held firm about the tender flesh of her wrist. She tried to look away and found that her gaze had been captured by his bold, arrogant stare and was no longer hers to command.

He regarded her steadily, those same sapphire blue eyes that chilled her with their sense of familiarity moving ever so slowly over her face.

Teresa shuddered. She *had* met him somewhere before, looked into those eyes before. She knew it. But where? When? And why couldn't she remember?

The seconds ticked by slowly, silently. Part of her wished fervently that someone would come and interrupt them, while at the same time she was horrified to realize that was the last thing she wanted.

"Careful," Brett said again, and released his hold.

She felt her flesh sting at the absence of his fingers and hurriedly lowered her arm.

His hand disappeared beneath the towel, and he closed his eyes and tilted his head back again.

Teresa forced herself to run the razor over his right cheek, along his jaw and up his throat, all the while praying that her trembling hand did not cause the razor to cut him. She had to finish. To get out of his tent. Away from this camp.

At the front of his chin, just below the left corner of his mouth, Teresa's hand slipped and the razor's edge sliced into his skin.

"Ouch! Dammit all." Brett jerked upright. He flung the towel aside and touched his chin.

Teresa stared at the gun in his lap.

Brett drew his hand back and stared at the glistening spots of blood that covered the tips of his fingers.

"Sorry," Teresa mumbled. Her stomach abruptly churned and her legs suddenly felt weak and unsteady. Panic seized her. She couldn't faint. Not now.

Not here. Her hands trembled. She closed her eyes and grabbed the edge of the desk. A wave of dizziness washed over her. She held herself taut and tightened her hold on the edge of the wood.

Brett wiped his hand on the towel and turned to glower up at her. "I think you'd better be . . ."

She swayed toward him.

Brett frowned, his mood having gone from dark to black. He wasn't in the mood for theatrics. "What's the matter—the sight of blood make you sick?"

She shook her head, then realized immediately that the movement had been a mistake. The room spun and her stomach turned upside down. She coughed. "Diz . . . dizzy. Maybe I'd . . . better go to . . . my own tent."

Brett swore under his breath, as angry now with himself as he was with her. If she was sick it was his fault for practically forcing that tobacco into her mouth. But if she was merely trying to escape she was going to be wildly disappointed; either way, she wasn't going anywhere. He'd made her do every demeaning chore he could think of in an effort to soothe the resentment and anger he felt at her probable betrayal, not only of her country but of her own brothers and it hadn't helped in the least.

Teresa took a step away from the table, only to fall forward toward Brett. He lunged forward and wrapped his arms around her. The anger he'd felt only seconds before left him. He pulled her toward him, into the circle of his arms and against the solid, strong wall of his chest, unconsciously offering both his strength and his warmth. Thoughts of suspicion and doubt, of betrayal and duplicity were instantly replaced by guilt and concern.

"Tess, what's the matter?" He touched a hand gently to her cheek, not even aware of having used the nickname he and Traynor had bestowed upon her when they were children. Her face was warm and flushed. "Tess? Tess, are you all right?"

She moaned softly. Her eyelids fluttered as she tried to look up at him and respond.

"Tess, answer me. Are you all right?"

She suddenly pushed away from him, dropped to her knees, and grabbing her empty stomach, experienced a violent case of dry heaves. Her body shook with one savage shudder after another.

Cursing himself soundly, Brett held her shoulders until she stopped.

"I . . . I'm okay," she mumbled softly, and attempted to stand. "I . . . I just haven't . . . had anything to eat for a while . . . and . . . not used to tobacco."

He felt her body tremble and sway. "You need to rest." Holding her tightly, Brett helped her to his cot. He'd been a stupid, thoughtless idiot. He knew she'd been riding for two days straight, day and night, with only short stops here and there to rest her horse and catch a little sleep. She was exhausted. And because of his own arrogant self-righteousness he'd forced her to play maid, barber, and chew a wad of tobacco.

Good going, Brett, he swore silently. Why didn't you just tie her to a tree and flog her? He looked down at Teresa who had curled up on his cot and had already fallen asleep. But flogging would be the least of her concerns if she was involved in helping her husband with his schemes.

No woman had been put before a firing squad yet, but there was always a first time . . . and Brett feared that the hatred his superiors had for Jay Proschaud just might spill over to his wife if she were suspected to be an accomplice in any of the things he'd done in the past two years.

Jay Proschaud was a dangerous man. He'd created a lot of havoc both in the Confederacy and the Union, hence a lot of people could be considered his enemies.

Unbuttoning the ragged and badly soiled jacket, Brett pulled it back, then thought better of taking it off completely. If he did that she'd realize when she woke that he knew her secret, even if she didn't remember him calling her Tess. Brett stared down at the slender body that lay on his cot. Even covered by the loose-fitting man's shirt and trousers, the lithe line of her body was evident to his appreciative eye.

It was very different from the last time he'd seen Teresa Braggette. A gangly, young girl's body had turned . . . He pulled a blanket over Teresa and tucked it about her neck before his imagination could take him any further.

"Stupid," he mumbled again, thinking back on what he'd done to her. He rose to his feet. Moving to sit behind his desk, Brett stared across the small interior of the tent at Teresa. "Stupid," he said again, and reached for the bottle of whiskey that lay tucked in his footlocker.

He wanted to capture Jay Proschaud more than he'd wanted anything in a long time, but that didn't excuse the way he'd treated her.

If she'd come into his camp as a lady, he liked to think he'd have treated her as such. But she hadn't, and he'd been forced to play her game or lose the lead that following her was providing. His best lead. He could only thank heaven that his man had seen what she was doing and warned him. Otherwise she might very well have succeeded in passing straight through the encampment.

It had seemed so ingenious, combining the two objectives: foraging out the strength of the Yankee troops camped near Petersburg, and intercepting Teresa Braggette.

Now he had to wonder if he hadn't put both their lives in more jeopardy than necessary.

Brett reached out to touch her cheek, then pulled his hand back abruptly. She hadn't given him any indication that she recognized him as the same young man who had been one of her brother's best friends. But there was no denying the look of puzzlement she'd turned on him several times. She sensed something, maybe a familiarity between them. She just didn't remember—yet, and all he could do was pray that she didn't, at least not until after they reached Richmond.

He straightened, but rather than turn away he continued to look down at her. How had she grown into such a beautiful woman in only a few years time?

Against his will, an old memory surfaced. Years earlier, while he and Traynor had been enjoying a brandy at the Exchange in the French Quarter, his friend had told him that he'd once overheard his little sister swooning over Brett to one of her friends. Brett had laughed. He'd been about seventeen at the time,

Teresa maybe eleven or twelve and all arms and legs. Certainly not the beauty she was now.

Turning away, he suddenly became aware of an uncomfortable tightening of the inseams of his trousers. "Damn." The curse echoed on the still night air. Hungering over Teresa Braggette was just about the last thing he needed.

He forced his mind to the more mundane, and safer, aspects of their situation. Even though she hadn't recognized him, he knew the longer they stayed in the Yankee encampment the more danger they were in. He knew he should get her out of there, yet at the same time he had to wait for his man to return with word that everything in Richmond was ready for them, and that they could actually get through the lines. There wasn't much point in starting out only to find themselves in the midst of a battle.

Brett poured two fingers of whiskey into a tin cup and drank it in one gulp. The amber liquor raced down his throat like fire, burning mercilessly, then turning into a soothing heat that spread warmth throughout his insides.

His gaze moved back to rest on Teresa. The ragged and soiled hat beneath which she'd kept hidden her hair had fallen off when she'd fainted. Long strands of ebony fanned out about her head like silk, a stark contrast to the frayed and well worn white sheet that covered his cot.

What was she? he wondered. His gaze remained fixed on her, the fingers of his right hand playing along the edges of the now-empty tin cup. A misled wife? A traitor?

He preferred to believe she was merely misled, her

judgment clouded by faith in the man she'd married. But he couldn't assume that, and the fact fed his fury at the entire situation. Why did it have to be *her* husband he was after? Why did he have to use her to get to the man? And why had Proschaud summoned her? Was it the first time he'd involved her in one of his treacherous plans? Or merely one of many?

The troubled thoughts refused to leave him. What if he found out she was a traitor like her husband? How could he protect her? Would he protect her?

If it turned out she was guilty, he had no choice but to try to protect her from the authorities—his own superiors—if for no other reason than she was Traynor Braggette's sister and Traynor had been his best friend for years. But how in the hell he could protect her if she was guilty of treason was a question that, at the moment, he had no answer for.

Brett pulled a cheroot from his pocket, thought better of lighting it, and dropped it onto the desktop.

He'd had an agent watching her for the past several months. He hadn't really expected anything to happen, but decided to be cautious and take no chances all the same. Then they'd intercepted Jay's letter. Brett had known instantly that she would go to her husband, not merely because he'd summoned her, but because of the veiled insinuation that one of her brothers was in trouble. It might be the truth; then again, it could be a ruse, manufactured by Proschaud to give Teresa an excuse to leave Shadows Noir and travel cross-country to Richmond. And Brett had no way of knowing the truth.

Rising and walking around his desk, he bent down

and picked Teresa's hat up from the ground. He hunkered down beside her, intending to tuck the long strands of hair back under the hat so she would not know her secret had been discovered. Instead his hand froze in midair as the glistening tresses covered his fingers.

It had been a long time since he'd felt anything so soft. Luxury and elegance were not a part of war.

Teresa stirred and Brett jumped, startled. He hurriedly tucked her hair up and under the hat, setting it onto her head as firmly as he dared and praying that his movements did not wake her.

He rose. If she wanted to terminate the charade when she woke, fine. Otherwise he had no choice but to continue it with her . . . to its conclusion. He only hoped the conclusion was one that didn't implicate her in the things Jay Proschaud had been doing for the past several years.

Brett took a step toward his desk, paused, and looked back down at Teresa. He'd noticed her watching him earlier. If she suddenly remembered who he was and blurted out the name Forteaux rather than Forsythe . . . Well, he didn't want to think of how he'd manage to get out of that one if any Yankees were close enough to hear. He probably wouldn't.

Brett poured himself another drink, this time sipping it slowly as he continued to look at Teresa. The last time he'd seen her she had been about thirteen. He'd been twenty. He remembered that because it had been the year he'd left to go abroad for his "tour." He and Traynor had planned on touring Europe together, but Traynor's father had refused to let him go. When Brett returned a year later, Traynor had moved away from the Braggette plantation and New Orleans, and there had been no reason for Brett to visit Shadows Noir anymore.

Again Brett realized how much Teresa had changed. He didn't really know the woman, only the young girl. His gaze bore into her as if he were trying to see past the flesh and blood and into her soul.

It had been almost two years since he'd seen Traynor. That was the first time he'd heard that Teresa had married Jay Proschaud. It had also been when he'd learned that his own sister, Suzanne, had married Travis Braggette.

Teresa groaned and rolled over. The sound jerked Brett's thoughts from his memories and forced his attention back to the present. He watched her for several long seconds, waiting for her to wake up. Then, reassured that she wasn't about to, he sat down at his desk and propped one booted foot on its corner. Luckily the hat remained firmly on her head.

Brett relaxed and allowed himself another few moments indulgence in old memories. Most of his friends had married—if not before the war, then during it. Even all of the Braggette brothers had married. Trace and Traxton had gotten roped in by the Sorbonte twins of Natchez, in spite of the fact that their father was accused of killing Thomas Braggette.

But Brett knew that none of the Braggettes really cared about what had happened to their father. From what Traynor had told him, even Eugenia wasn't concerned about the prosecution of her husband's murderer. Thomas Braggette had been a ruthless but popular politician. He had, however, offered no love to his family. Brett remembered all too well some of the cruelties Trace, Traxton, Travis, Traynor, and even Teresa and Eugenia had suffered at Thomas Braggette's hands.

It was no wonder that they had felt no grief over his death. But marriage was something he'd never thought of in conjunction with any of the Braggette brothers. The thought of any of the swaggering Braggettes tied to a woman's apron strings brought a smile to his lips.

Teresa stirred again and Brett forced thoughts of the past aside. His gaze moved slowly over her from head to toe as he tried to reconcile the woman who lay on his cot with the young girl he remembered last seeing at Shadows Noir.

She wasn't a gangly adolescent anymore.

Brett felt his body begin to harden as imagination took him where he shouldn't and didn't want to go. In spite of the dirty clothes that hung on her frame like oversized rags, the frayed hat that hid the lustrous, long strands of her dark hair, and the dirt smudges she'd intentionally wiped across her face, he could see that Teresa Braggette had grown into a very beautiful woman.

She was also his best friend's sister, another man's wife, and quite possibly an accomplice to the man he had been trying to capture for the past year—a traitor and a murderer.

Nevertheless, he could not deny the fact that he wanted her.

Six

Teresa woke with a start. She bolted upright and looked around the empty tent. Her temples ached, but that was the least of her concerns at the moment. Where was she? What had happened?

The tent flap suddenly flew open.

The realization of where she was returned with shocking suddenness. She jerked around to stare at the tent's entry. Sunlight poured into the cramped interior along with the Lieutenant, who was carrying a small tray laden with two cups, their hot contents sending steam swirling up onto the crisp morning air. The aroma of strongly brewed coffee instantly filled the tent and made Teresa's stomach growl, reminding her, embarrassingly, of how long it had been since she'd had anything to eat.

She watched him enter and walk past her. He was dressed in his uniform, everything buttoned and in place, unlike the night before when his jacket had been open and his suspenders had hung at his thighs. The dark blue fabric of his officer's jacket stretched taut across his shoulders and back and accentuated the ripple of muscle and strength that lay just beneath the tightly woven threads. His snug-fitting trousers with their gold corded outer seams disappeared into the same knee-high black boots she'd polished the night before.

He had an air of confidence about him that sent a shiver of trepidation up her spine. There was no doubt in her mind that Lieutenant Brett Forsythe was a man who took to command easily.

His hair, which she'd admired the night before, caught the light of the oil lamp on his desk and shone golden, as if to rival the fringed epaulets sewn to the shoulders of his uniform.

She had known few men with hair of that unique color, especially southerners. Most of the men she'd been allowed to associate with before her marriage had been Creoles, their families dating back beyond the founding of New Orleans, most able to trace their ancestry to France and its royals, as could her mother. Those men were dark, their skin burnished bronze, their hair, like her brothers and her own, as black as the night, and their eyes like obsidian.

Teresa stared up at him. There had been one, a long time ago, who'd had that same golden hair. A friend of Traynor's. She tried to recall the young man who'd been her brother's friend, but it was so long ago.

Her eyes narrowed with her thoughts. Was it possible that the Lieutenant . . . Teresa tore her gaze from him and looked down into her lap, but she could not force it to stay there. She looked back up at him. What would it be like to kiss this man? To be held in those arms that looked so strong? The thought was like a slap to her face, the shock of it almost as painful and real as her father's hand had been the many times it had slammed into the soft flesh of her cheek. But before Teresa could wonder about or even rationalize her musing, she remembered with sudden horror that she'd fainted. He must have put her on the cot and covered her up. Her hand flew to her hat to make certain that her hair was still covered. The other hand clutched at the front of her open jacket.

She stared at the Lieutenant's back as he walked directly to his desk and set the tray down on its marred surface, pushing several sheaths of paper aside in the process. Did he know? Had he realized during the night while she'd slept that she wasn't a man? Teresa practically held her breath, afraid to speak, afraid to draw his attention to her.

"So, Private . . ." Brett picked up both cups of coffee and turned toward her. He frowned. "Sorry, I forgot your name." He offered her one of the steaming cups. While she'd slept he'd had a long time to think about how to play this thing out. He'd infiltrated the Yankee encampment in order to assess their strengths. Now that he had that information and had sent it on with the agent who had been following Teresa, he could turn his mind solely back to the task of capturing Jay Proschaud. That meant sticking close to Teresa—he couldn't let her out of his sight. But they also couldn't leave the encampment, not until the agent he'd sent to Richmond to arrange things returned and assured him that everything was set and ready.

Jay Proschaud had escaped him twice before. It was not going to happen again. He stared down at Teresa, waiting for her to respond. He hadn't forgotten the name she'd given him, but he couldn't change his tactic with her either. He'd been brusque. He was an officer. She was masquerading as a private, and he had to treat her as such in order to keep up the charade.

Teresa looked up at him, totally stupefied at his asking her name. What had she told him? Her mind was a complete blank.

Her fingers brushed his and a tingling of warmth suddenly gamboled its way up her arm, leaving her almost more dumbfounded than she'd been seconds earlier. The sense of familiarity she'd experienced the night before while looking into his eyes washed over her again, yet she could not tear her gaze from his, as she knew she should.

Lord help her, how had she gotten herself into this mess? Teresa raised the cup to her lips and sipped at the coffee. Its heat warmed her insides while its content promised to partially satisfy her empty stomach.

Teresa glanced back up at him. She was playing a dangerous game, and if she had to lay odds on her progress, right now she'd have to say she was losing. Her hands trembled and she felt her heartbeat accelerate as fear slowly, steadily, engulfed her. She gripped the coffee cup with both hands to keep from spilling the hot liquid all over herself.

Brett felt a sudden and surprising jolt of awareness course through his body as their eyes met. If his mind had earlier registered the fact that Teresa Braggette was no longer a little girl, his body was just now discovering it in full force. And it was letting him know, in no uncertain terms, that it liked what it sensed was hidden beneath the dirt, grime, and baggy clothes. He tried to steel himself against the feeling, tried to tell himself that he had a job to do here, nothing more. It didn't work. His body continued to harden as his very sense of her presence heightened with each passing second.

The sensation was confusing, as well as new. He usually liked his women in silk and lace, smelling of expensive Parisian perfumes, adorned with precious stones or pearls . . . not dressed like a boy and smelling like a combination of river mud and the rotted remains of last week's dinner.

He pushed the troubling thoughts away and silently ordered his body to calm down. He felt pity for her. That was all. And concern. After all, she was his best friend's little sister. Brett had to use her, to deceive her so he could find out what Jay Proschaud and his organization was up to, but he still had enough honor left to prevent him from seducing her.

He forced himself to ignore the passionate gnawings within him. "Private." His tone was harsh and demanding, more so than he'd intended. "I asked you your name."

Teresa jerked her hat down onto her forehead. "Uh . . ." Lord, what had she told him? She didn't remember!

"Is that too hard a question for you, Private?" Brett snapped. He hadn't meant to be so curt, but realized it was the safest way.

"Uh, yes . . . uh, I mean no, sir," Teresa mumbled. She grabbed at her father's name. "Thomas, sir."

"Thomas," he repeated, and continued to look down at her, his eyes cold, hard, and empty.

Teresa nodded, forced the cup to her lips, and sipped at the coffee again. She wished a sudden storm would split the sky and send a bolt of lightning into the center of the tent. Then he wouldn't continue to stare at her so intently. She fidgeted on the cot.

"Thomas . . . what?" he demanded.

"Uh . . ." Thomas what? Certainly not Braggette. Think Teresa, think. She looked up at him. What would any of her brothers do in this situation? Probably throw a fist into his face, she thought instantly, but that was out of the question. Her fist would do him little damage and probably infuriate him to the point of hanging her. "Um, Thomas . . . ah . . ." She suddenly remembered the last name of an old beau, a man her father had refused to allow to court her. "Smithers, sir."

Brett moved back to his desk and settled into the wooden folding chair behind it. Sometimes he thought it would have been so much simpler if he'd have just joined the army and fought on the front lines instead of becoming a government agent. How many names had he used in the past three years? How many different personas had he assumed? How many people had he hurt while trying to serve his country and help to save it?

But as soon as feelings of guilt settled over him, he shrugged them away. He was doing what had to be done. His gaze moved back to Teresa and the last vestiges of guilt were replaced by the resentment he felt toward her for what he suspected she was doing. But if she was going to play the ruse she was going to have to get a lot better at it than this. "Smithers, uh? That's funny, I could swear that last night you said it was Smith."

Her heart plunged to her feet and her hands trembled. She looked down at the cup and saw the coffee splash softly against its sides. She had to play it out. It was her only chance. She looked back up at him. "Ah, no sir, Smithers." Now all she could do was pray.

Brett frowned. "I could have sworn you said Smith."

Teresa wished he'd go swear somewhere else. Anywhere else.

Brett reached for a sheath of papers in front of him. "I've got some paperwork to do. There's a biscuit and a couple of strips of bacon here on the tray for you."

Teresa looked at the plate. The mere thought of food made her mouth water. But she shook her head, not wanting to move nearer to him. He made her uncomfortable. Actually, to be truthful, he scared the daylights out of her, and it wasn't just because he was a Yankee officer. It was also because of the unwelcome and unwarranted emotions his nearness seemed to stir within her. She eyed the food and tried not to inhale the tantalizing aroma of the bacon. How long had it been since she'd eaten?

Not nearly as long as it's been since you kissed a man.

The thought almost made her choke on the coffee.

Brett glanced up. "It's going to be a long day, Private. I'd suggest you eat something. I might want you to accompany me on my rounds later."

Rounds? She didn't want to accompany him on his rounds, or anywhere else, for that matter. She wanted to leave . . . to be on her way. She *had* to leave. Her stomach growled.

Brett's brows rose slightly but he didn't say anything. Instead he looked back down at his papers.

Teresa pushed herself off the cot. There was no denying that she was hungry, and it didn't make sense not to eat when the food was right there. Anyway, she needed to keep up her strength if she hoped to escape him anytime soon. Keeping her head down, she hurried across the small room, grabbed a biscuit and several pieces of bacon, and shuffled back to the cot.

No sooner had she sat down than Brett stood. "I've arranged for you to stay with me."

Her head jerked up and she stared at him with eyes that she knew mirrored her alarm. But there was no help for it. *He knew!* He knew she was a woman and he was going to . . . going to treat her like . . . going to force her to . . . Teresa's heart hammered against her breast. Why else would he want her to *stay* with him?

Brett saw the look of stark panic that flashed across her face and felt a smug satisfaction. He'd purposely worded his announcement that way, just to see what she would do or say. Inside she had obviously reacted to the comment as a woman, while on the outside she was struggling to remain nonchalant. But the more he goaded her, the more he was beginning to believe that Teresa Braggette was no traitor, at least not intentionally. Nor did he believe she was attempting to spy on movements within the Yankee encampment. Her reactions to his harsh words seemed too innocent and real, yet it was more than that. It was the look in her eyes, a look that told him she lacked the cunning and guile her husband possessed in such abundance.

Nevertheless, he was still not totally convinced that she had nothing to do with Jay Proschaud's treacherous schemes. After all, hadn't Brett himself honed his own acting skills to near perfection?

"You'll be under my direct command now," Brett said. "I've been in need of an aide."

"But . . ."

His features tightened. "I'm offering you a way to stay off the front lines, Smithers." He glowered down at her. If she refused his offer she'd destroy her own cover. No man, no matter how loyal or gallant, would pass up a way to stay out of a bullet's path. On the other hand, if she accepted, he'd get what he wanted—a way to keep her close to him until they were in Richmond and his men were in place to watch her.

"But Lieutenant, I've got to . . . I mean, what about my own . . ." Teresa's mind searched frantically for the right words. Her own *what?* Captain? Outfit? Company? What was it she should say? She bit down on her bottom lip. No matter what she said it would probably be wrong. The man was baiting her, she was sure. But why? Did he know who she was? Or did he always act so pompous?

She dared to look up at him. The morning light shone through the entry flap and seemed to seek him out, spraying its pale glow about him. Once more, against her will, Teresa was struck with how attractive she found him. His blond hair was slightly ruffled, one thick lock falling rebelliously onto his forehead to lend him a rather roguish look contrasting drastically with the neat officer's uniform and highly polished boots. His dark blue eyes suddenly seemed filled with expression, though not the kind she would have liked to see there. Ice bristled from those sapphire depths and accentuated the features that were tight with what could only be anger.

Without warning she found herself yearning to run into his arms. Never in her life had she been so instantly and thoroughly attracted to a man, not even with Jay, and the sensation terrified her.

Brett settled onto his desk chair, his dark eyes fixed on her with an intensity that nearly made her squirm. She felt as if he could see right through her. "There's no one else you need to report to, Private." His tone was as near a snarl as she'd ever heard. "You're officially my aide now."

His aide. The words might as well have been a death sentence. Rage burned deep within her. Panic seized her heart. She couldn't stay here. Jay was waiting for her in Richmond, and he'd implied that one of her brothers could die if she didn't show up.

Teresa stood and faced him, squaring her shoulders. "Sir, I really must . . ."

Brett slammed a hand down on his desk.

Startled, Teresa jumped at the murderous look that suddenly glimmered from his dark eyes.

"It's settled," he growled.

"But . . ."

Brett wrote something on one of the papers before him and set it aside, but he didn't look up again. Instead he grabbed another sheet of paper. "As soon as you've finished your breakfast you'll accompany me down to the corrals. I want you to know which horse is mine so you can care for him personally. When we're done there I want you to bring my saddle back here. It needs a good cleaning and oiling."

His saddle. Thoughts of Jay, her brother, and escape momentarily fled her mind. Teresa's temper flared. Maybe she could use one of the saddle's stirrups to bash his head in. Then she could get out of this blasted camp and away from that hauntingly familiar face.

Then another thought struck her, offering just a bit of comfort. If she accompanied him to the stables she would know where StarDancer was.

For the next eight hours Teresa waited and watched for a chance to escape the Lieutenant. She struggled to maintain control over a temper that was threatening to mount beyond a thin veil of restraint.

He had not only insisted that she look at his horse, but then watched over her as he instructed her to inspect the animal's hooves, frogs, legs, withers, and hindquarters. Of course, what she was looking for she had no idea. She was used to riding horses, not taking care of them, other than to offer them an occasional apple or carrot.

Then he'd accompanied her back to the tent where he'd immersed himself in a pile of paperwork, stopping only occasionally when another officer entered the tent on some pretext or other.

All the while Teresa sat on the cot and cleaned and oiled his saddle, silently labeling him with every profanity she'd ever heard, she desperately wished she'd visited Madame Truseaux' shop before leaving

New Orleans. A voodoo curse or potion would have come in handy—maybe something that would turn him into a toad.

She'd no sooner finished with the saddle than he ordered her to clean the tent, then wash the sheets and blanket for his cot, then all his shirts, as well as polish another pair of boots. By the time evening settled over the camp Teresa's temper was near to bursting. She was Teresa Braggette of New Orleans, not his personal maid, horse groomer, military aide, or anything else!

But she didn't, because that would have been the stupidest thing she could do. It would spoil everything and then she'd never be on her way. Especially once they discovered she was a southern woman who had disguised herself as a man to slip past their lines. They'd put Rose Greenhow in a Yankee prison the first time she'd been suspected of spying. When she'd been caught again they'd exiled her to Europe. Teresa felt a spurt of courage and hope—she knew they'd never execute her, or any other woman, for spying.

There's always a first time, the little voice at the back of her mind whispered.

Her momentary good spirits deflated. Getting herself executed wouldn't do anyone any good, least of all herself. One of her brothers would die and Tyler would grow up without either a mother or father.

"Smithers, tell the sentry to bring in a tub and some hot water."

She jerked around and looked at Brett as his words broke into her thoughts. He had pushed his dinner plate to the corner of his desk.

Teresa slipped the last bit of biscuit and pork strip into her mouth.

"Now," Brett roared.

She jumped up and threw back the entry flap. "Arrogant beast," she murmured under her breath. If she had any luck at all maybe he'd drown in his blasted bath.

A sentry stationed nearby turned as she stepped from the tent. "Bring the Lieutenant a tub and some hot water," Teresa ordered, remembering only at the last minute to drop her chin and keep her voice low. "And hurry."

"Yes, sir," the sentry answered, and hastened from his post.

Teresa let the entry flap fall back into place and returned to her seat on the cot. She flung a quick glance across the room. A frown tugged at her brow. There was something about him, something that seemed to flit before her memory ever so briefly every once in a while when she looked at him. She knew it was as familiar as her own name, and yet too elusive to identify.

As if he had sensed that her thoughts focused on him, Brett raised his head and regarded her steadily. Teresa immediately felt both defiant and nervous. What was he going to order her to do now?

His night-blue eyes moved slowly over her face and the hard emptiness that normally dwelt behind his thick lashes suddenly disappeared, almost like a theatre curtain being drawn. Warmth, strength, and much more glistened from within those immeasurable depths.

For one brief, almost timeless second, Teresa forgot

all about her animosity toward him, the fact that he was her enemy, and she was virtually his prisoner and slave. She fancied that they were somewhere else—away from the war with its treachery and death—two people, strangers in the night, with no worries or cares, and no differences to hold them apart.

The thought mortified her. Cold, icy sanity washed over her in a rush, dissipating any remnants of fantasy that might still linger about the edges of her mind. She had no right to think like that. Not now. Not ever. And especially not about him, a man who represented the very force that was trying to destroy her world. He was a traitor to his own kind; a southerner wearing a Yankee uniform. He was despicable, and she didn't want to feel anything for him unless it was hate.

That, however, was not what she was feeling, and no matter how much she tried she couldn't lie to herself and say it was. She felt anger and resentment, but when she looked at Lieutenant Brett Forsythe, much as she didn't want to admit it, hate was the farthest thing from her mind. Her face flushed and she dropped her head, blocking his view of her with the wide brim of her hat.

Then the tent flap flew open and Teresa jerked around to stare up at two men. They carried a large, badly dented and scratched green slipper tub.

"Your bath, sir," one announced.

Brett tore his gaze from Teresa at the interruption. He had been fully aware that as they'd stared into each other's eyes, both had momentarily lost the emotional protection they held so tightly about themselves—and it was not something he could allow to happen again.

She had a unique way about her—pretending to be a man, yet looking at him as a woman. Sensuality clung to her, radiated from her, and made a mockery of her attempt to disguise herself as a soldier. But she obviously did not know that, and he had to continue to play her game. Too many lives depended on him. He looked at the two soldiers who had entered the tent. "Put the tub down there," Brett said, and pointed to an area at the rear.

They did as ordered and returned seconds later with several steaming buckets of hot water and towels.

"Will there be anything else, sir?" one asked.

"No." Brett had tried to turn his attention back to the papers on his desk, which were no more than his own coded notes, but he was too aware of Teresa sitting silently upon the cot.

The soldiers left.

Teresa stood. "I should lea . . ."

Brett rose and moved to stand beside the tub. He knew exactly what she thought she should do, and the opportunity to escape that it would allow her, and he had no intention of letting her leave the tent. "Soap's in my trunk," he said over his shoulder. He slid out of his jacket and began to unbutton his shirt. "There's also a wash brush in there." He shrugged the shirt over his shoulders.

Lamplight shone richly upon his lightly bronzed skin, creating deep canyons of shadow within the contours of his physique. His shoulders were as broad as she'd imagined them to be, vast landscapes of muscle—tight, hard, and well honed yet still sinewy and lean. When he turned to toss his shirt on the desk chair she saw that a fine feathering of blond hair covered the upper portion of his chest, a sprinkling of short, silky threads whose path narrowed dramatically as it disappeared beneath the waistband of his trousers.

Teresa felt her breath catch and tore her gaze from him. He was disrobing! She moved quickly, wanting to get him his soap and brush and get out of the tent before his hands dropped to the belt buckle at his waist.

She found them, slammed the lid of the trunk closed, and turned to hand him the requested items.

The belt buckle hung loose and the buttons of his trousers had been unfastened. Teresa watched, mesmerized, as his thumbs slipped beneath the waistband of the trousers and he began to push them down over his hips.

Seven

Teresa dashed toward the tent flap.

"Smithers."

She stopped, but didn't turn. Panic engulfed her as her heart beat frantically. She couldn't stay here. In a moment he would be naked, standing before her without a stitch of clothing. Fear lodged in her throat like a ball of cotton, dry and suffocating, threatening to cut off her air.

She'd never seen a man naked before. Not even Jay. They'd only made love twice, once before their wedding, and once on their wedding night, but on both occasions Jay had come to her in the dark. She'd only seen his silhouette. And barely that.

"Where do you think you're going?" Brett asked.

Where *was* she going? Teresa stared at the tent flap and tried to think of an answer. Her eyes stung with unshed tears. She was ruining her own plan. Her hands curled into fists and she dug her short fingernails into the fleshy palms of her hands. She had to think of an answer. Any answer. She blinked rapidly. "I . . . I thought I'd get you more hot water."

She had barely finished speaking when a soft thunking sound behind her caused her to jump and she realized something had fallen to the ground. Teresa swallowed hard and continued to stare at the closed tent flap, her back stiff, shoulders rigid. Something, instinct perhaps, told her the sound had been that of his metal belt buckle hitting the hard earth floor of the tent.

"Later," Brett said.

Teresa felt like screaming. She heard the sounds of water splashing against the tub's tin sides as he stepped into it. She closed her eyes—tight. If the Lord was ever going to help her out of a tight situation, He'd better do it now.

A slow, whispery hiss slipped from his lips as he settled his body into the tub and moaned in appreciation.

For one second Teresa forgot about escape and found herself wishing she could trade places with him. She would give just about anything to rid herself of these horrible, filthy, stinking clothes and settle her body into that lovely, steaming, hot water.

"Forget more water for now, Smithers," Brett said, interrupting her musings and jerking her mind back to the reality of the situation. "I've got enough. You can come on over here and scrub my back though."

Teresa started and struggled to stifle a shriek of disbelief and indignation. Scrub his back? Was he kidding? She ducked her head and turned to look over her shoulder, peering at him through the tiny space between her shoulder and the brim of her hat. He was looking at her expectantly, which meant he obviously hadn't been kidding. Teresa cursed silently. When she got hold of Jay she'd kill him for getting her into this, and she wouldn't be merciful about it either.

She turned, a sinking feeling beginning in the pit of her stomach, and walked back across the tent. She wouldn't look, that was all. She just wouldn't look at anything but his back. She'd keep her gaze glued to his shoulders. She'd stare at them, wash them, and rinse them for him, and then she'd leave—no matter what he said. Teresa picked up the brush and soap.

Brett leaned forward in the tub. "Start at the top, Smithers, and work your way down."

She stared at the wide expanse of muscle that was now slick with water. His skin was a surface of glistening bronze, rich and sensual, and she suddenly ached to touch him. Her fingers curled with tension in response to her thoughts, but it was not enough to stop her. She dipped one hand into the hot water to wet the bar of soap and then touched it to his back. A shiver rippled through her fingers and up her arm at the contact with his bare flesh. Mesmerized by the sight of him, intoxicated by the rush of feelings that gripped her at the innocent contact, Teresa moved the wet rag over his back, her eyes caressing the muscular spread of his shoulders, the curve of his neck, the golden waves of his hair.

"Ah, that's it," Brett said. He closed his eyes and let his head fall forward.

She made circles on his back with the soap, then moved the rag slowly, seductively over them, her fingers feeling his flesh even through the thin bit of cloth.

"God, that feels good."

Teresa jerked her hand away, his words suddenly penetrating the quixotic haze she had momentarily allowed herself. She didn't want to make him feel good. Teresa stared down at him in horror. She didn't want to make him feel anything at all.

"Don't stop," he said, his voice husky and deep.

She picked up the scrubbing brush and touched it to his back. This was safer. At least she didn't have to actually touch him.

Another moan slipped from Brett's lips. If this wasn't heaven then it was as close to it as he'd been in the last couple of years. He relaxed further. At the moment it was very easy to ignore the fact that she was his best friend's sister. It was even easier to forget that he strongly suspected she was guilty of treason. But it was becoming difficult to ignore the gnawing hungers raging deep within his body as it constantly reminded him of how aware he was that Teresa Braggette, beneath the dirt and grime, had grown into a very attractive young woman. And it had been some time since he'd been with a woman.

She set the brush on the nearby trunk and Brett settled against the back of the tub's raised rear panel. "Front," he said simply.

Teresa stood beside him but made no move to follow his orders. He looked up at her.

She stared down at him, her eyes full of disbelief.

Desire and anger waged war within him. He wanted her, there was no use denying that, but try as he might he could not totally forget that she was a traitor's wife, and quite possibly a traitor herself—to everything he believed in, everything he and her brothers had put their lives on the line to defend for the past four years. It was no excuse for the way he'd been treating her, yet he couldn't help it. Brett clenched his teeth, hard. Much as he hated admitting it, even to himself, he knew he had to continue to treat her harshly for fear of what might happen between them if he didn't.

"Front?" she finally echoed. "You . . . you want me to wash your front?"

"Yes, Smithers," he growled, forcing his tone to be cold and brutal. "I believe that's the order I issued." He propped his arms up on the tub's rim to give her full access to his body, including the lower portion, obscured from sight only by the soapy film floating on the water.

Teresa's gaze remained riveted on the opaque surface, wanting and yet not wanting to penetrate its murky depths, knowing she had to follow his orders. A sharp gasp shook Brett when she picked up the soap again and hesitantly touched it to his chest. Fire rippled through his flesh, igniting every male cell with a sudden, desperate need as her hand slipped into the water and slid over the taut muscles of his stomach. His body turned hard and rigid as desire burned hot in his groin.

He stared at her as she kept her eyes averted, her face turned away as much as possible. God, had it been so long since he'd enjoyed the pleasures of a woman that he would lust after one clothed in filthy rags and looking about as sensual as his sentry?

But even making the effort to continually remind himself that she was his best friend's sister, another man's wife, and that she might be voluntarily working with both Proschaud and the KGC didn't lessen the need simmering within him and stoked to fury by her touch.

A long-forgotten sense of home and warmth invaded him as he looked at her, attacking the inner sanctuary of solitude that was his bulwark against a world that had turned ugly and was desperately, brutally trying to destroy itself.

Unable to stop the wild imaginings of his mind, and afraid he was about to lose all self-control, Brett gripped the sides of the tub and abruptly pushed to his feet. Water sloshed over the high tin rim.

Sputtering as a soapy spray covered her, Teresa jumped to her feet.

The foolishness of his move hit Brett the moment he saw her face. She stared at him in shock, her mouth agape, her eyes as big as saucers. Brett looked down. "Damn it all to hell!" He hadn't stopped to think about the fact that he was naked. Worse, that he was so aroused by her caresses it would be obvious even to a blind man. Stepping from the tub, he quickly grabbed for one of the towels that lay on the trunk.

Teresa watched him, horrified and fascinated. Streams of water ran down over his body, transformed by the light of the lamp to cascading rivers that glistened silver as they snaked over the golden landscape of his torso. The thin, twisting rivulets moved over, around or between every curve of sinew, every muscle.

His flesh was a rippling plane of bronze, burnished to perfection. The light of the lamp touched the blond curls that covered his chest. They glinted gold and drew her gaze. She had averted her eyes while he disrobed, but now she found she couldn't—nor did she want to. Her gaze followed the path of those silken strands as they moved down in an ever-thinning line, over the rippling landscape of his ribs and the taut surface of his stomach.

He stood proudly, watching her and not moving.

Her gaze jumped to his legs which were well muscled, yet long and lean. His hips were slim.

But the hard, swollen member that protruded from a thick mass of blond curls just below his stomach was what her gaze kept returning to time after time. Her eyes repeatedly defied the command of her mind to look away, her legs refused to run, her pulses refused to slow.

Teresa became quite still, suddenly unable to breathe. The blood in her veins roared in her ears, her heart hammered frantically, wildly, within her chest. Never in her life had she seen a man like this, or known a man could be so beautiful.

Brett snapped the towel he'd grabbed and wrapped it around his waist, tucking one end into the other to hold it in place.

The abrupt movement startled Teresa from her trance. She jumped, blinked rapidly, and felt her cheeks burn with embarrassment at the realization of how blatantly she'd stared at him. But worse, at how wanton she'd suddenly found her thoughts.

Brett grabbed his shirt and slipped it on without drying himself off, then glanced back at her. "Go ahead and take a bath, Smithers. The water's still hot."

Teresa's gaze snapped up to meet his. "Take . . . take a bath?" She clutched at the front of her shirt.

"Isn't that what I just said?" he barked. Brett cursed softly. He was so damned angry with himself he could barely think. That had been the stupidest thing he'd ever done. If he hadn't been so outraged with himself he might have laughed at the expression his act had brought to her face. But as it was, he didn't find it amusing. Once he'd thought of himself as a gentleman. Obviously, considering how he'd been treating Teresa, the war had changed that. A scowl creased his face and fury filled his heart. If his honor as a gentleman was found lacking because of his duty to his country, then so be it. There was no honor in being a traitor, yet he was beginning to feel no honor at being the one to catch a traitor. At least not this traitor. "No sense wasting the water when it's still hot." He glanced coldly at her. "Anyway, by the looks of those clothes, you could do with a little soap and water."

"Oh, no, sir, really." She took a step back and dropped her gaze to the ground. "That isn't necessary, really." The words were a lie, maybe the biggest she'd ever told in her life. She wanted to bathe. Lord, how she wanted to, but she couldn't take her clothes off in front of him! Unless that was exactly what he wanted. Her eyes darted up to meet his again and her chin rose in defiance. Could it be that he knew the truth and wanted to see her disrobe? Wanted to humiliate her before he denounced her?

Brett grabbed his trousers but paused to stare at her before putting them on. "If you're going to be my aide, Private, the bath *is* necessary. You stink."

"Oh!" No man had ever talked to her that way. A sharp retort formed on her lips, only to be swallowed. Someday, when there was no longer any reason for this horrid disguise, she'd find Lieutenant Brett Forsythe and . . . and . . . Fury washed over her in roiling waves. She didn't know what she'd do, but she'd think of something, some way to get even.

But at the moment she had to think of a way to get into that tub without disrobing in front of him.

"I . . . ah . . . maybe I should . . ." Her mind searched for a means of escape while she tried to convince herself that her secret was still secure, in spite of the situation. Yet at the same time she was very much aware of him.

His gaze locked with hers. One brow soared upward in question as his eyes seemed to darken at her hesitation.

He knew what she was thinking, and what she was afraid of. But she didn't know that he knew who she was, and for the time being it was best to keep it that way. How many times had he played this game with others? Knowing, because of his contacts and intricate chain of informants, everything they knew, what they were about to do, how they thought, what they wanted. Most times he enjoyed the game of cat and mouse, but this time was different. This time he wasn't enjoying it at all.

Brett swore silently. Using Teresa to get to Proschaud was about the lowest thing he'd ever done, yet he didn't have a choice. Proschaud had to be stopped, and that was the bottom line.

"Is there some reason you don't want to bathe, Private Smithers?" His tone was purposely harsh and goading, even threatening, and he saw her flinch from fear. He wasn't immune to the guilt his actions caused, but knew it was better this way, for both of them. If he allowed himself to drop his guard, to feel compassion or understanding even for one second, something could happen between them that shouldn't. She was definitely a woman, in spite of the horrible costume she'd chosen to wear. Taking her would be easy—if he allowed it to happen, which he wouldn't.

"I . . . uh, well . . . I . . ."

Brett reminded himself that her actions, if she was Proschaud's accomplice, could be directly responsible for the deaths of many young men. Some were even his friends. It helped to harden him against her and chase away the desire burning in his groin. "Don't people bathe where you came from, Smithers?"

Teresa stiffened. "Well, of course we bathe," she snapped, momentarily forgetting to keep her voice low and deep.

"Good. Then get to it." He pulled his trousers on and discarded the towel, then yanked the suspenders up over his shoulders and grabbed his jacket. "I've got to go and talk with Captain Laelswood. If you finish bathing before I return, oil my holster and belt."

Oil his holster and belt? Teresa glared after him as he stepped past the flap and let it fall closed behind him. Is that all he thought of, finding work for her to do? She'd oil his holster and belt all right. Maybe so good that it would slip down around his ankles and trip him so he'd break that Yankee neck of his.

Several seconds passed before she moved, then she glanced down at the still bath water.

The tent flap suddenly flew back.

Teresa jumped.

The sentry stepped into the tent. "Lieutenant said to give you these." He laid a clean shirt and a pair of trousers on the cot. "One of the other guys was washing them for the Lieutenant but he said to tell you to wear them."

Teresa nodded and the man left. She walked over to the cot. Clean clothes. Lord, but it would feel good to put on clean clothes, even if they were men's clothes. She glanced down at her filthy garments. They smelled so bad she could barely stand herself. It was a wonder the Lieutenant could bear having her in the same tent with him.

Teresa hurried back to the tub and ripped the dirty clothes from her body. Just getting them off felt wonderful. She removed her camisole and pantalettes hesitantly, glancing warily at the tent flap every half-second, afraid someone would suddenly appear and see her. No one did. She tossed the hat down next to her underthings but left her hair pinned up in a mass of curls. Throwing one last look at the entry flap, she hastily stepped into the tub and sank down until she was submerged in water to her chin.

"Oh, saints be praised," she murmured softly as a sigh of contentment slipped from her lips.

The soothing warmth penetrated her flesh, caressed her tired muscles, and massaged the soreness from her bones. Two days and nights in the saddle had left her aching everywhere. Teresa laid her head back upon the raised rim of the tub and closed her eyes.

Now this was heaven.

An hour later Teresa woke with a start. The water was nearly cold and one side of her hair had come unfastened so that long black curls lay loose upon her bare shoulder.

Something had startled her into wakefulness. Her heart raced. She gripped the sides of the tin tub. But what? What had caused her to wake so abruptly? She frowned and listened to the silence, straining to hear something.

"Yes, two dinners, Private, and leave orders with your counterpart that I don't want to be disturbed otherwise." The deep voice boomed loudly against the silence of the night.

Teresa bolted away from the raised rear rim of the tub and twisted around to stare in horror at the closed entry flap. The Lieutenant was back and he was about to enter the tent. Teresa felt a rush of panic. If he came in now he'd see her naked. He'd know the truth. She scrambled from the tub. Cold, soapy water splashed over its rim and soaked the surrounding ground.

Shivering almost uncontrollably, Teresa grabbed the clean shirt and trousers from the cot and frantically tugged them on over her wet skin. A shudder rippled through her, as much from fear as from being chilled. "Oh, Lord help me," she pleaded softly. She rammed the hat back onto her head and hastily tucked several rebellious locks under it, then crammed her feet into the scuffed and worn boots she'd stolen off the dead soldier.

She was just grabbing for a jacket the sentry had brought with the shirt and trousers when the tent flap was drawn back and Brett entered.

"I had James burn your old clothes." He had meant to keep his gaze from hers, to walk directly to his desk and look over the entries he'd recorded in his journal earlier. Instead he paused just inside the tent and allowed himself, just for a moment, to enjoy the unexpectedly erotic image she unwittingly projected.

She was dressed in the clothing he'd had the sentry bring her, a pair of Brett's own trousers and a spare shirt, but she had yet to cover herself with the baggy jacket, and obviously unbeknownst to her a lock of long black hair had escaped the quickly donned hat and lay curled upon her shoulder. Its tip touched the soft swell of one breast, starkly evident through the crisp white of his shirt.

Brett felt a sudden and powerful urge to close the space between them, to reach out and lift that glistening black lock of hair and let it slide slowly through his fingers. He wanted to cover her breast with his hand, feel the hard tip of her nipple press against his palm. Her eyes were wide as she stared back at him, their gray-blue depths swirling with emotion, not the least of which was fear. The thick, dark lashes that surrounded those eyes and the gracefully arching brows that curved above them were a vivid contrast to the silken ivory of her skin, while the pert, upturned nose was all a man really needed to see to know that Teresa Braggette was a woman of sass, spirit, and temper.

And she was a woman he should not have any thoughts about other than that she was going to lead him to the traitor he'd been trying to capture for over two years. He moved past her to sit at his desk.

Teresa clutched the jacket to her breast and waited,

fraught with tension and expecting him to turn and scream that he knew she was a woman.

Instead he began to shuffle through a pile of papers, not even bothering to look up at her. "They smelled so bad that after another few hours in the company of those rags I'd probably have lost my sense of smell."

She wanted to be angry with him, to feel fury at his insolent tone, but she couldn't. She was too glad to be rid of those clothes even to work up a pique at his arrogance. Teresa hurriedly jerked on the jacket and buttoned it over her bosom.

Their dinner arrived a few minutes later. Brett made no attempt to draw her into conversation so they ate in silence. Afterward, while he sipped at a cup of coffee, he again leafed through the papers on his desk.

Teresa sat on the cot trying to clean the dead soldier's boots.

Suddenly Brett rose.

Teresa jumped at the abrupt movement.

He looked at her and then quickly averted his gaze. "I have to speak with Captain Laelswood again. I'll be back shortly." He walked to the entry flap. "You might as well stay here and relax."

Teresa stared after him, surprised at the abrupt departure. Then she breathed a sigh of relief. At least he hadn't found something else for her to polish or oil. A spark of hope ignited within her. She rose and walked to the tent flap, moving slightly aside to peek out. The sentry stood only a few feet away, but she'd been fairly certain that would be the case. She couldn't escape, but she could do something else.

She turned around and moved to the foot of his cot, then kneeled before the trunk that sat there. She'd seen a stack of papers and a notebook in it when she'd retrieved his soap and brush earlier.

Teresa took a deep breath and prayed that Brett wouldn't return until she was done and the sentry would not find a reason to enter the tent. She flipped open the trunk's lid and hurriedly began to rifle through its contents until she found the notebook. Pulling it out, Teresa sat back on her haunches and eagerly flipped through its pages. Excitement quickly turned to disappointment, hope to despair. The pages of the notebook were covered by writing but it was all in code. The papers were merely expense ledgers, a few old newspaper clippings, and some sheets of unused writing paper. She replaced the notebook and was about to close the trunk when she saw the corner of what appeared to be a letter protruding from beneath a folded shirt.

Teresa pulled it out and held it up. The name written across the front of the envelope was Ben Morgan but that's not what held her attention. She didn't know the name, but she did know the handwriting. It was Jay's, she was certain of it. He had a most unusual script, which she'd always admired for its graceful curves and flourishes.

"Make certain you stay alert tonight, Private."

As if touched by fire, Teresa snatched her hand from the trunk and the letter fell onto one of Brett's folded shirts. Her gaze snapped up and toward the tent flap.

Eight

The tent flap opened and Brett stepped inside. "Goodnight, Private Simms," he said over his shoulder, and let the canvas flap fall behind him. He looked across the room at Teresa and she suddenly realized she was still kneeling down before his trunk.

"I . . . I was just going to put the brush and soap back into your trunk."

"Good." He moved around his desk and sat down. "Those things aren't too easy to come by anymore."

The tent flap flew open and the sentry stepped inside. He saluted Brett. "Sir, I have the other cot you requested."

Brett looked up. "Set it up over there." He pointed to a spot just to the right of the entry flap. "And take this tub and water out, would you, Simms?"

"I'll help," Teresa said. She stood. This was what she'd been waiting for: a chance to get away.

"No, I have something else for you to do, Smithers," Brett said.

His words stopped Teresa in her tracks.

She looked at him, wanting nothing more at the moment than to pick up the inkwell on his desk and bash him over the head with it. *Something else for her to do.* He always had something for her to do.

Frustration with him, with the situation, nearly overwhelmed her. She had to get out of there and go to Richmond.

The sentry set the cot up in the corner of the tent opposite Brett's cot, then turned and, picking up the pails that had earlier been used to carry in hot bath water, dipped them into the tub.

Brett smiled and Teresa started. She'd seen that kind of look before. It was the kind a man gave a woman when he was thinking about . . . No, that was impossible. He wouldn't look at a man like that. And he did think she was a man. Her heart slammed against her breast. Didn't he?

She felt a moment's spurt of panic and pushed it aside. Of course he thought she was a man. He'd most likely have her instantly carted off in leg irons if he even suspected the truth. Or have her flat on her back in his bed. That last thought brought with it a shiver of fear that threatened to explode into uncontrollable panic.

"Sleep."

Teresa looked at him in surprise. "Sleep?" she repeated.

"Yes. The something else I have for you to do . . . sleep. Neither one of us got much last night. I'm thinking of taking a reconnaissance ride tomorrow, but an aide who's asleep in his saddle won't do me any good."

"A reconnaissance ride," Teresa echoed. Where? She wanted desperately to ask and yet knew she couldn't. It wasn't a private's place to question an officer. She didn't want to ride anywhere with him. Then the foolishness of her resistance dawned on her.

Accompanying him on a reconnaissance ride might just provide her the opportunity to escape.

Brett rose and moved around his desk toward her.

Teresa took a step backward, her thoughts jerked back to the present. Tomorrow she might escape, but tonight she still had to play the charade. She looked up at him and suddenly wished she hadn't. His eyes met hers for a few seconds, then dropped to travel over her body. Teresa felt her breath catch in her throat. A gentleman did not look at a lady that way. She opened her mouth to issue a sharp reprimand but the words hadn't even formed in her mind before she snapped her jaws closed. *A gentleman did not look at a lady that way.* The words echoed in her mind over and over.

She felt her hands tremble and clasped them together behind her back. The silence between them spun out as each regarded the other.

His gaze dropped and Teresa knew instantly that drawing her arms behind her had caused her breasts to push against the jacket front. She instantly unclasped her hands and crossed them over her breasts.

A hint of a smile, or smirk, pulled at one corner of his mouth.

A gentleman did not look at a lady that way. The words kept repeating in her mind, stoking the already mounting panic that filled her body. But his blatant look was also stoking something else within her, causing her to feel things she shouldn't feel, think of things she shouldn't think of, yearn for things that were totally impossible.

Panic overrode common sense. She turned away

from him and stumbled toward the tent flap. "I . . . I think I'll get some coffee."

Moving with more speed than she'd thought possible for a human being, Brett came around the desk and closed his hand around her arm before she had taken more than several steps.

Reaching for the tent flap, her arm stopped in midair, then dropped to her side. He jerked her around to face him. Sparks of anger glittered in his eyes. "I'll decide if and when you leave this tent, Private," Brett said, the words sounding harsher than anything he'd ever said to her.

Teresa stared up at him. The lamplight at his back left his face swathed in shadow, but not enough so that she couldn't see the hardness that had gripped his features.

Her heart beat in thick, uneasy strokes. His face was only inches from her own, and as they stood there Teresa became more aware of him than ever before. She felt the soft caress of his breath on her cheek, warm and smelling slightly of brandy. The scent blended with the faint odor of horses and leather that clung to his clothes.

She tried to pull away from him, not really wanting to yet knowing she should, but rather than release her, Brett's hold on her arm tightened and he jerked her toward him. Her body brushed against his, her breasts touching the hard wall of his chest. She felt the heat of his body radiate through hers, like fire touching her skin.

As abruptly as he'd grabbed her, Brett released her. He spun on his heel and returned to the chair behind his desk. "Go to bed, Smithers," he ordered gruffly.

But bed was the last thing on Teresa's mind. She sat on the cot, her head down, but not so much so that she wasn't able to glance furtively up at him from beneath the wide brim of her hat.

An hour or so later Brett tossed his shirt onto the trunk at the foot of his cot, turned, and sat back down. He raised a booted foot toward Teresa. "Since you haven't gone to bed yet, give me a pull, Smithers."

She rose from her cot without raising her head to look at him. He watched her as she knelt before him, took hold of the boot and yanked it from his foot. She then proceeded to do the same with the other one. She was either struggling to control her temper or her tears, he wasn't certain which.

He felt a wave of guilt, then quickly brushed it aside. He had a job to do and he was doing it. He might be acting a bit more harshly than he'd intended but there was no help for that. And there was nothing to feel guilty about. Hell, if anyone should feel guilty it was her. She was not only married to one of the most despicable human beings ever to walk the face of the earth, but she had most likely betrayed her own country as he had. Brett lay back on his cot, releasing a long, slow sigh and closing his eyes. What would her brothers think once this was over if it was proved that Teresa was a traitor to the Confederacy?

Not for the first time since she'd walked into his tent, Brett silently cursed the fates that had placed him in this situation. And along with that he cursed himself. Even now, lying on the hard and narrow length of his cot, his mind filled with the probability of her betrayal, his body was hard with the unreasonable desire he felt for her. It was ridiculous. He had never been so instantly attracted to a woman in his life. Perhaps it was just the excitement of being closer to capturing Jay Proschaud than ever before. Or maybe it was merely that he hadn't been with a woman for a while. There were a hundred things he could call to mind to excuse the hunger gnawing at his insides, but they would all be lies and he knew it.

He wished fervently that his agent would return from Richmond and tell him everything was ready. Then they could leave the Yankee encampment before it was discovered he didn't belong there at all. He could breathe easier once they were on their way, both because he could keep more of a distance between himself and Teresa, and because his plan would be moving toward its culmination, toward capturing Jay Proschaud at last. Brett turned his head and looked at Teresa lying on the cot across from him. How would she react when she found out who he really was? *What* he really was?

Brett turned and stared up at the canvas ceiling, illuminated now only by the soft glow of moonlight that filtered through its worn threads. Jay Proschaud was a traitor, but not because he'd done any favors for the Yankees. He was worse than that. In his zeal to further the Confederate cause, the small faction of Knights of the Golden Circle that he commanded had killed almost as many Confederates with their sabotage efforts as they had Yankees. And not all of them were soldiers, or even men. He tried to turn his thoughts in a different direction and blot out the images of the women and children who had suffered or been killed because of Jay Proschaud, but it didn't work. He couldn't forget their tearful faces. He would never forget.

Teresa lay with her back to Brett and stared at the canvas siding. The night was cold. A folded blanket had been placed on the cot earlier and she'd drawn it over herself. It offered a little warmth, but not enough to completely ward off the night's chill. The minutes dragged by. If she could get to StarDancer, she could escape. Minutes later she heard Brett's breathing turn soft and steady.

Teresa rose slowly, taking every precaution to be as quiet as she could. The last thing she wanted to do was wake him up. She pulled the tent flap aside and peeked out. The sentry was standing only a few feet away, smoking, and obviously quite alert. Teresa fumed in frustration and returned to the cot. Why was everything going wrong? All she wanted to do was get to Richmond, make certain her brother was safe, and go back home. Was that so terrible? So much to ask? She began to rock back and forth, boredom joining her frustration. She stared at Brett again, trying to remember where she'd seen him before, why he looked so familiar.

It was a terrifying feeling, knowing that you knew someone and not being able to remember the circumstances. Had it been a pleasant encounter or an unpleasant one? Was he one of those horrid Union soldiers who had occupied New Orleans three years before? Perhaps he was one of the very officers who had dragged her into General Butler's office and complained that she wasn't being "respectable enough" toward him?

Teresa almost snorted in disgust. Respectable! That

little escapade had almost gotten her branded a prostitute by that insufferable, ugly little commanding officer. But worse, a few days later she'd once again turned her nose up at a Union officer's advances and had again been hauled into General Butler's office. That time she'd told him in no uncertain terms that he had no right to order her to be nice to anyone, including his filthy Yankee officers. The man had turned a very unpleasant shade of purple and bellowed an order to his aide to take her to Jackson Square and have her shot.

Her gaze moved slowly over Brett's face. The only thing that had saved her life that day had been another Yankee officer. He'd talked to the general and convinced him that it wouldn't look good to put a southern woman before a Union firing squad. Even an impertinent southern woman.

Teresa sighed and rubbed her fingers over temples that had begun to throb. Lieutenant Forsythe wasn't that man. The Union officer who'd saved her life had been shorter and older, maybe forty or fifty, with a close-cropped beard and mustache riddled with gray.

Frustrated and out of patience, Teresa shot to her feet, her troubled thoughts and the headache that was quickly becoming intolerable making her forget the need for caution and silence. She glared down at Brett. So who was Lieutenant Brett Forsythe and why did he seem so blasted familiar? She felt like slamming her fists against his chest. Where had she met him? Where? Teresa stared down at him. Was it really possible that they'd met and he didn't remember either?

She glanced at the trunk at the foot of his cot and

remembered the letter she'd seen there. She was sure the handwriting on the envelope had been Jay's. But why would the Lieutenant have a letter Jay had written to someone else?

Because he'd intercepted it. The answer came to her mind almost instantly. She looked over at him. Why did she find herself not wanting to believe that when it so obviously made sense. The Lieutenant was a Yankee. Jay was a southerner and though he wasn't fighting in the Confederate army, Teresa had no doubt that whatever he was doing it was something to help the South and its cause. Whatever else Jay might be, she had no doubt that he was loyal to the South. Unlike Lieutenant Brett Forysthe.

Teresa frowned and nibbled at her lip. She had to know what was in that letter. It could be very important. But did she dare try to get to it now, with the Lieutenant in the tent? Her eyes darted back to look at him again. She didn't have a choice. If she didn't try now she might not get another chance.

Moving quietly, Teresa crept to the foot of his cot and knelt before the trunk. Hardly daring to breathe, she raised its lid, then glanced at the Lieutenant to make certain the faint rustling sound of her movements hadn't awakened him.

His breathing remained deep and steady.

Teresa reached inside the trunk and pulled out the envelope. She wasn't made for this kind of daring. Her hands were trembling almost uncontrollably and her heart was beating so fast she feared it might burst from her breast. She looked down at the envelope. The handwriting across its front was large, thick, and executed with a flourish. No two people could write so identically. It had to be Jay's. But the addressee was unknown to her. Ben Morgan. San Francisco, California.

She started to open the envelope, paused, and looked back at the addressee again. Ben Morgan. Teresa prowled through her memory. The name seemed vaguely familiar. Perhaps it was one of her father's business associates. She stared at it. But why would Jay be writing to him? And why would a Yankee officer have intercepted the letter unless . . . ? The frown that pulled at her forehead deepened. Unless it had something to do with the Knights of the Golden Circle.

She didn't know much about her father's affiliation with the secret organization, but she knew that her brothers had all joined at one time, and just as quickly disassociated themselves with the Knights. Had Thomas Braggette, before his death, taken Jay into that organization? Was that why he hadn't joined the army when the war broke out, because he was working with the KGC?

Teresa tried to remember what she knew of the Knights of the Golden Circle, which wasn't much. What she did know was that none of her brothers had anything good to say about it.

But sitting here speculating wasn't getting her anywhere. It was just wasting time. She opened the envelope, pulled out the letter, and unfolded it. It had been written by the same hand that had addressed the envelope. Her gaze darted to the bottom of the page—Jay's signature was scrawled at the end of the letter.

She'd been right—it was a letter from Jay. She

looked back at the Lieutenant. But why did *he* have it? Teresa hurriedly read the words Jay had written.

Ben,
Have everything under scontrol. Have written Teresa. She'll come. Project on. Meet us at the hotel in Richmond on April 2. Carlsberg managed to procure the supplies we need for the transfer. He found them in Boston and has transported. My trip to New Orleans was not as successful.

Teresa's fingers tightened their hold on the letter. Jay had been in New Orleans. Fury, hot and explosive, roiled within her breast, filled her blood, and left her wanting to scream. He'd been in New Orleans and not only had he not contacted her, he had not even come by the house to see his own son!

She forced her anger back and read on.

The blockade has prevented our cargo from leaving port, thereby further stalling the return supplies. We may have to change our plans there. I've managed, however, to make the necessary arrangements for our task in Richmond. All should go as planned. Hope you managed to get your end squared away in Virginia City.

Virginia City? Again Teresa stopped reading and sat staring at the words her husband had written. Travis was in Virginia City. Did the two have any connection?

Her mind pondered the question while her gaze returned to the letter.

See you in Richmond.
Jay Proschaud.

Teresa stared at the signature, looked up at the sleeping Lieutenant, then back at the letter. What was going on? Before reading the letter she only wondered why Lieutenant Forsythe had it. Now a dozen other questions filled her mind. What was the project Jay referred to, and why was he letting someone else know that she was coming to Richmond? She looked down at the letter again, re-reading the words. Her gaze stopped abruptly.

My trip to New Orleans was not as successful.

Her fingers began to curl about the paper as her anger grew, but the soft crumpling sounds it made as it was forced to fold in upon itself suddenly sounded ear-splittingly loud. Teresa stopped, frozen in place. She glanced toward the Lieutenant again. He hadn't stirred.

Sighing in relief, she straightened the letter, replaced it in the envelope, and returned both to the trunk. Teresa hurried back to the cot and lay down. What did it all mean? Jay was up to something, that much was clear. All too clear. And he'd implicated her in whatever it was.

April 2. That was only a few days away. But whoever Ben Morgan was, he wouldn't be meeting Jay because he hadn't gotten the letter requesting that he do so. That meant Jay's plan, whatever it was, wasn't going to work.

A more alarming thought suddenly struck her. How would that affect her brother? Would he still be in danger?

Teresa tossed and turned for the remainder of the night. It wasn't worry over what Jay had gotten himself into, however, that kept her from getting any rest. She honestly no longer cared about him. There was no love left in her heart for the man she'd once thought she'd spend the rest of her life with. She was worried about her family, and what Jay was dragging them into. One of her brothers, herself, and her son, Tyler. They could all suffer because of Jay, and she was the only one who had a chance to stop him. If she could only find a way to get out of the Yankee encampment, away from Lieutenant Forsythe, and make it to Richmond!

When Brett woke it was still dark, but he heard the familiar sounds of men already emerging from their tents, restoking fires, making coffee, and frying biscuits. It was a soft rustle of sound just beyond the thin canvas wall of his tent and would have been comforting—*if* he was supposed to be here. Sooner or later someone was bound to find out who he really was. Or maybe who he really wasn't. He could only hope that when that happened he was long gone from the camp.

He inhaled deeply but didn't stir. The tantalizing smell of fresh biscuits filled his nostrils and just about made his mouth water. One thing he'd say for the damned Yankees, at least their troops had food most of the time. Brett stretched. Damn, but sleeping on a cot no wider than his own shoulders wasn't exactly the most comfortable way to spend a night. If it wasn't so cold he'd almost rather sleep on the ground. He glanced across the tent's small interior to Teresa's cot.

The dilapidated slouch hat she'd worn ever since entering the encampment was pulled down tight over her forehead, no doubt to keep her hair safely tucked inside. A thin wool blanket was pulled up almost to her nose.

Brett smiled. He'd had a few thoughts on how they could have kept each other warm last night, especially after he'd almost re-entered the tent before she'd finished her bath. She didn't know that he'd seen her . . . but he had, and now he almost wished he hadn't. The sight had thrown his libido into a tailspin of desire that he'd been hard put to control ever since. That exquisite sight—the smooth, ivory color of her flesh, the soft curve of her bare shoulders, and the glistening curls of her black hair—had been almost more than he could resist. He had, but not because he'd wanted to.

He could no more take advantage of Teresa than he could his own sister, Suzanne. At the thought of his sister, an unexpected but pleasant memory swept through his mind. If anyone had told him five years ago that his sister would be married to Travis Braggette he'd have told them they were crazy. After deserting her at the altar, Brett had been certain that Travis was the last man on earth Suzanne would ever talk to again, let alone marry. Obviously he'd been wrong.

Brett sighed, but whether in relief or envy even he wasn't certain. His sister had married and most of his friends had gotten married. Maybe there was something to it that he hadn't considered. But no sooner had the thought entered his mind than he scoffed at it. Marriage. It was the one thing he'd vowed never to experience. It wasn't that he didn't believe in it. He did. He just didn't see himself living out his life with only one woman when there were so many in the world whose company he could enjoy.

Teresa stirred and a soft moan slipped from her lips.

Brett turned to look at her and as quickly looked away. What the hell was he doing thinking about marriage? He had more important things to think about. Anyway, even if he did decide he wanted to marry someday, there was certainly no reason to debate it now.

Teresa sat up. She rubbed her eyes and stretched, pushing her arms out wide and momentarily rolling her head over her shoulders. Then she saw Brett watching her. "Oh." Her arms flew down to cross over her breasts and she shot to her feet. "I'll . . . I'll get you some coffee."

She ducked out of the tent before he could respond.

"Simms," he called a split-second later.

The sentry hurried into the tent.

"Follow Smithers and make certain he knows where to go to get my coffee. And how to get back here."

The sentry gave him a questioning look, then hurried to follow his orders.

Brett growled softly. Coffee hadn't exactly been what he'd been yearning for while watching her. He had tried like hell to hide the fact that he knew she was a woman, but from her reactions to him sometimes he'd swear that she was fully aware that he knew she was playing a charade.

He sat up and ran a hand through his hair. What the hell did she see when she looked into his eyes? He threw his blanket aside and rose.

He was up and dressed by the time Teresa returned, but then he'd slept in everything except his boots and jacket. He accepted the coffee gratefully, his chilled fingers closing around the tin cup to absorb some of its warmth. Until that very moment he hadn't even realized he was cold.

Brett sat down behind his desk and looked at Teresa, who resettled herself on her cot. She'd pulled her hat low again, trying to hide as much of her face as possible. He could tell her it didn't matter, that she didn't have to bother with the disguise any longer because he knew the truth. He sighed. Of course he wouldn't do that. Teresa was the best lead to Jay Proschaud that Brett had ever had, and he wasn't about to do anything to jeopardize that. Anyway, he had absolutely no proof that she was not only Jay's wife, but also his accomplice. Brett had uncovered a string of other women Proschaud had used over the years to further his schemes, so why not his own wife?

Brett sipped at the hot coffee. He sat back and was just about to ask Teresa to get them some breakfast when a sentry entered the tent carrying a tray of freshly cooked biscuits and crisp strips of bacon. The man placed the tray on Brett's desk, saluted smartly, and left.

Brett looked at Teresa. "Where's yours?"

She looked down at her coffee. "I'm not hungry."

Brett shoved a piece of bacon into his mouth, chewed and swallowed it, then followed that with a sip of the steaming hot coffee, all the while continuing to stare at her.

The sentry re-entered the tent.

Brett tore his gaze from Teresa. "What is it, Simms?" he barked. He hadn't meant to sound so gruff but the whole situation was beginning to wear on his nerves.

"Excuse me, sir, but there's a gentleman here to see you."

Brett frowned. Was this good or bad? "A gentleman?" he questioned.

"Yes, sir. A Mr. Emerson Wilkins, sir."

Brett's features remained calm and stoic, but his insides were taut with anticipation. Wilkins was back, hopefully with good news. Brett nodded to the sentry. "I'll speak to him outside. Thank you, Simms."

The sentry saluted and left the tent. Brett turned to Teresa. "I'll be back in a moment. Stay here."

She offered no response.

Brett stepped from the tent and looked around. A man stood a few yards away, his hat pulled low, his collar turned high. Brett quickly approached him. Greetings were quick and hushed. They moved toward a tall oak tree that grew just beyond where the last tent was staked.

"I was beginning to think you weren't coming back," Brett said, only half jesting.

"I thought about it."

Brett looked at Wilkins quickly. The man's face remained stolid.

"Richmond's got some right good-looking females up there. Good whiskey, too."

Brett chuckled softly, the tension easing somewhat at the man's words. "So what's the situation, Wilkins? Is he there?"

"Yeah, he's there. Waiting for her at the hotel just like you figured."

Brett nodded. "Good. Are the others set up?"

"Yep. Everything's ready. Just waiting for you and her to show up."

"Then we'd best be getting her there. Go on up the trail about a mile. We'll meet you there in half an hour."

The man nodded and was gone almost before Brett had finished his sentence.

Brett walked back to the tent. "I'll need my horse saddled, Smithers."

"Yes, sir," she mumbled, but didn't look at him.

"Saddle yourself one, too, and pack enough rations for a week for both of us. You'll be accompanying me."

Teresa's head shot up and she stared at him through wide eyes. "Accompanying you?"

"Yes."

She couldn't go with him on some stupid reconnaissance ride. She had to get to Richmond . . . to

Jay, and find out what was going on . . . what was threatening one of her brothers.

"I've arranged for you to be my permanent aide."

Permanent aide. Teresa glared up at him.

"You do have a horse, don't you, Smithers?" He looked at her sharply. "If not, requisition one."

"I have a horse," she said begrudgingly. At least she thought she had a horse, unless one of these lowlife Yankees had stolen StarDancer and deserted with him, which she wouldn't put past any of them.

"We'll be leaving in about half an hour. Have the sentry go on down to the corral and get our horses. I need to pack up a few things here."

Hope sparked in Teresa's breast. "I can get the horses, sir."

He gave her a hard look. Brett knew exactly what she was thinking, and for that reason alone he wasn't about to let her out of his sight. "No. We'll go to the corral together, when I finish packing my papers."

Teresa busied herself rolling both their bed blankets and tying them with a few strips of leather he handed her from his desk.

"Good. We're ready," he said. "Let's go."

Teresa felt a wash of despair that was followed quickly by apprehension. Jay's note had said it was a matter of life or death. She had to get to Richmond. Instead, she was being forced to traipse off to an unknown destination in the company of some blasted Yankee Lieutenant.

She eyed the gun settled snugly in the holster at his waist. The safety flap was unfastened.

Teresa bit down softly on the inside of her bottom lip. Was she fast enough to grab the gun, pull it from its holster, and hit him over the head with it?

Nine

For the next few hours they rode nonstop. Brett took the lead with Teresa riding directly behind him on StarDancer. She glanced over her shoulder as they traversed a gully. The soldier who had met with Brett earlier, Emerson, brought up the rear but she had yet to actually see his face. He wore his hat pulled low onto his forehead and the bottom half of his face was covered with whiskers.

If this was a reconnaissance ride, as Brett claimed, she found it extremely peculiar that they weren't trying to sneak up on any fortified Confederate positions or even seek them out. They rode mainly under cover, remaining within the shadows of dense forests, sparse copses of willows, and pines or wild scrub brush whenever possible. But it seemed to Teresa that they were avoiding everyone, Yankee and Confederate alike, rather than seeking them out or taking note of their positions.

She glared at the back of Brett's head and rained a series of silent curses down on him. All she'd wanted to do was pass through his crummy camp without bothering anyone. That's all. Just pass through and go on to Richmond. So how had she gotten stuck being his aide? And why . . . not to mention when . . . had she started thinking of him as Brett rather than Lieutenant Forsythe? Her anger burned hot. He was her enemy, a handsome one, she'd admit, but her enemy nevertheless. And he had all the charm and honor of a rattlesnake, which she'd do well to remember above all else.

They rode through a small but thick growth of brush and emerged into a wide meadow. Brett reined in as their cover disappeared behind them. The others did likewise. Teresa watched him as his gaze moved slowly over the landscape; satisfied that it was safe, he nodded and nudged his horse forward.

She had absolutely no hope of getting away now. If she tried to make a run for it she had no doubt Brett or Emerson would catch her. StarDancer was fast, and if the terrain hadn't been unfamiliar it would be no problem to outrun the other two horses. In fact, at the moment Teresa hadn't the faintest idea where they were or even in which direction Petersburg or Richmond lay. That meant escape was totally out of the question . . . at least for now.

They kept off the roads and continued to travel through dense areas of brush and trees, which confused Teresa even more. Before leaving New Orleans she overheard that Lee was struggling to defend Petersburg, because if that city fell the Yankees would march on to Richmond, the Confederate capital.

Teresa remembered the large Yankee encampment they'd just left . . . and which she would be returning to if she didn't manage somehow to get away from Lieutenant Brett Forsythe. She looked at him riding ahead of her and frowned. This wasn't a simple reconnaissance ride. She'd never been on one and had very little knowledge of military strategy, but something told her this ride was not what he claimed it to be.

Brett reined in again at the edge of a small clearing. The sun was directly overhead, yet the sprawling branches of the surrounding trees left the glen mostly in shadow. Teresa watched Brett. His eyes scanned the area, piercing the duskiness of the surrounding copse, moving over every bush and rock, studying each tree. Finally he appeared to relax. "We'll rest here for a little while." He slid from his saddle and led his horse into the sunlight of the clearing.

Teresa and Emerson did likewise.

Brett walked across the clearing. "Emerson, give the horses some water," he said over his shoulder.

Teresa approached Brett. "Where are we heading?"

Brett turned his head at her approach, frowning in annoyance at her question. "A ways up the road."

The feeble hold she had on her temper suddenly slipped away. "Oh. Well, that's really informative. *A ways up the road.*" She threw her hands up and began to pace. "So, Lieutenant, I suppose if I happen to be killed out here you'll just bury me *a ways up the road* and that will be the end of that." She kicked at a small rock with the toe of her boot and sent it skittering across the clearing. "Just do me a favor and write my mother, would you? I'll dictate it now so you'll know what to say. Dear Mother, sorry to inform you of this but your beloved child is dead and buried *a ways up the road.*"

Brett stared at her as if she'd lost her mind, which Teresa realized with sudden horror was exactly what she'd just done. Engulfed in a wash of dread she glanced from Brett, whose hard features and cold eyes were almost unreadable, to Emerson. He merely shook his head, spit a wad of tobacco onto the ground, and grabbed the reins of her horse.

Privates didn't act like that, say things like that, to a commanding officer. No one had to say it, she knew it. And she'd done it anyway. Teresa waited for one of them to denounce her, if not as a private about to meet his Maker, then as a woman they'd surely label as a spy. Her eyes darted from one to the other.

Emerson ignored her, busying himself with the horses. Brett merely stood watching her, an indolence to his stance. She swallowed hard. "I'm sorry. I just meant . . ." *Think,* she ordered her brain. It raced frantically in search of something intelligent to say. "I . . . well, I thought . . ."

Brett shifted position, obviously impatient.

Teresa bit the side of her lip. "I mean . . . well, I could . . ." *What?* she nearly screamed at herself. And then the answer rolled off her tongue as if it had been there all along. "I thought I might be of more help to you, sir, if I knew where we were going and why. You see I had relatives up this way and . . ."

"I don't think so, Smithers," Brett bit out brusquely. Turning his back to her, he threw down his knapsack and settled himself on the ground, using his sack as a pillow.

Teresa bristled, unnerved by his retort. He didn't think so *what?* That she could help? Or that she had relatives here? She glared at him and began to pace the small clearing. What did it matter what he meant anyway? It wasn't as if she had any intention of helping him even if she could, which she couldn't because she was totally lost.

Brett crossed his arms over his chest and closed his eyes.

Teresa paused. Was he going to sleep? Here? Now? A sudden and intense sense of familiarity washed over her as she stared down at him, so strong that it nearly rocked her off her feet.

"We have a lot more riding to do," Brett said from beneath his hat. "I'd suggest you try to get some sleep."

Trembling, Teresa moved to sit beside a small bush several yards away from where Brett lay. Sleep was out of the question. Even relaxing was something that, right now, she couldn't do. Her body was suddenly as taut as a dry twig, and ready to snap just as easily. What was there about him that gave her this overpowering feeling that she'd met him before? She slammed a fist onto the hard ground, then winced as pain shot up her arm. Why couldn't she remember?

Brett watched her from beneath the brim of the Yankee officer's hat he'd pulled over his face. Teresa looked almost as tired as he felt. But then they'd been in the saddle for seven hours. He had been pushing them hard, but he wanted to get to Richmond as soon as possible and they had a lot of miles to cover.

He'd known ever since intercepting Jay's letter to Teresa that he was on the right trail, and this time he wasn't about to lose it. He still wasn't exactly sure why Jay Proschaud was in Richmond, what diabolical scheme he had planned, or why he'd sent for his wife, but Brett was determined that this time the man wasn't going to escape capture. That's why he'd arranged for Teresa to be watched, even though it made him feel like a louse. That had been bad enough, but having to delay her in the Yankee camp until things were arranged in Richmond and Emerson returned with word that they were ready had been worse. Brett had spied on a lot of people, but he'd never thought he'd be spying on a Braggette.

His gaze moved over Teresa from head to foot. Brett was a man who had always enjoyed women, and they had always been more than willing to allow him that pleasure. His mother wanted him to settle down and marry, but her relationship with his father had not exactly been a loving example of what he could look forward to should he ever grant her wish. They were both good people, and good parents, they just weren't a good husband and wife. And Traynor's parents had given him an even worse look at what two people could do to each other once the bliss of matrimony faded. Brett had never let a relationship go on for more than a few weeks and he had never allowed his emotions to get away from him. But he couldn't deny that Teresa was a woman he would like to get to know a whole lot better, in spite of it all.

Brett started and bolted upright. Those were the kind of thoughts that could get him in trouble and cause him to drop his guard. Love them, use them, and enjoy them . . . but never get attached to them. That's what he believed. And until this war was over that's exactly what he'd continue to believe. Maybe even longer.

He looked back at Teresa. He'd definitely like to enjoy the pleasures his best friend's little sister obviously had to offer a man, especially after having caught a glimpse of her while she was bathing. Brett settled back against the tree. But that wasn't going to happen—because he wasn't going to let it. Not even if the opportunity arose.

Cursing himself and everything that had happened in the past few days, Brett sat up and pulled a cigarillo from his jacket's inside pocket. A quick flick of a lucifer to the heel of one boot turned its tip to flame. He cupped it with both hands and held the sputtering fire to the end of the tobacco. He should be trying to get some rest, not dwelling on impossible thoughts of physical pleasure. Especially with a woman who was out of his reach in more ways than one.

Almost murderously his gaze swept to where Teresa sat. Damn her to hell, he thought savagely. Why couldn't she have married someone else? Or at least stayed at home where she belonged. His life would be a lot less complicated.

Taking a long, deep draw of the cigarillo, Brett turned his gaze to the still leaves of the surrounding trees, the faint sounds of the animals who made their home within the tiny grove, and the warm sunlight that shone down on them all. It all seemed so peaceful, so serene. Who could guess, sitting here, that war raged only a few miles away? That men were savagely killing each other. And for what? So that southerners could own slaves? So that northerners could continue to force their dictates on people whose way of life was so different from theirs it was like night and day?

Brett swore softly. Neither reason was good

enough. And yet they continued to fight. And he fought. Not because he believed in slavery . . . not because he hated northerners . . . but merely because he was loyal to his state, to his home. Southerners had a right to their beliefs, to their way of life, to their honor, just as everyone else did.

The cigarillo lost its appeal, the brandy-soaked tobacco suddenly tasting repugnant. With a violent twist of his wrist Brett threw it down and ground its burning tip into the earth with the heel of his boot.

But it wasn't the war that had soured his mood so completely. Or even the reasons for it. He'd thought he could handle the situation concerning Teresa with all the cool reserve he had managed to exert during all of his other assignments. But he'd been wrong.

Several hours later, just before the sun was ready to sink beyond the horizon and Teresa felt as if she were about to fall out of her saddle from exhaustion, they stopped again.

Brett turned to Emerson. "It's time," he said simply. Teresa looked at him in puzzlement. Time? Time for what? She desperately wanted to ask, but after her earlier outburst she knew the best thing to do was remain silent. She turned to look at Emerson, but the grizzled, older man ignored her, as he'd done ever since they'd first laid eyes on one another.

Emerson nodded in acknowledgment of Brett's words.

Dismounting, both men removed their jackets and began to pull other garments from their saddlebags.

Teresa slid from StarDancer's back to the ground.

The long hours in the saddle had left her legs weak and shaky. She bent and stretched, then turned back to watch the two men. It took only a matter of minutes before she realized they were changing from their uniforms into civilian clothes. What were they going to . . . ? The thought died abruptly in her mind. Reconnaissance. He'd said they were going on a reconnaissance ride, and he'd told the truth. They were going to spy. They were going to attempt to spy on Confederate troops, but not from a distance. They were going to get up close. That's why they were putting on plain clothes. They were going into a Confederate encampment or town to pass themselves off as civilians.

Her temper flared. Civilians. Well! If they thought she was going along with this little ruse they both had another think coming!

Teresa stomped to Brett's side, fury burning within her breast. "Lieutenant, if you think I'm going to go along with you to spy . . ."

He turned.

Something in his eyes made her realize instantly that she'd been about to make another mistake. Teresa nearly bit the tip off her tongue as she clamped her mouth shut in mid-sentence. Lord, had she lost her senses altogether? She couldn't refuse to accompany him to spy on Confederate troops. Not if she didn't want him to find out who she was—or rather who she wasn't.

Suddenly another thought came to her. She could act as if she was going along with his plans and when they were in or near a Confederate camp she could scream her head off and give them away.

Excitement and a sense of impending satisfaction replaced her fury and she felt like smiling. She looked back up at him. His gaze caught hers and held, blue melding with gray, stripping away the barriers between them, destroying the walls and differences to leave nothing but two people, two lonely souls who felt an almost overwhelming attraction to one another, along with a responsibility to fight it.

In that instant Teresa realized the depth of what she felt toward Lieutenant Brett Forsythe. She didn't want to feel that way, hadn't thought she did feel that way, but at that moment she could no longer deny it any more than she could deny her help to a brother in peril.

Nothing was going the way she'd planned. Nevertheless she knew that she didn't want to put Brett Forsythe's life in jeopardy, didn't want to ride into a Confederate camp and denounce him as a Yankee. The mere thought suddenly made her eyes sting with tears, which in turn stoked the fury that had almost been smothered by the shocking realization of her true feelings toward him.

She would not feel that way toward a Yankee!

Pulling her gaze from his, she spun around and marched to where StarDancer was tethered. The horse was contentedly munching on a crop of grass. Teresa grabbed his reins, jerking them free of the limb she'd looped them around earlier. She had no intention of riding docilely beside Brett while he spied on Confederate troops. Neither did she intend to complacently continue with the pretense of being his aide. One of her brothers was in trouble and needed her help and she'd wasted enough time dancing around these damned Yankees. She would get away from them if it was the last thing she ever did!

Brett's gaze bored into Teresa's back. So, she thought he was getting ready to spy on Confederate movements. And she didn't want to help him. The thought set well. Not that he still wasn't suspicious of her motives, but her near refusal to cooperate assured him that she didn't recognize or remember him. That should have made him feel good, reassured him, and it did—somewhat. But there was a part of him that smoldered with an unreasonable anger at the thought that she didn't remember who he was. That she could look into his face, into his eyes, and have no recollection of him whatsoever galled him to the core. Anger more than reason or need stirred his tongue and colored his harsh tone. "Private Smithers."

Teresa stopped only a few feet from where Star-Dancer stood and looked back at him.

"We're going to make camp here for a few hours. Since you seem to have so much energy, why don't you gather some firewood and make us a pot of coffee?"

She wanted to tell him to gather the firewood himself—to make the coffee himself—to go straight to hell and burn until he was nothing but cinders. But this time she knew better than to let it slip from her tongue.

Brett's eyes bore ruthlessly into hers. He knew what she was thinking—it was etched clearly on her delicate features and glistened from within the mesmerizing gray-blue depths of her eyes. But he said nothing. He merely looked at her, suddenly wanting all the hostility between them, the antagonism and even the secrets, to go away.

He was tired of war, of secrets and deception, and he didn't want to do it anymore. The situation with Teresa had propelled him toward that realization, which he'd been trying to ignore and deny for months. But his honor and loyalty would not allow him to concede.

How had she stirred these feelings within him? he asked himself angrily. It wasn't merely her beauty, which she was trying so desperately to conceal. He'd known other beautiful women, and they had given him pleasure without trying his patience. Teresa aroused urges he would rather forget for now. There was every possibility that she was a traitor—she was married—and she was his best friend's sister. More times than not in the past few days he'd found himself caring less and less about those things and dreaming more and more of what it would be like to hold her in his arms, to taste her lips against his, feel the heat of her exquisitely shaped body.

He wanted her. Dear God, he wanted her more than he'd ever wanted any other woman. It was unexplainable and unreasonable.

Ripping his gaze from hers, Brett pulled another cheroot from his pocket, bit off one end, and spit the tiny plug of tobacco onto the ground. His body felt suddenly as if it was tied in knots, the fire in his gut almost unbearable. Why did he feel this way about *her?* Fury blended with the pangs of unsatiated passion. He had every reason to despise her. Every reason to hold her in disdain.

He snapped a lucifer against the heel of his boot.

The tiny match broke in half, its sulphured tip falling unlit to the ground. Brett swore softly and glanced up at Teresa.

The soft glow of twilight had settled over the clearing and over her, accentuating the feminine curves of her delicate face, the long column of her ivory-hued neck, the soft curve of her shoulders. Everything that she was trying so hard to disguise.

Brett tore his gaze away and reached into his pocket for another lucifer. What the hell was wrong with him?

His eyes fastened upon her again, but this time he did not look away, this time his gaze searched hers, needing to see beyond the physical facade. She was playing a game, but was that all there was to her actions? Or were her coy looks not so much naiveté as strategy.

A shiver rippled through Teresa's body and she found herself unable to move. His gaze held hers, but this time it wasn't a gaze of antagonism or even challenge that she met. Suddenly she saw a warning in those deep blue eyes that were looking at her so intensely. And something more, something that surprised her: loneliness. For one brief millisecond it seemed to emanate from him, and then was as quickly drawn back behind the cloak of arrogance he wore so well.

Teresa felt a sudden urge to drop her disguise and reach out to him. She could tell him the truth. This was a man she could trust, a man who would help her, protect her, love her.

She reacted instantly to the thought, feeling as if she'd been struck by lightning. It shook her to the core and left her momentarily dazed and confused. Trust *him?* She nearly laughed aloud as she tore her gaze from his. The words shrieked through her brain like a runaway train. The thought that she could trust him, that he would help or protect her, was insane. But the other . . . Her temples suddenly throbbed. Love? The thought was ludicrous, and completely uncalled for.

Had her mind turned to mush from the day's hard riding? Had she been bounced in the saddle once too often and lost all capacity for rational thought? Brett Forsythe was a Yankee—the embodiment of everything she despised in the world.

"Smithers, are you going to daydream or find some firewood before our light is completely gone?"

Teresa snapped from her reverie. Nothing like a little ruthless reality. She nodded her acquiescence while she inwardly fumed and, putting ladylike sensitivities aside, called him every vile name she could think of. Someday someone would have to teach Lieutenant Brett Forsythe some manners.

She began skirting about the bushes for enough bits of dried twigs to build a fire. What was she going to do? She couldn't let him spy on Confederate troops. That could result in disaster beyond imagination. Men would be killed. Maybe some of her friends. Teresa froze—maybe one of her own brothers. She suddenly felt so helpless. What if the opportunity to betray him didn't present itself? What could she do?

Then again, what if it did? And what did this so-called reconnaissance trip have to do with the letter from Jay she'd found in Brett's trunk . . . if anything?

Teresa picked up another twig and crammed it under her arm where several others were already nestled. Lord, how had she gotten mixed up in all of this? She cursed softly, but she didn't have to search far for an answer. Jay. It was all his fault.

A thought came to her that made Teresa stop dead in her tracks. She spun around and stared at Brett. He'd settled himself on the ground and was leaning back against a large rock, his eyes closed. Could this have all been arranged? What if it was no accident she'd run into him? What if, somehow, he'd known she was coming? Maybe he wasn't just an ordinary army lieutenant. Maybe he was a spy or some special secret government agent whom Lincoln had sent to watch her as a way to get to Jay. She frowned. But was Jay that important? She didn't know.

She felt something hard beneath her foot, looked down, and saw that she'd stepped on a piece of old tree limb that had been half covered by leaves. Bending to pick it up and add it to her growing cache, Teresa froze. Terror gripped her in such a vise she felt the air leave her lungs and her heart slam against her ribcage. If he knew she was coming, if this whole thing—her meeting him, being appointed his personal aide, accompanying him on this trip—if it was all arranged, then he knew who she was, knew she wasn't a soldier . . . or a boy . . . man . . . male . . . Panic mingled with terror and nearly choked her.

"Smithers?"

Teresa turned, totally prepared to see him pointing a gun at her head, ready to confront her with the truth. Instead, Brett had settled himself on the ground. His head lay on his saddle and his hands were folded across his chest. He looked at her. "How about building that fire? It's starting to get cold and I could sure use a cup of coffee right about now."

She hurried to pick up several more twigs.

Brett drummed his fingers upon his chest. His emotions were in a turmoil, which did nothing for his mood. Never before had he felt the wars of indecision battle within him as they did now. What the hell kind of spell had she cast over him? He had a job to do—a duty to perform. What he didn't have was time to act like a sex-starved coxcomb. Yet that's exactly what a part of him was doing. Lusting after her as if he'd never had a woman in his life. And she was parading around in his clothes! The whole thing was preposterous.

He watched her walk to the center of the clearing and kneel down to arrange the twigs into a pile. She couldn't even walk like a man. Her hips swayed gently, back and forth with each step, as if in open invitation. A parade of whispered curses danced from Brett's lips. He tried to avert his gaze and found he couldn't. There was nothing else about that he cared to look at.

The legs of the trousers were too long, and she'd been forced to roll them up at the cuffs. But it wasn't the legs or the cuffs his gaze had settled on, but rather the firm, rounded curve of her derriere, blatantly outlined by the trousers' snug fit.

She took a lucifer from the box he'd given her earlier and struck one against the heel of her boot.

Its tip erupted into flame and she held it to the pile of dried twigs.

The match went out.

Brett twisted his mouth to keep from smiling.

Teresa lit another lucifer.

It extinguished before she was even able to get it to the twigs.

Brett bit down on his bottom lip, but remained still and made no effort to help her.

Another match blew out before she could get it to the wood.

"Blow on it," Brett said finally, knowing that if he didn't offer her at least some advice he might never get his coffee.

Teresa turned to look at him. "Blow on it?" she repeated, obviously confused.

"Softly."

Teresa struck another match. It remained alight as she moved it to the pile of twigs. Bending over it she blew, ever so softly, at the tiny flame. A few minutes later she had a campfire and a pot of coffee brewing. The fragrance made her stomach growl and reminded her that she hadn't eaten anything since having a biscuit and a few strips of bacon that morning before they'd left camp.

She glanced at Brett. Had he bothered to bring any food, or had that been her responsibility? Teresa cringed. If so, he would soon be barking at her because she hadn't brought any.

Brett sat up and pushed to his feet—a movement, Teresa noticed, that was as effortless and graceful as that of a cat. She watched him walk to his horse and untie the leather thong that held his saddlebags closed.

The familiarity came back in a rush. She stared at him, half afraid, half mesmerized. Brett turned and walked toward her. She noticed then that he was deep in thought, a faraway look in his eyes. But whatever those thoughts were, she realized as she watched him, they weren't pleasant. The golden brows that arched so gracefully above his eyes were scowling, and the mouth was pulled thin and taut.

Teresa swallowed convulsively and poked at the fire with one of the twigs.

He closed the distance between them with several long strides. Teresa started as he neared, suddenly feeling as if a graceful but predatory assailant was silently, steadily stalking toward her . . . its quarry. The feeling of helplessness, hopelessness, was overpowering. And yet so was the almost overwhelming allure she could not deny he held for her. There was something about Brett Forsythe that beckoned to her, that threatened to cause her to do things she would not normally do, and that frightened her as much if not more as the sense that this man was not a stranger to her.

He terrified her and attracted her. He was her enemy and he was the dark stranger of her dreams—the lover who came to her in the night when she was alone, who promised that someday the future would be filled with sunshine again . . . and promise.

Pausing beside her, Brett drew the cheroot from between his lips and tossed it into the fire. It sputtered momentarily, then the sweet smell of brandy and tobacco melded with the fragrance of the burning willow wood. He hunkered down beside her. "Here."

Struggling to emerge from the haze of imagination she'd momentarily allowed herself, Teresa merely stared at him, his curtly spoken word and its meaning lost to her.

Brett's brow furrowed and he stared at her quizzically. "Smithers." He jabbed her arm. "Here."

Teresa looked down. A tin cup was in his hand. She took it from him.

Brett turned away and poured coffee into the cup he held in his other hand. When Teresa made no move to hold out her cup, he turned to Emerson, who had hunkered down opposite him, and poured coffee into the man's proffered cup.

Both sipped at the steaming liquid.

Emerson rose and moved back to where he'd been sitting a few feet away.

"Nice going, Smithers," Brett said and took another swallow.

"Thank you," she mumbled, remembering to keep her voice low and her head tilted down. He was too close.

Brett took another sip. "You'll make someone a right fine little housekeeper someday, Smithers, if they like coffee."

Emerson laughed and raised his cup toward them, as if in salute to Brett's comment.

Teresa froze. Was there a hidden message behind that remark? She looked at him, expecting to see confrontation in his eyes, a gleam in those icy blue depths that told her not to bother because he already knew what she'd been trying desperately to hide. But there was nothing there but amusement.

Instead of relief, she felt fury. The man was absolutely obnoxious. An arrogant beast who knew how to do nothing more than order her around or taunt her with cloaked comments and veiled insinuations. Her fingers curled around the empty tin cup he'd given her, squeezing down hard. If she were truly his aide she'd probably poison his food or split his head with the butt of a rifle. She'd slit the strap of his saddle so he'd fall off and break his neck. Or maybe she'd just punch him in the nose.

Or kiss him.

The thought came out of nowhere and nearly caused her jaw to drop open in shock. Kiss him? Teresa's mind skittered about frantically as it tried to find out why the thought had cropped up in the first place. But rhyme and reason were nowhere to be found. And neither was an excuse.

She found him attractive, that was undeniable. But she was also *attracted* to him. She was married. Well, no, not really. Not anymore. But that didn't matter anyway. And he was a Yankee! Not to mention one of the most infuriating men she'd ever met. She poked the stick at the fire again, a little more savagely this time. Attracted to him—hah!

But the thought nagged at her. What would it be like to kiss him? Be held by him? Snuggle into the safe harbor of those strong arms, feel the warmth of his body, his strength and virility envelop her?

Stop it. Teresa shook with the effort she had to exert to stem the traitorous and unwelcome thoughts. She'd admitted to herself that she felt something for him, something she didn't want to feel, but she'd also decided it was ridiculous. And most likely only there because she was alone in enemy territory and afraid. He was a Yankee. He was filth. Handsome or not, he was a rotten Yankee and no Yankee was ever going to touch her!

But the thoughts wouldn't stop and with every passing second that he remained hunkered down beside her, she became more sensitive to his presence, more aware of the fires that simmered between them.

Brett tossed the remains of his coffee onto the fire. It sizzled and steamed but kept burning. Then he walked back to where he'd been lying earlier and resettled himself on the spot, pulling his hat down over his eyes and folding his hands beneath his head. "Get some sleep, Smithers," he said from beneath the hat. "We'll be heading out again in a little while."

Teresa looked at him. If they were in enemy territory, shouldn't one of them keep watch?

"I'll keep the first watch," Brett said.

Teresa flinched and stared at him in shock. Could he read her mind? With a deep sigh Teresa lay down beside the fire. The air was still crisp with spring and colder than she was used to in Louisiana. With the setting of the sun and the earth shrouded in darkness, the crisp air was quickly turning cooler.

Suddenly a deep, grumbling roar penetrated the night. Teresa nearly jumped out of her skin. She bolted up and stared into the darkness beyond the fire's glow.

"It's only Emerson," Brett said from beneath the hat he'd pulled over his face.

She glanced at him, and then turned to glare at

Emerson. His snores were enough to wake the dead. But that wasn't why she couldn't go to sleep. She turned to look at Brett again. His breathing seemed soft and steady. Maybe he was asleep.

She could sneak away now. She knew she could. But even if she did—then what? She didn't have the faintest idea where they were. What good would it do to get away from them and then spend days wandering around the countryside trying to find her way to Richmond, most likely ending up right back in a Yankee encampment?

She lay back down. At least if she stayed with Brett she'd be led toward a Confederate camp. Teresa felt certain of that. Otherwise, why had he changed into civilian clothes? He was going to spy on someone—that seemed evident—and it certainly wasn't one of his own. Since he was a Yankee that meant it was a Confederate troop he was out to watch, and that's just where she wanted to be, in the company of her own kind.

"Traitor."

Brett's softly muttered comment penetrated Teresa's consciousness and brought her bolt upright again. At first she thought he was speaking to her and her heart jumped into her throat. The brim of his hat obscured his eyes, but she felt certain they were still closed. And his breathing was still steady, another indication that he was asleep.

"Justice . . . this time . . . Knight."

Night? Teresa frowned. He was talking in his sleep but his mumblings weren't making any sense. Justice during the night? Is that what he meant? He was probably just dreaming and dreams didn't usually make sense.

"Proschaud."

Teresa's heart nearly stopped beating. Her breath caught in her lungs and her hands trembled. She rose to lean on her elbow and stared at Brett, willing him to say more and at the same time terrified that he would.

He rolled onto his side and tucked his hands beneath his arms. The hat remained over his face.

Proschaud? Was he talking to her? She squinted against the night, straining to see beneath the hat. Did he know? Was he merely teasing her by muttering her married name while pretending to be asleep? Her breathing turned ragged at the fear mounting within her. She shook her head. No. It couldn't be that. She hadn't used her married name for the past several years. She was Teresa Braggette. Even Tyler used the Braggette name.

She sat up. So, if Brett was taunting her, and if he really was talking in his sleep, he must be referring to Jay. But why? Teresa's mind was ajumble with questions. Was Brett specifically after Jay for some reason? What could Jay have done to the Yankees to make them want to capture him badly enough to send someone after him? And was she part of their scheme? Was she their bait?

Thoughts of Tyler filled Teresa's mind and tears sprang to her eyes. If Jay was doing things against the Yankees and was caught, they'd most likely hang him. She shuddered. Their son would grow up under the stigma of his father having been executed as a traitor.

"No," she mumbled softly. The word had been spoken as little more than a whisper against the night, yet her hushed tone held more conviction and force than it ever had. Whatever Jay Proschaud was, whatever he had done, he was still the father of her child, and if protecting Tyler meant she had to protect Jay, then she would.

Ten

Brett watched Teresa through barely parted lashes. The lowered brim of his hat blocked any moonlight from touching his face and shrouded it in shadow. It gave him the advantage of being able to see Teresa without her knowing it, and without her being able to see him.

She thought he was talking in his sleep and that's exactly what he wanted her to think. He'd been mulling over in his mind what to say and how to bait her, but when it came right down to it, mentioning her husband's name was really all it had taken. Now Brett was certain, after the thread of horror he'd seen on her face, that with a little loosening of the invisible leash she would lead him directly to Jay Proschaud. All Brett had to do was be careful that he didn't lose her before then.

As if his thoughts had been overheard, he watched Teresa push to her feet. Hunched low to the ground, she crossed the small camp to where the horses were tethered. They whinnied softly and Brett saw her freeze in place, waiting for the animals to recognize her and calm down. She glanced over her shoulder toward where he and Emerson lay, supposedly asleep. As if reassured that her movements and the horses' snorting hadn't wakened them, she bent and hurriedly picked up her saddle. She moved toward StarDancer and, throwing a blanket over the large gelding's back, hefted her saddle up.

Brett surged to his feet. He wasn't ready to let her make a break for it, especially not now while it was too dark to be sure he could follow her successfully. And the timing was all wrong. They were still too far from Richmond, which meant that losing her trail was a distinct possibility. "Going somewhere, Private Smithers?" he asked, walking up behind her.

A shriek escaped Teresa's lips and she spun around. She made a grab for the hat, feeling it fall askew at her sudden movement and realizing with horror that she'd failed to pull it tight over her tucked-up curls. But she was too late. It flew from her head, grazed her shoulder, and fell to the ground. With her hand still in midair and thick waves of ebony hair cascading over her shoulders, Teresa stared up at him.

It was a moment frozen in time. Neither moved nor spoke. Brett saw panic flash into her eyes and noticed the trembling of her shoulders. He felt a surge of guilt at having startled her. He had meant to confront her, not scare her. But more than the guilt, he felt desire suddenly sweep through him like a firestorm. It was insane, irresponsible, unreasonable, but it was there nevertheless, threatening to overwhelm him, to make him do things he knew he would regret. Staring down into those gray-blue eyes, seeing the slight trembling of her bottom lip, Brett wanted to pull her into his arms. He wanted to hold this woman, make love to her . . .

His shoulders stiffened at the traitorous thoughts.

No matter how hot his body grew with desire, there was still some small thread of reason left in his mind. You can't do this, it warned. And finally, he listened.

Brett swallowed hard. He wanted her body, not her. He'd gone too long without a woman in his bed, but he'd rectify that situation while they were in Richmond. For now he would hold himself in check and maintain control over the emotions threatening to tear him apart. He had a job to do, and he damned well intended to do it. And that job did not include seducing his quarry's wife . . . or being seduced by her.

Through a haze of shock and fear, Teresa continued to stare up at him, waiting for the fires of hell to rain down on her head. Everything was ruined. Her secret, her plans to meet Jay, and her hope of rescuing one of her brothers from whatever trouble threatened him. Tears of anger welled in her eyes, bringing with them a feeling of total helplessness and defeat. Her brother. Four handsome, beloved faces flashed into her mind and she knew she couldn't bear it if anything happened to any of them. Especially because of her. She nearly groaned aloud.

"You . . . you don't understand," she croaked when he didn't speak. "I mean, it's not what you think. I . . . I need to get to . . ." She stopped, shocked at seeing something in his eyes she hadn't expected to see, something that frightened her more than the wrath she had expected. Desire. It burned hot. Brilliant embers of heat danced sensuously within the sapphire depths that had turned almost as black as the night. It flamed fierce, like a volcanic inferno, hot, swirling, abrupt—and threatening.

The sight was as captivating as it was terrifying. It promised more than she'd ever even dared to dream, yet threatened more than she feared she could handle.

A shudder of apprehension rippled through Teresa's body. The look in his eyes and the expression on his face were more intense than any she'd seen since their meeting only a few short days before. It told her everything about him, and it told her nothing about him.

"We're on our way to Richmond," Brett said finally, interrupting her thoughts and shattering the spell that had held her in its grip.

But if his words were meant to soothe or reassure, they did just the opposite. Horror etched itself in every delicate curve of Teresa's face and flashed cold in her eyes. He *had* known. The thought screamed in her mind and seized her heart in a punishing, icy grasp. He had known all along. Terror invaded every cell of her body, every length of fiber, bone, and sinew. It had been a trick—all of it. Instinct and a sense of survival overcame her terror. Teresa's arm swung up and back down, her outstretched palm flying toward the side of his face.

Brett caught her wrist, thwarting her attempt to strike him. The fingers of his right hand curled around the slender flesh and bone and jerked her arm down. Once his hands had been the soft flesh of a gentleman's, but the rigors of war had turned him hard and firm. His grasp was as strong and unyielding as steel and held her in an implacable grip, yet exerted only enough pressure to control, not hurt.

"You beast," Teresa shrieked in outrage. "Filthy Yankee beast." She tried to yank her arm free, failed, tried again, and then swung out in desperation with the other. This time her hand curled into a fist as it neared its target.

Brett caught her right arm as easily as he had her left and held both in an uncompromising grip. "No," he growled softly, and jerked her toward him. He had known she would try to run at the first opportunity because it made sense; it was what he would have done if the situation were reversed. She wanted to get to Richmond. And he had known that she would be angry if he foiled her plans. He had been prepared for that. Brett had not, however, anticipated that she would lash out at him like a crazed lioness.

Teresa twisted away, writhing furiously against the restraint of his hands. "Let me go, you horrid cretin." She swung her hips and jerked her arms, trying desperately to break his grip. Several of the buttons on her jacket popped off and fell to the ground.

Teresa paid no heed. "Let me go," she demanded again. Long black tendrils whipped about her face as she fought against him. Her breathing had turned ragged as she gasped for each breath and poured her energy into struggling against him.

She threw her body to one side. The heel of her boot sank into the ground and Teresa's ankle twisted beneath her weight. Pain shot through her leg as she fell forward and slammed into his chest.

Brett grunted as her elbow rammed into his stomach and forced the air from his lungs. He felt a hot burning upon his flesh, but whether it was his own body's reaction or the touch of her flesh to his, he didn't know.

"Let me go," she demanded, and tried to push away from him again.

Though he damned himself for noticing, Brett couldn't keep his eyes from straying to her breasts, crushed against his chest and heaving from exertion. "You don't know how much I'd like to do just that," he said, his voice deep and drawling against her ear. It was both a lie and the truth. He wanted to let her go—his mind told him it was the sane thing to do . . . the safe thing to do. But he wanted to keep her near him, to press her body against his until there was no space between them, to feel her lips beneath his, the touch of her flesh, the warmth of her body.

She tried to pull away but Brett jerked her closer. "I'd like to let you go, my spirited little rebel," he said softly, each word a slow, seductive murmur, "but not just yet." He was taunting her, but he was torturing himself. His words were purposely suggestive, and though he had meant them to startle her into submissiveness, their hidden meaning tantalized him as much as they were meant to scare her.

Teresa glared up at him for a split second. What was the matter with her? She stiffened, furious at him, at herself, at everything. She didn't want this. Not now. Not with him. Her hands trembled, yet not from fear, but from the desire that had begun to smolder within her, from the aching need she felt to reach out to him, to touch him gently and lovingly. Teresa nearly groaned in despair as the realization of what she really felt and wanted struck her, along with the impossibility of it all. She'd only been trying to save one of her brothers and do what was right. So why was everything going wrong? How had she gotten into this mess?

The answer to that question loomed immediately in Teresa's mind: Jay. It was all his fault. How she was going to get out of the situation, however, remained a question with no answer, except that she knew there was a part of her that would never escape—the part that had become attracted to a Yankee officer with hair as gold as the sun and deep blue eyes that, she felt certain, could look into her soul.

Teresa stiffened against the feelings churning within her. Another time, another place, and maybe things would have, could have, been different between them.

Tears stung her eyes and she rapidly blinked them back. The last thing she wanted to do was cry. Or, more to the point, let Brett see her cry. She squeezed her eyes shut. Only the sound of her heavy breathing stirred the quiet night air. It felt good, being cradled in his arms like this, her body pressed to his.

Teresa's eyes shot open and she tried to pull away from him again, twisting her body to one side and yanking at his hold on her. Then she heard the sound of ripping fabric, of thinly woven threads being pulled away from each other.

Teresa froze, horrified, and looked down at her shirtfront. Three of its five buttons had ripped loose. She looked up quickly but felt no surprise at seeing that Brett Forsythe's gaze had dropped to her bosom.

"Well, well, Private Smithers," he said as one golden brow soared skyward.

Indignation returned twofold as she watched him stare down at the subtle swell of her bosom above the lace edges of a white camisole trimmed with blue silk ribbon.

Brett's face lit with a sly smile meant to tease her as well as put the fear of God into her. "And just what other delectable little treasures have you been keeping from me?"

"I . . . I . . ."

Reluctantly Brett's gaze left the tantalizing sight of her exposed breasts and moved upward. Their eyes met. He knew he should feel guilty, but guilt was the farthest thing from his mind. And at the moment, so was honor.

His gaze dropped again. Something hot and not altogether unwelcome stirred deep within him as his eyes once again roamed over her pale ivory flesh.

This was not the reaction of the honorary big brother he had always thought himself to be toward Teresa Braggette. This burning hunger growing deep within him was the reaction of a man consumed by desire. It was ridiculous, unbelievable, and unacceptable. Yet there was no denying it. But then he was no longer a youth, and she was no longer a child.

A slow fire began to invade his loins. It spread outward from his groin and left behind a sweet, torturous ache that was all too familiar and yet surprisingly more intense than any he'd ever felt.

Her eyes glittered dark and defiant, gray to blue to fathomless black. Brett felt the fury and outrage, the indignation she held around herself like a protective veil.

His best friend's sister was definitely no longer a

little girl, and if the stirrings tearing at his insides meant anything, his body had definitely discovered that brotherly love was not what he felt toward her.

She glared up at him, her head thrust back, chin lifted. "My brothers will kill you if you so much as lay a hand on me, you filthy Yankee," Teresa spat.

Brett smiled. If nothing else, her words reassured him that she still didn't know who he was. He thought of telling her, and immediately rejected the idea. "Kill me, huh?" He laughed and watched her scowl intensify at his reaction to her threat. Actually, she didn't know how true her words most probably were. Regardless of the fact that her brothers were his friends, Brett had a sneaking suspicion that *they* just might consider killing him if he tried anything with their little sister.

Brett's gaze moved slowly over her face, assessing each line and curve. He knew what he wanted. It was wrong, but he wanted it anyway.

Teresa suddenly experienced the eerie sensation that his gaze was plunging past the exterior of her flesh, beyond the blood that moved through her veins, the bones that made up her body, and seeing directly into her soul, into her innermost self. She felt her breath catch in her throat. No one, not even Jay, had ever looked at her like that, had ever cared enough to look at her in quite that way.

"No more fight in you, Smithers?" Brett whispered softly, not lessening his hold on her.

"Plenty," Teresa said, but the word came out a hushed whisper, turning it seductive rather than rebellious or threatening. And she didn't try to pull away.

She knew she should be angry with him, indignant and even insulted, but she wasn't. Instead, she felt tossed on a sea of turmoil, a hurricane of emotion that made her want to reach out to him, and at the same time shy away. He mesmerized her . . . and he terrified her. He was her sworn enemy, and he was a man whose embrace she desperately wanted to know. He was everything she should fear, and at the moment, everything she wanted.

The effect he had on her was startling and held her spellbound against her will. It warmed long-dormant desire and mocked the warning signals that had begun to flash within her mind. But looking away from him—pulling away from him, was out of the question, and at the moment beyond her ability.

Almost against her will, Teresa's gaze moved over his features as they stared at one another, neither moving nor speaking. Her eyes hesitated, fighting to recall something, anything, about him. Lieutenant Brett Forsythe was not a man most women would forget. He was not a man most women would *want* to forget. Something she knew she should not acknowledge blazed in his eyes, hot and scalding, beckoning to her, daring her, commanding her to respond.

Her heart pounded madly, fear and excitement sending her pulses racing. The urge to give in to him, to surrender to the unreasonable and surprising heat and need building within her body was almost more than she could control. Where had this compulsion to know him, to be held by him, come from? Why did her flesh suddenly ache to know his touch, her lips yearn for his kiss. Why?

Teresa tried to look away, and couldn't.

Brett felt her hesitation and recognized it for what it was—not the hesitation a woman might feel about accepting a man's advances, but rather in spurning them. They matched his own feelings. Resisting the urges building within him was suddenly something he felt incapable of doing, and if he was honest with himself, he didn't want to resist them. All the arguments he'd been using on himself since the moment she'd stepped into his tent suddenly seemed unimportant.

He was a man and she was a woman, and he wanted her. Everything else be damned. Later he could deal with the consequences of Jay Proschaud, her brothers, his lack of honor and momentary lapse of duty. All he wanted now was to taste her lips, feel her body pressed to his, and experience the sensation of her arms holding him close.

That she was his best friend's sister, another man's wife, and quite possibly a traitor to the cause didn't matter—not now. An hour from now, a day from now, it would matter. He needed, just for a moment, to feel wanted, needed, and maybe even loved. His head lowered toward hers.

The realization of what he was about to do, of what she wanted him to do, swept over Teresa with the force of a tidal wave. With a gasp she jerked away from him, her eyes wide, her throat dry. Passion, masquerading as love, had betrayed her once, and she had paid dearly for the mistake. She did not want to go through that again, especially with him. Brett Forsythe was virtually a stranger and her enemy. Yet even as her mind told her to run, to flee from him as fast as she could, she remained still, her heart not listening, her body not obeying. Loneliness, regret, and pain had been her constant companions for so long . . . would it really be so bad to abandon them just for a little while, to feel the soothing comfort of a man's arms around her, his strength supporting her, his kiss reassuring her that she was still a woman, still alive?

Teresa unconsciously leaned away from him. She wanted him, too, and that was the damnation of it all.

"Don't fight me, sweetheart." His voice was a silky, seductive murmur that caused her to flush at the bittersweet affirmation that fighting him was really the last thing she wanted to do.

"Or yourself," he added in a whisper. Brett released her wrists then and slid a hand to her waist, pulling her closer as his arm wrapped around her. His other hand moved to her face, the tips of his fingers skipping ever so lightly across the curve of her cheek. The touch sent a delicious shiver coursing through her body that left her trembling in his arms. She had never reacted to Jay like this . . . never.

His fingers moved along the line of her jaw and slowly slid down the curved column of her neck.

Teresa nearly moaned in frustration. She didn't want to fight him or herself, but she knew, in the back of her mind where reason and logic struggled to resist the magic of his touch, she had to. A flash of familiarity swept through her again. Where? Her mind screamed. Where had she met him before? How did they know one another? Teresa tried to twist away, forcing herself to ignore the apprehension growing within her. But more threatening, more urgent, and harder to ignore, were the heated yearnings his closeness stirred to life. Yearnings she feared, in a few seconds, she would no longer be able to control.

His fingers on her neck, so sensuous, so teasing, caused her to shiver.

He smiled.

"I'm not fighting myself," she retorted finally. "Only you." Teresa pushed against his shoulder with the heel of her hand. "Now, if you have even an ounce of gentlemanly honor, let me go."

Instead of releasing her, Brett wrenched her closer. "I'm not a gentleman, remember?" he goaded. "I'm a Yankee." His arms wrapped around her waist and held her so tightly that she could hardly breathe.

Teresa glared up at him. His face was so close. All she had to do was lean forward, just a bit, and her lips would touch his. She stiffened against the traitorous thought. "I don't want this."

"No?" He smiled, a taunting curve of his lips that piqued her anger yet stirred her excitement. "Your eyes tell me different."

He was going to kiss her. She knew it. Felt it. And, God help her, she wanted it.

Suddenly Brett paused and his hold on her relaxed.

Teresa felt a wave of disappointment. She could escape from him *if she wanted to.* So why didn't she? The accusation echoed in her mind. Why didn't she?

The fact that she remained within the circle of his arms, unresisting, stripped the last thread of self-restraint from Brett's mind and soul. She wanted him as much as he wanted her. His mouth came down on hers, hard and savage. His kiss blatantly sought her acquiescence, demanded a complete and total surrender, and promised more than she had ever hoped to experience.

His tongue traced the line of her lips, then forced them open and plunged between them, filling her mouth like a hungry inferno, searching for more to devour, more to inflame. Her body reacted swiftly, simmering fires turning to a hungry conflagration, needing, yearning for his touch.

Teresa was suddenly a hostage of her own emotions and desires, flinging reason from her mind. Shockingly, as his arms tightened about her and his hands splayed upon her back, she felt her body respond to the onslaught of his kiss. It pressed toward him, silently answering the intense surge of emotions his nearness and embrace had aroused.

Nothing had ever felt so right or so good. Her eyes closed and she relaxed, her arms slipping up to rest on the broad expanse of his shoulders. Unconscious of her own movements, she pressed tighter to him, womanly curves fitting instinctively, perfectly, to his male body.

His mouth offered her an ecstasy she had never known, his body offered a world of passion she had never charted. She knew it was wrong, but, oh God, how she wanted him to continue! Yet memory of the past, of treachery and betrayal, of a pain so deep she still believed she could never overcome it, proved stronger than desire and she tore her lips from his.

"No, p . . . please," Teresa breathed against his mouth. She knew with a certainty beyond question that if he didn't stop kissing her, she was going to lose complete control of herself. "Stop. Please." A tear of anguish slid from the corner of her eye. "Please. I don't want this. Really. I don't want . . ."

"Yes, you do," Brett growled softly. "Just as much as I do." His lips brushed across hers, then slid over the delicate line of her jaw and slipped ever so lightly, tantalizingly, down the long column of her neck to press against the pale flesh revealed just above the lacy edge of her camisole.

Teresa couldn't breathe, couldn't move beyond the passionate assault of his lips and the hammering urgency of her own desires. She was lost to him, she was helpless, and for the first time in her life she didn't care.

His arms tightened their hold on her, bringing her closer, and Teresa was suddenly aware that this was what she had wanted from the very minute she'd first seen him.

And now she knew he had wanted it, too.

Reality threatened to sweep from her mind, from her life, and leave her alone with this dark stranger, this man who was both rogue and dream lover. Her mind told her to beware, to pull away and run. But her heart commanded that she stay, no matter who or what he was, that she remain in his embrace and return his kisses.

She did not know him, yet she knew that she did. Somehow, somewhere, sometime. She knew him.

As much as there was passion, Teresa felt a loneliness in his kiss and embrace that matched what she had lived with for the past four years. This, almost more than the passion that engulfed her body, drew her to him and fed the fires of her soul. But total reason had not deserted her. She forced herself finally to push away from him. "No," she said softly, and gasped for breath. "Please, Brett." She shook her head. "No."

He looked down at her, neither releasing his hold nor forcing further attentions on her.

Teresa remained standing within the circle of his arms, looking up at him and trying to decide whether to break away or slip her arms around his neck and pull his lips back down to hers.

His eyes burned with the passion that still held his body in its fiery grasp. But what frightened her more was the reflection she saw in his eyes, a reflection of her own passion. For one brief moment, she yearned to answer the call of those eyes, to allow herself the luxury of just one more kiss. But she couldn't.

Once before she'd let the sweetness of passion rule her heart and her mind . . . and both she and her son had been paying the cruel price ever since. She would never let that happen again.

Suddenly, as they stood looking at one another, each fighting their own demons, their own passions and memories, shots rang out in the distance, shattering the peacefulness of the night.

Eleven

Teresa bolted from Brett's arms as the sound of another shot shattered the night air. She ran blindly, her instinct born of panic. But it wasn't the sound of gunfire that spurred her flight—it was thought of the man whose arms she'd just fled. The gunfire had merely jerked her back to reality, giving her the impetus to run. Now, getting away from Brett was the only thought on her mind.

Unfortunately she was wearing the boots she'd taken from the dead soldier and they were holding her back. The sole of the right one suddenly split away, curled under, and nearly tripped her, while the rough leather insides of both boots scraped against her thin stockings and rubbed her ankles raw.

Pain engulfed her feet with each step she took but she wouldn't stop. She had to keep going. A huge bush loomed up in the darkness before her. Teresa swerved to dash around it.

Another shot sounded in the distance.

She cringed.

A dead limb, obscured from sight by the inky shadows and hanging directly in her path, slapped against her shoulder. Its brittle appendages caught on the rotting threads of her jacket and jerked her off balance.

Teresa gasped and stumbled.

Brett's hand clamped down on her shoulder. "Just where in the hell do you think you're going?" Fury turned his voice to a snarling growl.

She tried to jerk free of his grasp, failed, and twisted about to glare at him. "Let me go, dammit," she cried, fighting tears and the fear of what would happen if he tried to kiss her again. She didn't want to look up at him, was scared silly of what might happen if she looked up at him, yet she couldn't help herself.

She struck out at him, instinct overriding thought.

He caught her wrist.

Teresa lashed out with the other as if fighting for her very life, which she suddenly realized was exactly what she was doing—her life and the life of one of her brothers.

His quickly raised arm warded off the blow.

She tried again and Brett grabbed her other wrist.

Fury replaced fear. He was no gentleman. He'd proven that when he'd tried to force his attentions on her the moment he'd discovered she was a woman. If she'd been a man masquerading as a soldier and suspected of being a spy or traitor, or a member of the Knights of the Golden Circle, he'd have put her in irons at the very least. Instead he'd kissed her. But he was a Yankee . . . why expect anything else? She was just as angry with herself, however, because she'd responded to his advances like a wanton trollop.

"Don't touch me," she yelled and writhed against

him. "Don't you dare ever touch me again, you beast."

He held her arms against his chest. "Stop it."

She tossed her head, sending waves of black hair whipping about her face, then stood on tiptoe to glare up at him. "Don't you . . ." Teresa stopped, the rest of her words caught in her throat. The feeling of familiarity was too strong to ignore, so intense that it left her mouth agape and her body shuddering. Her mind, her thoughts, spun in confusion. It was as if they were re-enacting a scene they had already played once before. Just like this, but some other time. Looking up at him, hating him yet attracted to him, and demanding that he not touch her.

Teresa shivered. It felt so familiar, like some sort of *déjà vu,* yet she knew they hadn't done this before. She'd remember if she'd met him before. She'd remember because . . . The thought stopped her short and sent a chill of alarm racing through her. No. She had never kissed him before—never stood within his arms or felt the heat of his flesh warming hers, making her feel things that were so deep, so strong.

That she definitely would have remembered. Tears of rage and confusion stung her eyes. She fought for self-control. "Let . . . let me go," she whispered hoarsely. Fear made her act that way. Her body had merely been seeking solace, instinctively searching for some kind of reassurance, not passion. The need to be safe, to be comforted had caused her to respond to his kiss. Or maybe loneliness, but she wasn't attracted to him. She couldn't possibly be. He was a Yankee, and that said it all.

Her fingers curled into fists, short fingernails purposely digging into the soft flesh of her palms, as if by causing herself physical pain she could stop her runaway thoughts.

His eyes narrowed and flashed with irritation. "Fine, I'll release you and I won't touch you again . . . as long as you do exactly what I tell you to."

Any hint of caution flew from Teresa's mind at his arrogant words. "Do as you tell me? Hah! Why should I?"

Brett felt an insane urge to take her mouth again, to silence her defiance by covering those sensuous lips with his own. Insolence glistened in her eyes, swirling gray permeated by midnight blue, daring him, challenging him, as if she knew exactly what he was thinking and wanted to do.

He felt her resistance, the stiffness of her spine, the tension in her arms, and knew the moment he released her she would either run or slap him. "We have a long ride ahead of us, Smithers," Brett said with a mocking glint in his dark eyes. "Don't make it any harder than it has to be."

"Why shouldn't I?" Teresa retorted as one black brow soared upward.

Thoughts of desire fled from his mind. He bristled at the blatant defiance she threw at him and prepared to override and meet her challenge. Then he saw the fear that lurked behind her insolence, the uncertainty that she was trying so valiantly to hide. Suddenly the years slipped away and Brett remembered another time when Teresa Braggette had looked up at him in just this same way. He'd been about to go fishing with Traynor and she'd wanted to go. He'd said no and she'd thrown a fit, then disappeared in a sulk. A few minutes later she'd pelted him with several eggs she'd stolen from the plantation's henhouse.

He'd been fourteen and thought of himself as a man. She'd been about six or seven, and in his eyes, nothing more than a nuisance. "Brat" was what he'd called her more times than not. Brett had picked her up and given her a thorough dunking in a horse trough.

He suppressed the smile that tried to curve his lips at the memory, replacing it with an expression even more somber than it had been seconds before. The past was dead and gone. He only regretted that there wasn't a horse trough available to him now. Teresa Braggette might not be a pigtailed little girl anymore, but she was definitely just as defiant.

"Because you might not like the consequences, Miss Smithers."

Teresa's eyes grew wide and she gasped in surprise. "You'd . . . you'd force me to . . ."

In an unconscious movement Brett's gaze raked over her again, skipping from her face to her breasts. Let her think the worst of him. Maybe then she'd cooperate. And he could keep himself under control.

He sighed.

Teresa started at the small sound that slipped from his lips and her eyes narrowed in suspicion.

"No, I'm not going to force myself on you, Smithers, if that's what you're afraid of."

Teresa thrust her chin out toward him. "I'm not afraid of anything, least of all a Yankee cretin."

"Really?" Brett felt a devilish urge sneak up on

him. "What if I decided to kiss you again—would you be afraid of that?"

"No."

It would have been so much simpler if he'd just been able to let her continue on her way through the encampment and then followed her. At least then he'd only be wrestling with the damned fact that she was Traynor's sister and on her way to meet a traitor—not struggling to maintain some semblance of command over the fires of desire.

But letting her go on unescorted had been, and still was, impossible. There was no way he could take the chance of losing her trail out here in the open countryside, not when it was a near certainty that she would lead him to Proschaud. Anyway, Proschaud's note had merely instructed her to get to Richmond. It hadn't said where he would meet her so Brett had to assume either she already knew, or she knew where to wait until Proschaud showed up. Either way, Brett's men were there, too, ready and waiting.

Once they arrived in Richmond he would give her the loose rein she so desperately wanted. Teresa would bolt then without a doubt, but Brett would have enough agents around so her trail would be covered from every conceivable angle.

"Maybe you *should* be afraid of me," Brett said finally.

"I don't think so," Teresa snapped haughtily.

"Then you're a fool."

Teresa yanked her arms in an effort to pull away from him.

"Forget it, you're not going anywhere," he said,

purposely instilling an edge of impatience into his voice.

"You have no right to hold me a prisoner. I haven't done anything."

"You impersonated a soldier."

Teresa's heart hammered furiously. "That's not a crime."

"Oh, isn't it?" The smile remained fixed on his lips, an arrogant satisfaction glistening in his dark eyes.

Teresa's eyes locked with his. It was useless to try to escape, but she would not willingly give him the pleasures he so obviously craved. She grew stiff and her eyes narrowed, daring him to try anything. His fingers on her arms were like talons of steel.

She bristled at her own thoughts. She was not his prey. Nor did she intend to be his victim . . . as long as she could control her own mutinous emotions. "Okay, so shoot me," she dared.

"Don't think the thought hasn't crossed my mind."

Several more shots rang out in the distance and both turned to glance toward the horizon to the south.

If she didn't find a way to escape him everything would be lost. Teresa bit gently into her bottom lip. Maybe she could bribe him. The Braggettes still had plenty of capital tucked away, thanks to Trace's insistence that they not invest all their funds in the plantation.

She turned back to Brett. "Lieutenant, perhaps we can come to some kind of arrange . . ." Teresa stopped at seeing that he'd already dismissed the shots and had turned back to look at her. But it was where his gaze had strayed that sparked her temper. "Get an eyeful, Lieutenant?" she drawled.

Brett's gaze rose insolently upward until it met hers. There was no apology in his eyes, either for where they'd strayed or for the thought that act had conveyed to her. "Yes, thank you, a very nice eyeful in fact, Miss Smithers. Or is that really your name?"

"Smithers," Teresa said curtly. "I told you that."

"Smithers?" he echoed. His brows rose slightly.

She squared her shoulders. "That's what I said."

He nodded. "Not very original, but I guess it will do . . . for now."

"Yes, Lieutenant, it will." Anger had always been Teresa's ally when fear threatened to overpower her. Out of habit she fell back on it this time. Unfortunately, it didn't work. Her voice was filled with indignation and her body stiff as a board, but inside she was a mess of confusion, anxiety, and uncertainty. Had she really broken some stupid Yankee law by masquerading as a soldier? Or was he lying? Either way it really didn't matter. He obviously wasn't about to let her go. But what did he plan to do? Lock her up? Or would he keep her his personal prisoner?

Teresa's pulse accelerated. She would not submit to his demands.

"Smithers," Brett repeated, breaking into her thoughts.

She looked up at him and was once again assaulted by an overwhelming sense of familiarity. So strong now that it was almost terrifying. She knew him. Lord, there was no doubt of that in her mind any longer. But from where? Her mind sped through the past, hopping from one memory to another, discounting and discarding, while she grew more frustrated and frightened by the moment.

"I don't know who was firing those shots, Miss . . . Smithers," he said.

The smile that curved his lips agitated her further. She wanted to slap it off. At the same time she nearly groaned aloud at realizing a part of her also wanted to kiss it off.

"But I don't intend to wait around any longer to find out," he continued.

Before she had time to absorb his meaning, let alone think of a response, he jerked her around by the arm and pushed her into motion.

Teresa immediately dug her heels into the ground.

Brett felt his temper flare. "I'd appreciate it if you'd be a little less trouble and a lot more cooperative, dammit." He forced her to move forward.

Teresa sniffed. "I can think of absolutely no reason to be cooperative with a Yankee." She pushed at the leafy limbs of a bush protruding into her path.

"I assume, then, that you're intent on getting us killed."

"Not both of us, Lieutenant." She smiled up at him. "Just you."

Several more shots rang out in the distance and Brett paused abruptly. He hadn't been that concerned about them the first time, but they seemed to be getting closer.

As before, an intense silence followed the blasts. The normal sounds of night were absent—all had been stilled by the threatening sounds.

The short hairs on the back of Brett's neck rose slightly. Obviously there was a skirmish going on, but what was it? He didn't intend to stick around long enough to find out—just in case.

He turned his attention back to Teresa and the path.

She released the limb she'd been holding. It snapped back, but this time Brett caught it with his hand rather than his chest. He glared at her. "You don't give up, do you?"

"Never," Teresa said and, tossing her head, marched away.

Brett followed, scowling. If the situation weren't so dire he might find her attitude amusing. As it was he found it gave him cause to worry. He felt his anger turn away from her, away from himself, and in another all too familiar direction—Proschaud. Just thinking about the man made his blood boil. Jay Proschaud was a menace, as was the organization that had spawned his initial efforts of subversion. It wasn't a certainty, but Brett felt pretty secure in his suspicion that Jay's sabotage endeavors in the last few months had not been directed through the normal channels of the Knights of the Golden Circle, but rather through a faction of radicals that had split off from the secret organization.

The Knights supported the South, and Brett had once been a member, as had all the Braggette brothers, and he knew there were things even the KGC wouldn't do. Allowing innocent women and children to get caught in the crossfire and be maimed or killed was one of them.

He'd been a fool ever to join the Knights himself, and maybe Proschaud had been the same: young and eager to do something more glamorous than join the Confederate Army. But Brett had gotten out of the

KGC before he'd crossed the line. Proschaud had not. He'd crossed it, double-crossed it, and crossed again. Now he was a threat to both sides. His sabotage efforts against the Union had taken many innocent lives and destroyed property that was of no consequence to the war effort. He'd stolen for the mere sake of stealing, or perhaps it had been for self enrichment. One thing was certain: it hadn't been for the Confederacy.

Both sides wanted him. He'd be charged with treason and sabotage no matter whether the Union or Confederacy captured him, and sent to prison, probably for the rest of his life. And Brett wouldn't be surprised if even the regular units of the KGC wanted him, but they'd most likely want him dead. Dead men don't tell tales.

Brett's thoughts were suddenly interrupted as something rustled in the bushes to their right. He reached out and grabbed Teresa, nearly jerking her off her feet as he yanked her back against his chest.

"What the . . . ?"

"Shhhh." He strained to see into their moonlit surroundings.

An owl hooted.

"Great," Teresa snipped. "I'm traveling with a Yankee who's afraid of owls."

Brett released her and they walked on.

"We should reach Richmond sometime tomorrow," he said into the silence that had enveloped them.

Teresa glanced over her shoulder at him. Why was he telling her that? She'd asked where they were headed earlier and he'd basically told her she didn't need to know.

"What was your reason for traveling there?"

Teresa looked back at him again. What was he doing? Was this some sort of attempt to get information out of her? "I never said I was going to Richmond."

"I guess I just assumed it."

She stopped and turned to confront him. "Well, you assumed wrong."

"Did I?" He stared pointedly at her. "You went to a lot of trouble to disguise yourself in order to pass through the lines. Rose Greenhow used to do that, and it worked—for a while."

Teresa's eyes widened at his mention of Rose Greenhow. Everyone knew that she'd been caught spying on the Yankees several times. Her heart nearly jumped into her throat. She held her arms tight to her sides and whirled around, stomping away in the direction of the camp. The last thing she wanted him to see was how nervous his comment had made her. She was fairly quaking inside, and that did little to soothe her temper, which she was barely hanging onto. "Just what are you trying to say, Lieutenant?" she threw over her shoulder, hoping the quaver she felt in her body wasn't evident in her voice.

"Nothing," he mumbled.

Teresa stopped and spun around to face him.

Brett nearly tripped over her and swore softly.

Teresa rammed clenched fists onto her hips and glowered up at him. "Are you accusing me of being a spy?"

He met her blazing gaze. Anger and indignation sparked from the blue depths of her eyes, but fear shone brilliantly from within the misty gray. Brett felt a swift flash of guilt and shrugged it aside. As a man that was abominable, but as an agent of the Confederacy it was his duty. "A spy? Well, now that you mention it, yes, the thought has definitely occurred to me, Miss Smithers. Or whatever your real name is."

"Hah! I didn't know Yankees were capable of thought." Teresa spun around again.

Brett grabbed her arm, nearly jerking her from her feet as he yanked her back around to face him. "Am I wrong?" he challenged.

Her eyes raked over him in scathing contempt, and she spoke with deadly calm. "Wrong? You're a Yankee, Lieutenant Forsythe. What difference does it make, really, if you're wrong or not? You'll believe whatever you like."

He ignored her derision. "Why were you going to Richmond?"

"I never said I was, Lieutenant. You did."

"Then if you weren't trying to get to Richmond, where were you going?"

The question stopped Teresa cold momentarily. Where was she going? She'd never been good at spur-of-the-moment lies, which was one reason she had never been able to get the best of any of her brothers. Or avoid half of her father's punishments. She shuddered at the recollection of Thomas Braggette and the scowling face that was so much a part of her childhood memories.

But worse than that memory, at least at the moment, was the fact that she really didn't know the geographical layout of the cities north of Louisiana. Especially this far north. She'd only made it by sheer luck and a good map given her by a neighbor who used to live in Richmond. Panic threatened to overtake her. What was near Richmond? She tried to recall what other places had been marked on the map as reference points.

Think, Teresa, she ordered herself. Think, think, think. What else was in that direction? Where could she have been going? She blurted out the first and only answer that popped into her mind, "Washington."

"Washington?"

She saw the disbelief in his eyes and instinctively thrust out her chin. The man was an infuriating beast who seemed able to spark her temper faster than anyone she'd ever known. Not to mention the fact that she was getting tired of being called a liar, even though lying was exactly what she had been doing ever since they'd met. Teresa met his gaze, incorporating as much defiance and indignation into her own as she could muster. "Yes, Lieutenant, *Washington.* You have heard of it, haven't you? It's your Yankee capital."

"I know what it is, Miss Smithers," Brett growled threateningly. "I even know where it is." Her answer had thrown him, and if she was telling the truth they had trouble. Big trouble. His men were set up in Richmond, not Washington. "What I want to know is why you were going there."

"To see a friend—not that it's any business of yours."

"To see a friend," Brett repeated, skepticism etched clearly on his face. "Kind of a dangerous trip for a woman to make alone just to see a friend, isn't it?"

"Who said I was alone?"

She had him there. The only way he could declare that he knew for certain that she'd been traveling alone was if he confessed that he'd had a man following her the entire time, and he couldn't do that. "What's your real reason for heading up north, Smithers?"

Teresa eyed him coldly. "What's your real reason for wearing blue, Lieutenant, rather than gray?"

He ignored her challenge. "Perhaps there's more to your visit than merely going to see a friend."

"And perhaps there's not."

"Why should I believe that?"

He didn't miss the wariness that gleamed from her eyes.

"Because it's the truth."

"Your friend must be pretty special."

"Yes, he is."

"He?"

Her gaze jumped to meet his, then darted away. "I didn't say he, I said she."

"No, you said he."

"Well, I meant she." Teresa's fingers tightened around a handful of trouser leg.

Brett felt an unreasonable but definite stab of jealousy. He wanted her to trust him, to plead for his help and tell him that Jay was in Richmond, that he was planning another heinous act and had somehow forced her to respond to his summons. Instead Brett straightened his shoulders and looked down at her—long and hard, and forced himself to face the truth. It didn't matter what he wanted because it wasn't going to happen that way. She'd just said the person she was going to see was special, and he knew that person was Jay Proschaud. Brett felt his insides roil. She was still in love with Proschaud.

Twelve

The shots were definitely closer now, but still far enough in the distance so that Brett wasn't all that worried. If he had wanted Teresa to be quiet on their return to camp, however, he might just as well have wished upon a star—for all the good it would do.

With only moonlight illuminating their surroundings, Teresa tromped ahead of him through the copse, stepping on dry leaves, snapping twigs beneath her feet, and savagely slapping bush and tree limbs from her path. And all the while she muttered under her breath. He couldn't make out what she was saying, but he had no doubt the acrimonious remarks were directed solely at him.

But it didn't matter. He was salving his anger by allowing himself the momentary indulgence of enjoying the view directly ahead of him. Her trousers were a bit baggy, but not enough to camouflage the sensual sway of her hips or the firm, round curve of her derriere as it rose first on one side, then the other with each step she took.

Spurred by the memory of their kiss, his imagination took a detour from the mundane, everyday thoughts and strategies of war and ventured onto a much more dangerous battlefield. What would it be like, he wondered, to run his hands over those provocative female curves, to experience the feel of Teresa Braggette's hot, naked flesh beneath his fingertips? To taste her total, unresisting passion?

Brett's fantasy began to affect him. He felt his body start to harden at the path his thoughts had taken. Cursing softly, he tried to redirect them but found that impossible given the delectable sight still in front of him. The inseam of his trousers, already a snug fit, began to tighten further.

A few feet ahead of him Teresa pushed aside another tree limb, ducked past, then released it. The leafy bough snapped back.

Brett looked up just in time to see it coming. "Son of a bitch," he cursed sharply, and raised his arms to ward off the blow, but it was too late. The flying limb slammed against his chest and the air in his lungs rushed past his lips. The world suddenly took on a dazzling array of swirling colors and the stars that had been in the sky dropped to dance crazily in front of his eyes. He gasped for air and stumbled back several steps in an effort to maintain his balance and remain on his feet. The heel of one boot came down on a half-buried rock, his ankle twisted, and his weight jerked to the left. Sputtering a string of obscenities, Brett flailed the air with his arms.

Teresa paused, glanced back over her shoulder, and grinned wickedly.

Brett stood bent over, hands on his knees, hastily gulping air. He glared up at her, and for the briefest of seconds Teresa's grin faltered and the feeling of devilish satisfaction deserted her. Had she really hurt him?

He saw the smug little smile that curved Teresa's lips and wished fervently for a horse trough. Just for a moment, that's all it would take. He gulped in another lungful of air and began to feel as if he'd live.

If she didn't act like a lady, did he really have to act like a gentleman? The thought intrigued him, though he knew better than to pursue it. He had more important things to tend to. Remembering his lascivious thoughts before being nearly catapulted into space, Brett wondered if she had read his mind and known he had practically undressed her with his eyes.

"Oh, I'm *so* sorry, Lieutenant," Teresa cooed, her tone falsely sweet. Her smile widened. "I didn't mean to hurt you."

"Hurt me? No, I'm sure you didn't mean to do that. You were probably trying to kill me," he snarled.

Teresa's eyes widened in a feigned expression of shock and she clapped a hand to her breast. "Oh, Lieutenant, however could you say that?"

"Well, I don't know, Smithers. I guess I just have a hard time trusting a southern woman who dresses like a man and pretends to be a Union soldier."

Teresa's expression changed to one of resentment and challenge. "What about a southern gentleman who joins the Union Army, Lieutenant? What kind of trust does he deserve?"

Their gazes locked while the attraction smoldered between them, drawing them to one another in spite of themselves.

Brett was the first to look away, anger at both her and himself overriding the feelings of lust he'd had only moments before. He shook his head and pushed to his full height. It wasn't only his bruised ego that needed salving, or his temper that needed calming. His overheated libido, along with a ridiculously zealous imagination, was definitely creating a problem for him. Especially since the cause of both was totally out of reach. Brett Forteaux and Teresa Braggette. He almost snorted aloud. The mere thought was ridiculous. There was nothing between himself and Teresa . . . never had been . . . never would be . . . never could be. And he'd mentally tick off all the reasons why . . . as soon as he could remember what in the hell they were.

He rolled his shoulders to get out the last kinks, and looked around. The world was normal again, their surroundings varying shades of blackness, the stars back in the sky where they belonged.

Teresa tossed her long hair over her shoulder and walked away.

He watched as the dark waves fanned across her shoulders and back like a luxurious ebony veil and bounced softly with each step she took. He wondered what it would be like to let those silky strands slide through his fingers, to feel their satin smoothness tumble onto his chest and tangle with the mat of blond curls there. Brett instantly slammed a lid down on his wayward thoughts. What was the matter with him? He'd just come close to getting his head knocked off while daydreaming like that—if he kept this up he'd have to figure he was unconsciously trying to commit suicide.

Silently damning her impudence and his stupidity, he followed her, his hands curled into fists and his jaw clenched tightly. How in the name of all that was saintly could he desire Teresa Braggette? Especially the way she was made up. Without that hair cascading over her shoulders anyone would have thought she was a young man . . . a very slightly built, whiskerless young man, but a young man all the same. Which meant he must be crazy. Either that, or he'd gone too long without enjoying the pleasures of a woman. He tried to think of the last time he'd been with a woman . . . couldn't remember . . . and decided that was the answer. He was only feeling this . . . this desire for Teresa because it had been much too long.

Brett cursed the string of circumstances that had put him in this position in the first place—the Knights for their lies, and himself for believing them, even for a little while. He cursed Jay Proschaud for being such a fool—or a devil, he didn't know which—and Teresa for being foolish enough to marry the man. She should have known better. Done better.

And lastly he cursed Eugenia Braggette for having such a beautiful daughter.

He could have kept up the string of silent expletives except that ahead of him Teresa broke from the shadowed copse and walked into the small clearing where they'd made camp. Brett followed instantly, almost on her heels. He'd noticed minutes earlier that the shooting in the distance had quieted again, meaning that the skirmishers were on the move, had stopped to reload, or one side had achieved victory and the fighting had ended.

The thought that whoever had been shooting could be on the move, and possibly coming in their direction, bothered Brett more than he wanted to admit. He glanced at Emerson, who stood lounging lazily against a tree on the opposite side of the clearing. A cheroot dangled from one corner of his whiskered lips, while white wisps curled gracefully into the air from the glowing tip of the burning tobacco. He had his thumbs hooked around the well worn and frayed red suspenders under his coat.

Brett glanced about quickly and saw that everything had already been dismantled and packed. The horses stood tethered nearby, saddled and ready to go.

"Hear those shots?" Emerson asked Brett.

Brett nodded. "Yeah, I figure it's a couple of skirmishers. Either that or someone trying to hunt down a meal." He ignored Teresa as she stamped across the clearing and flounced down on a rock near the horses. "I don't think they're near enough for us to be concerned, though." He glanced back over his shoulder in the direction he calculated the shots had come from. "On the other hand, I don't think we should wait around here any longer and find out I'm wrong."

Emerson nodded and pushed away from the tree. "My thoughts exactly." He smashed the cheroot's burning tip against the worn heel of his boot and slipped the butt into his shirt pocket. He glanced at Teresa from beneath a snarl of bushy eyebrows, then looked back at Brett. "What about her? She okay?"

Teresa glared at Emerson. "I'm fine, no thanks to your Lieutenant. And don't talk about me like I'm not here."

Emerson ignored her and continued to look at Brett for an answer.

"She's not hurt," Brett said, his tone harsh, "but

she's not exactly in a mood to cooperate either, so watch her. I'll ride point." He looked long and hard at Teresa, but his next words were still directed to Emerson. "If she tries to bolt, grab her and hogtie her to the damned saddle."

"Why not just do it now?"

Teresa stared at the older man, his words about tying her to the saddle completely flying past her as she realized he wasn't at all surprised to discover she was a female.

A frown cut deeply into her forehead and her eyes narrowed as she contemplated the situation. Had he already known? The thought was unsettling. How could he have known? He'd been asleep when she'd struggled against Brett and her shirt had ripped open. And even if he hadn't been asleep, the scuffle had been too far away for her torn shirtfront to be visible to Emerson, especially in the dark.

Fear, cold and gnawing, crept into her veins. It seemed impossible that he'd known, and yet she felt with dreadful certainty now that he had. If Emerson had known she was a woman then Brett had known, too—before her shirt had ripped, before her hat had fallen off. Brett had known and said nothing. He had treated her like a man, like a regular soldier. Her eyes settled on Brett, while cold, hard fury settled into her bones.

Teresa fumed, remembering how he'd made her clean his boots, and just about everything else in his tent. Never in her life had she been so furious, not even when Jay had left her. It was unreasonable, but true. Fury filled every cell in her body, hot and explosive. Brett hadn't treated her like a soldier, he'd treated her as if she were a maid. His own personal maid.

She whirled to face him. "You knew!" The words hung on the air, dripping with indignation.

Brett, checking the cinch of his horse's saddle, paused and turned to look at her. "Pardon me?" he said, turning the polite remark into a snarling challenge.

"You knew I wasn't a soldier . . . wasn't a man," she accused.

"You're right. You're much too pretty, Miss . . . Smithers, to be a man."

The compliment did nothing to soothe her pique. If anything it only intensified it. "Bastard," she hissed.

Brett stifled the relief that swept through him as Teresa stalked away. She still didn't know that he was aware of her true identity. He swung easily up and into his saddle. Things were status quo, his plan could still work. He looked down at her. "Actually, I do have a legitimate mother and father, Miss Smithers, so that curse doesn't really apply." He grinned wickedly as she scowled. "I'm sure, however, that as we ride you'll be able to think of something more appropriate to call me later."

"Son of a . . ."

Brett eyed her sharply. "That one doesn't work either." He grabbed her reins and swung his horse around. "My mother is really quite charming."

"Well, she certainly bungled the job of raising you," Teresa snapped.

One golden brow soared skyward. "War changes all of us. It causes us to do and say things we wouldn't normally even consider." His gaze bore into hers. "Doesn't it, *Miss Smithers?"*

She didn't miss the emphasis he put on her assumed name. Teresa stiffened and thrust her chin high as she mounted her horse. "A true gentleman would never forget how to treat a lady."

Brett snorted. "Let me know when we encounter a lady, Miss Smithers, and I'll be certain to show you just how gentlemanly I can be when I try." He was goading her and enjoying every minute of it. Guilt be damned. This was a hell of a lot safer than letting his imagination and his body dwell on other things. He couldn't resist one last comment. "And a true lady, I think, would never utter some of the words you use so easily." Before she could respond, Brett turned away and touched his heels to the flanks of his horse. The animal moved forward instantly. Teresa's mount followed, having no choice since Brett had a tight grip on its reins.

Teresa stared at the back of Brett's head and wished fervently that she had something to split it open with. The man was an absolute beast. She'd never met anyone so insufferable. "A *true* gentleman treats every woman as a lady," she said to his back.

Brett glanced over his shoulder but didn't respond.

They traversed a small stream but Teresa paid it no mind, the soft splashing sounds of the horses' hooves in the shallow water not even penetrating her thoughts.

They were beasts. All of them. Every damned Yankee! Uncouth, filthy beasts. They'd marched into New Orleans, forced people from their homes and took them over, stole their silverware and jewelry and destroyed their other possessions. And their commander . . . Teresa nearly scoffed aloud as her memories of General Benjamin Butler brought on a wave of disgust. He had declared it law that any southern woman in New Orleans who scorned the attentions of a Yankee be declared a prostitute!

Memories flew through her mind, none of them pleasant. She'd come close to being branded with that label, and she would have worn it proudly rather than accept the attentions of one of those filthy cretins. Her gaze moved over Brett's back. Was that where she knew him from? Had he been one of *those* Yankees?

If he had held her before, if he had made her feel as warm and protected then as he had now . . . Teresa curled her fingers into fists and hit them against her thighs, trying to force her mind elsewhere, to distract it from the traitorous thoughts it seemed so bent on recalling. If he had made desire warm her blood like he had when he pressed his lips to her neck just a short while ago . . .

"Stop it!"

Brett swiveled in his saddle.

Teresa clamped her hand over her mouth. She hadn't meant to say that aloud.

"Stop *what,* Miss Smithers?"

"Uh, nothing. I was just thinking and it . . . ah . . . popped out."

Brett turned back around.

Teresa chided herself and her thoughts instantly returned to her earlier thoughts. He hadn't made her feel anything when he'd kissed her. Nothing. It had only been her own loneliness that made her believe his arms offered warmth, her own fear that made her see protection when there was only danger. And desire? Teresa scoffed softly. That was ridiculous. She would never, ever feel desire for a Yankee, especially a Yankee who was also a southern traitor. In fact, after her experience with Jay she wasn't even certain she wanted to feel desire for any man again.

Teresa's gaze bore into the back of Brett's head. She hated him. The first chance she got, she'd bash his brains in and run like the devil.

It had been dark when they broke camp. That had been hours ago, but it was still dark. If weariness was any indication, it should have been light long ago.

They'd been riding at a slow, steady lope. She'd ridden all of her life, but never for such long periods, and never with her body constantly gripped by tension and fear. She was already fatigued beyond belief, the continual battle to remain alert proving almost more exhausting than the ride itself.

Had she been a fool to respond to Jay's letter this way? The question had been haunting her for hours, ever since she'd begun to suspect that her capture by the Yankees was not what it seemed to be. That fact answered her question. Traveling halfway across the country in answer to her former husband's summons had been a mistake. But how could she have done otherwise when he'd insinuated that one of her brothers' lives might be in jeopardy if she failed to come?

The old fury swept over her in a blinding flash. Jay Proschaud was just about the last man on earth she ever wanted to see again. She couldn't think of anything much more despicable than a man who would sneak away from his pregnant wife on their wedding night, except a turncoat Yankee who would force his attentions on a captive enemy.

As if he knew she'd been thinking of him, Brett turned. "You all right?"

Teresa looked away. "What do you care?"

Brett resettled himself in his saddle. "I guess I don't."

With a whispered profanity, Teresa let her thoughts return to Jay Proschaud. He hadn't even had the decency to leave a note of explanation or farewell. And he'd known she was carrying his child, had known it for several months before the wedding. That was the part that puzzled her. If he hadn't wanted to marry her, to give their child his name, why had he gone through with the ceremony?

Honor? She nearly choked on the thought. As far as she was concerned, Jay Proschaud didn't have any honor. Teresa shifted on the saddle and flung the memories aside. What did it matter anyway? She wasn't in love with him now, if she ever really had been, and he was no longer her husband. She'd seen to that. Jay Proschaud could rot in hell or swing at the end of a Yankee rope for all she cared. And God help him if he'd lied to her.

"Watch out for the bramble," Brett called out.

His comment broke into her thoughts and Teresa looked up at him. His jacket was dark and blended well with the night, but he wasn't quite the dark spectre she felt he was trying to be.

The needle-covered ground beneath the pine grove

they were riding through was a patchwork of light and shadow as moonlight filtered down through breaks in the leafy growth. Whenever they rode through one of these thin moonbeams, his blond hair would shine like gold.

Teresa hated herself for noticing. More, she hated herself for enjoying it, yet could not deny herself the sight.

Brett twisted around in his saddle, stood in the stirrups, and looked past her to Emerson pulling up the rear. "Everything all quiet back there?"

The older man nodded and spit a wad of tobacco juice onto the ground before answering. "Yep."

"We shouldn't have to go much farther, I'd say."

Emerson spit again. "Nope."

Brett looked at Teresa. "Are you all right?"

Her eyes darted to meet his. There had been a gentleness in his voice she hadn't expected, as if the question and his concern were actually sincere. She slapped the thought aside. Sincere? He probably only wanted to get her off guard again.

But as much as she told herself he was a blackguard, there was a part of her that couldn't forget what it had felt like to be in his arms, to be kissed. But more importantly, how it had made her respond.

She tried again to rid her mind of the memory and found it difficult to do. She'd lived with loneliness for so long it had become like a constant companion, cold and threatening. Yet at the same time it was a comfortable feeling because anything else, any other kind of emotion, was too dangerous. Love, need, passion—the acceptance of those feelings, allowing herself to indulge in them—meant taking the risk of being hurt, and she didn't think she could bear to go through that type of pain again.

Teresa stiffened unconsciously. She didn't have to take that risk. And she wouldn't. Trace would come back to Shadows Noir after the war, and her other brothers would visit often even if they didn't return to live at the plantation. Tyler wouldn't have a father, but he would have four wonderful, loving uncles.

Brett maneuvered his horse down the slope of a deep gulley, and StarDancer followed immediately.

Teresa clung to the saddlehorn and pressed her feet against the stirrups to keep her balance.

"Careful," Brett called back.

She looked up at him. The sense of familiarity was still there but now it didn't bother her as much as it had. He only reminded her of someone and she would remember who that someone was in time. But it wasn't really important. They'd be in Richmond soon and then she'd probably never see Lieutenant Brett Forsythe again.

The thought should have filled her with joy. Instead she felt a sudden and intense sadness sweep over her.

They rode for several more miles without speaking, the only sound the faint clop-clop of their horses' hooves upon the soft earth and the occasional rustle of a night creature skittering about. There was also the more disgusting sound of Emerson spitting out a mouthful of tobacco juice.

Several times Brett raised a hand as a signal for them to stop, and Teresa would find herself suddenly listening for any sign of someone approaching. But there never was anyone there. She'd watch Brett, too, and notice the way he'd sit in his saddle like a statue, still and unmoving, his eyelids half-closed as he squinted against the night, attempting to penetrate the shadows of the surrounding terrain.

After a few moments he'd signal for them to continue on. They didn't talk much now and she assumed it was because they were in Confederate territory. Several times she thought of screaming for help but squelched the idea. What would be the purpose? Brett claimed they were headed for Richmond, and that's exactly where she wanted to go.

And she knew she was probably safer on the trail with two men than she might be alone. And there was no guarantee that if she screamed and some Johnny Rebs came to her rescue they would be gentlemen. She had no delusions that all southerners were gentlemen, though it was a nice thought.

Once they caught sight of Richmond, however, she'd find a way to escape Lieutenant Brett Forsythe if it was the last thing she did . . . which she sincerely hoped it wouldn't be.

Teresa wiped a hand over her face, leaving a small dirt smudge on her forehead. She was tired, sore, and brain-weary. And if she never saw another Yankee uniform, or another Yankee, it would be all too soon.

She glanced at Brett and her mutinous thoughts forced her to wonder if there wasn't at least one Yankee she wouldn't be so unhappy to see again after the war. But as quickly as the thought developed in her mind, she rejected it.

Lieutenant Brett Forsythe was the last man she ever wanted to see again—next to Jay Proschaud.

Dawn broke over the horizon quietly, a glow of pink-tinged gold that crept slowly across the land. It steadily chased away the chilly darkness and left only a few dusky shadows hovering about the landscape. War was nowhere in evidence in either sight or sound. Teresa felt as if she hardly dared to breathe for fear the magical peace that had befallen them with the breaking of a new day might be cruelly dispelled.

Brett turned around in his saddle. "We'll be arriving soon."

She realized immediately he wasn't talking to her, but to Emerson, keeping his eyes as well as his words averted from her.

"Look sharp and keep alert. We haven't run into any problems yet and there's no indication we will. But things can change in a minute and we won't have an update on the situation until we make contact with Handel, so there's no telling what we're riding into."

"Right. You want me to hang on to her?"

Brett's gaze shifted to Teresa.

She shuddered as her eyes met his. The man who had held her in his arms and looked down at her with warmth and passion was nowhere in sight. This man's eyes held the chill of an ocean storm, while his facial features had turned as hard and cold as ice.

"No, I'll keep the reins," Brett said, "you just keep an eye on her—and on my back. Once we reach town we'll head straight for Gracen's place."

Thirteen

"Gracen's place." Teresa repeated Brett's words beneath her breath. She didn't know who Gracen was, or where his place was, but it was a start. If she could manage to get away from the Lieutenant and that grizzled old coot, knowing where she was running from was better than knowing nothing. And the information just might help her get to where she wanted to be.

Jay's letter hadn't been as specific as she'd have liked, but he'd given her enough clues to figure out where he wanted her to go. At least, she hoped she'd figured it out.

It had been years since she'd been to Richmond with her family, but during their courtship Jay had mentioned on numerous occasions that while on business trips with his father they'd stayed at the Hotel Spotswood, near the Capitol Building.

Teresa assumed that was where he wanted her to go since he hadn't stated otherwise. It was all supposition, of course, but she assumed that Jay hadn't been more specific in case his letter was intercepted, which she was beginning to suspect was exactly what had happened . . . by one Lieutenant Forsythe. But if she was right, the Lieutenant had forwarded Jay's letter on to her, unlike Jay's letter that she'd found in the Lieutenant's trunk.

They mounted a small knoll and Brett signaled for them to halt.

Teresa's heart suddenly skipped a beat and began to hammer against her breast. The city of Richmond sprawled in the distance, the roofs creating a jagged horizon. It was much bigger than she'd imagined. Her hopes plummeted momentarily. How would she ever find her way around?

"The city of seven hills," Brett said softly.

She looked at him quizzically.

He caught her gaze and smiled in spite of himself. "Richmond is built on seven rolling hills. I used to come here with my father."

"Your knowledge of the South must come in handy, now that you're in the Union Army," Teresa said coolly.

"You'd be surprised."

Teresa bristled. "I doubt it."

Brett eyed her pointedly. "I don't."

She tossed her head, sending her hair sliding across her shoulders, and then turned away. "Humph. Nothing a Yankee would do would surprise me."

Brett turned to Emerson. He pointed to the left. "If I remember right, that's Manchester," he said, indicating the small township on the opposite bank of the river. "Right?"

Emerson leaned slightly to one side and spat tobacco juice onto the ground, then straightened and nodded to Brett. "Yep. Conners and Dellows were waiting there when I checked. Said when we arrived to get word to them and they'd meet us at Gracen's place."

Brett nodded. "Good."

Teresa stood slightly in her saddle. Richmond's Capitol Building was clearly evident beyond the buildings that lined the river's edge. If Richmond was similar to New Orleans, she knew they'd be warehouses, shipping depots, mills, and machine shops. The tall, pillared Capitol sat on the city's highest knoll, a flag flying proudly from its roof, no breeze stirring the air to ruffle its folds.

It had been a long time since Teresa had visited Richmond with her parents but not so long that she didn't remember some of its landmarks. And even if she had forgotten them, the same neighbor who had drawn her the map had also reminded her where certain things were.

Approximately a block west of the Capitol she recognized the unmistakable spire of St. Paul's Church reaching up into the sky. Her gaze took in the entire landscape, moving rapidly from one end of the city to the other. It was bigger than she remembered, and more widespread.

If memory served her right, and she prayed that it did, Jay had said that the Spotswood Hotel was near the Capitol Building.

She glanced quickly at the Lieutenant. He had brought her to exactly the place she wanted to be, but why? Had he intercepted Jay's letter and brought her here so she would lead him to Jay? The thought troubled her. What could Jay possibly be doing?

Teresa knew most Yankees were crazy, but purposely riding right into the middle of enemy territory was absolutely too much. Worse, into their capital city. Unless . . . she bit her bottom lip. Unless he had planned this whole thing, which would mean she'd been the bait all along. But for what?

She would have to try to find out before she escaped. It was the only way to sabotage his plan. She glanced over at him.

He pulled a small notebook from his breast pocket and began to read one of its pages.

Teresa's heart nearly flip-flopped at the thought that suddenly filled her mind. Was it possible that Brett was after one of her brothers? The idea sent a shiver up her spine. She clenched her hands into tight fists to keep them from trembling.

That had to be it. They were after one of her brothers. Jay had never been one for heroics, but her brothers . . . that was a different story. She remembered her mother saying once that their deeds sometimes went beyond bravery right into foolhardy.

Her mind tripped frantically over what she knew of her brothers' activities. Traynor was still running the blockade and bringing in supplies from Bermuda. Travis was in Nevada, sending what money he could to help the cause and searching for his wife Suzanne's missing brother. Trace was stationed in Richmond as a special aide to President Davis, and Traxton's cavalry unit was always nearby.

Her hands began to tremble as another, more ominous thought took root in her imagination. The President. What if . . . She tried to force the thought away, but try as she might, it would not dissipate.

Teresa took a deep breath and forced herself to face the idea. What if Brett planned to use her as a way to get past the guards at the Capitol Building? And past her brothers? The blood nearly stopped within her veins; turning chill with fear. What if his plan was to assassinate the President of the Confederacy . . . Jefferson Davis?

"Emerson, we'll split up here."

His voice jerked Teresa from her thoughts. She jumped in the saddle, suddenly back in the present. Her gaze shot to Brett.

He leaned forward to look past Teresa. "I'll go directly through town and on to Gracen's. You check yourself into the Spotswood Hotel and make contact with Handel. After both of you check things out, leave Handel in town and come out to Gracen's."

Teresa looked at Emerson. He merely nodded at Brett and, pulling on the reins of his horse, turned the animal aside and rode away.

Check into the hotel? She watched as Emerson rode toward another knoll. Why were they splitting up? Why was Emerson checking into a hotel? And who was Handel? She swallowed hard, suddenly afraid of the answers to her own questions. What was Emerson supposed to check out? Jay? Her brothers? The President?

She turned to look in the direction he'd ridden but there was no sign of him. Teresa looked back at Brett. He'd told Emerson to check into the Spotswood Hotel, the same one she was supposed to go to and await Jay. Did they know that? Was that why Emerson and this Handel person were there?

Teresa felt panic mounting within her breast and fought to control it. Not yet, she told herself. She couldn't lose control yet. There was too much at stake and she couldn't be certain of what they knew, or even what they were planning to do.

Teresa's fingers tightened on the saddlehorn. She glared at Brett, even though he paid her no mind. He would have another think coming if he planned to use her to get to the President. Or to one of her brothers. He could have Jay, but not the others.

She inhaled a long, ragged breath. She had to know more about his plan. Her mind zipped along at a frantic pace. If she stayed with him and delayed her escape, maybe she could learn more of what he hoped to accomplish in Richmond. That way, once she did get away she would be able to warn Trace or Traxton.

Brett looked at her. "Miss Smithers, we're going to ride through town and on to the home of a friend of mine. Put your hair back up under your hat until we get through town. It'll be safer that way."

"For who, Lieutenant?" Teresa taunted, unable to help herself.

"You," he said bluntly. He slipped the notebook he'd been looking at back into his pocket. "When we get to my friend's place I'd appreciate it if you could find it in yourself to act like a lady." His features remained stoic, his voice cool. "If you know how."

Her brows rose slightly at the barb. "Well, I'll do my very best, Lieutenant," she said, "but only if you'll try to act like a gentleman . . . that is, if *you* know how."

"I'll do my very best, Miss Smithers," Brett said, mimicking her words and urging his horse forward with a tug on his reins.

"That will be an interesting change," Teresa snapped.

Ten minutes later they were crossing the James River on the Mayo Bridge, the only footbridge for several miles and the only entrance to the city from the south other than two railroad trestles.

The steady rhythm of the horses' hooves upon the thick wooden planks echoed softly in the still afternoon air. They passed several carriages, and each time one neared Brett glanced at her, as if warning her to remain quiet. His face remained stoic, his eyes calm, yet she sensed a tension in him that made her nervous. She had no intention of screaming for help or trying to run from him—not until she found out for certain what he was up to. But, of course, he had no way of knowing that.

Teresa glanced to her left and saw Tredegar Iron Works on the shoreline slightly upriver from the bridge. Huge stacks of black cannonballs littered the grounds like giant pyramids, while dark gray smoke billowed from the building's tall stacks.

Brett and Teresa moved down Fourteenth Street toward the Capitol and turned left on Main Street. The city began to look more familiar as they passed the Exchange Hotel, the post office, and the bank. Brett maneuvered the horses onto Tenth Street, then Bank, and Teresa looked up to see that they were passing directly in front of the Capitol.

She looked at the Lieutenant, puzzled. Why in heaven's name was he taking a route that led them past the Confederate Capitol? Did he want her to scream? To try and run? Her mind searched frantically for an answer, for some rhyme or reason to his actions, and found nothing but more confusion. She looked back at the elegant building. Trace might be in there, right this minute. Perhaps Traxton, too. The urge to break away and charge her horse up the curved drive was almost overpowering. Instead, she sat stiffly in her saddle and reminded herself that she needed to find out what Brett was up to.

She glanced at Brett but he seemed to be paying no mind to either her or the Capitol and its guards. More curious, he didn't even seem nervous about being in enemy territory.

Teresa looked back at the building as they neared the corner and began to leave it behind. It was three stories in height and topped by an ornately trimmed portico. In the center of the portico was a huge fan window which was in turn framed by two half-fan windows. Their panes caught the afternoon light and reflected its shimmering brilliance.

The knoll upon which the building sat had obviously once been a lush blanket of green grass. But war had taken its toll here, too. The grass was full of weeds and the trees around the boundaries of the property and along the walking paths heavy with unpruned limbs laden with Spanish moss.

She turned away from the building as they crossed the corner street leaving the Capitol behind, and took a deep breath.

"I wouldn't scream, if I were you," Brett said.

Teresa looked at him quickly, instantly recognizing the hard gleam in his eyes. She felt an instant flash of rebellion. "And just why not?"

"Because you never know what might happen." He smiled, but the curve of his lips conveyed only a smug satisfaction. "Someone might believe you were in need of rescue, Miss Smithers. Shots could be fired, and someone would most likely get hurt. Perhaps someone . . ."

She looked back at the two guards standing at the entrance of the drive that led up to the Capitol building.

". . . you care about very much," he went on.

She tossed her head and snorted softly. "Obviously we're not talking about you."

The smile widened. "Obviously." Brett saw the annoyance that turned her eyes dark and fathomless, saw the fury that held her shoulders stiff. But he also saw something else . . . resignation, and this last allowed him to relax a bit. Whether she thought his threat was directed against her, one of her brothers, or even Proschaud, he didn't care. It had worked to keep her compliant, and that's all he needed at the moment.

If she'd screamed he had no doubt he would have been assailed by the two guards and just about any other man within earshot. A southern woman screaming for help was not something a gentleman ignored.

Brett rubbed his temple. He seemed to have had a constant headache ever since the plan to intercept Teresa had been formulated.

If she caused any trouble while they made their way through the city, his plans to capture Proschaud and put an end to his atrocities would be ruined.

Deep, throbbing drumrolls of pain slammed at his temples.

The Confederacy couldn't afford to allow Proschaud to continue. Once he might have thought he was doing good for the cause, but now he was nothing more than a threat to everything it stood for.

Brett glanced at Teresa, then touched his heels to his horse and spurred the animal into a faster pace. The quicker they got out of the city, the safer he'd feel.

Three horsemen turned the corner ahead of them and began to approach. Brett's gut clenched with the tension that suddenly gripped his insides and caused his fingers to tighten on his horse's reins.

Traxton Braggette rode one of the lead horses and was thoroughly engaged in a conversation with the man riding beside him.

It was over. He glanced quickly at Teresa. She had her head turned away and hadn't noticed her brother riding toward them. But she would. Any minute she'd turn back and see him. Then she'd call out and it would all be over.

Brett's mind searched for an escape, a way to save his plans. But there was none. They were in the center of the block. If they turned around it would look suspicious and draw Traxton's attention. And there was nowhere else to go. There were no alleys between any of the buildings, and since they were in the business district, no carriageways.

Brett jerked the brim of his hat down low over his face, hurriedly raised the collar of his jacket, and tucked his chin down inside of it. He glanced at Teresa. "Pull your hat down over your forehead," he ordered gruffly. "Now!"

She jerked around, startled.

"I said *now,*" he commanded again.

Instead, Teresa looked up the street. Brett saw her face light up as she recognized her brother. Her hand moved upward.

"Don't," he warned, "or they'll die."

Teresa paused and looked at Brett, shock and horror reflected in her eyes.

"I mean it," he bluffed. "Say or do anything to make them notice you and I'll kill them." To emphasize his threat, Brett reached a gloved hand to the Navy Colt that lay nestled comfortably in the holster at his hip. With his gaze riveted on hers, he moved his thumb so that it flicked off a small thong of leather that looped from the holster to the gun's hammer, encircling it and acting as a safety.

He saw Teresa flinch and hastily pull the brim of her hat down so that her face was almost totally obscured. She slouched low in the saddle. "When this is over, Lieutenant," she hissed, "I'll . . ."

"When this is over, Miss Smithers," he said, cutting off her rejoinder, "I hope you'll forgive me. Until then, make one move to call out to those soldiers and their deaths will be on your head."

Two miles and half an hour later Teresa was still silent, which was beginning to make Brett edgy. If he'd learned one thing about the "grown up" Teresa Braggette, it was that she wasn't the silent type. He shot her a furtive glance from beneath the brim of his hat, which was still riding low on his forehead, more now to block the brightness of the afternoon sun than to hide his face. She was staring straight ahead, her hands clasped around the thick saddlehorn, her shoulders still stiff, her back straight.

She appeared thoroughly uncomfortable and totally defiant, but it was the look in her eyes that made him even more nervous—fury fairly shone from those gray-blue depths.

Brett shifted position in the saddle and shot her another glance. Determination. To do what? Escape? One corner of his mouth pulled upward. If that was what she was thinking then he had nothing to worry about because once they settled into Gracen's place that's exactly what he wanted her to do—escape.

Moving across a small bridge that spanned Shockoe Creek, they rounded a curve in the narrow road and Lance Gracen's plantation came into view. A sigh slipped from Brett's lips, but it was from exhaustion rather than relief. The past few days he'd found it necessary to remain constantly alert. His body was strung taut with tension, and it wasn't over yet.

Brett pushed the brim of his hat up with his thumb and looked at Teresa. He didn't want to think of what her brothers would say, how they'd react if it turned out that Teresa was in collusion with Proschaud. They'd hate her for it and hate Brett for bringing her in. He nearly groaned aloud at the prospect. The scandal about Thomas Braggette's murder would be nothing compared to what this could be. The Confederate government was ready to charge Proschaud with treason and would not hesitate to do the same to his wife if they thought she was guilty.

They approached the plantation's drive and, looking down the winding path as their horses moved past a pair of tall iron gates, Brett could almost forget there was a war going on.

But he knew better. Brett's gaze scanned the sprawling terrain. The afternoon sun reflected off the large, deep green leaves of a magnolia tree near a curve in the drive and lent the air a comfortable warmth.

"Is this your friend's place?" Teresa asked, breaking the silence that had hung heavy between them ever since they'd left town.

Brett turned to look at her. There had been no hardness in her tone, no coldness or accusation in her words, and just for a moment he remembered the woman he'd held in his arms and kissed.

The memory instantly fled when his gaze met hers. Teresa's tone may not have been cold or hard, but her eyes were, and they reminded him of another time and place, another episode in his life that had been just as harrowing as this was proving to be.

Several years ago, when he'd still been a loyal member of the Knights of the Golden Circle, he'd been ordered to travel to England on their behalf and procure arms, among other things. It had been the dead of winter and the sea was choppy, constantly spraying the ship with an icy foam that seemed to permeate the heavy planks of the deck and slip into the very bowels of the vessel. The air had been frigid, night and day, never warming, even beneath the sun's rays.

When they'd finally neared England's shores a fog had rolled over the water's surface, a freezing, mind-numbing coldness that melded with the icy blue waters. It was something he would never forget. There had been a wintry bite in the air that had pierced his flesh and penetrated his bones.

Now those unmistakably gray-blue Braggette eyes reminded him of that same winter's fog, that icy blue sea and its penetrating coldness. The effect was the same as it had been that day several years ago when he'd stood on the deck of the ship and tried to see England's shores.

He had been filled with anxiety and a sense of dread then, just as he was now.

"Lieutenant?"

Her voice pulled him from the murky gloom of his memories. Brett wiped a hand over his eyes, as if the gesture might eradicate the unwelcome trepidation he'd begun to feel.

"Lieutenant?" Teresa repeated. "Are you all right?"

He stared at her for a long moment, wanting to tell her to turn around and go home, to forget about meeting Jay Proschaud. He'd posted agents to watch Trace and Traxton. To the best of his knowledge neither Traynor, nor Travis was in any danger, despite what Proschaud had written her. Brett opened his mouth to tell her that, then closed it again. He couldn't. More innocent people, on both sides, would die if Jay Proschaud wasn't caught. And Brett still wasn't certain that the veiled threat against "one of her brothers" was the only reason she'd come. Perhaps that was merely a ploy to throw someone off if the letter were intercepted—a way to make Teresa appear innocent of any involvement in her husband's activities.

Fury and frustration filled him. He had to play this thing through until he knew, one way or the other, where Teresa's loyalties lay. Brett passed a hand over his eyes again. "Just a headache," he said to Teresa, repositioning his hat and focusing his gaze on the road. He didn't want to look into her eyes anymore, didn't want his body to feel what she made it feel, or his mind to remember what those gray-blue depths made it remember.

But even as he tried to convince himself that the stirrings Teresa's nearness caused within him were nothing more than physical hunger, he forced his mind to remember why he'd had her watched in the first place, why he'd assigned an agent to follow her, why he'd intercepted her in the Union encampment, and why he was bringing her to Lance Gracen's plantation.

A parade of obscenities danced silently through his head as tragic images from the past replaced thoughts of pleasure and passion. His heart contracted at the flood of personal memories that invaded his thoughts but he forced himself to face them, as he had every night since the day he'd heard the news about his sister.

Tears stung Brett's eyes and blurred his vision as thoughts of Suzanne filled his mind. Because of the secrecy required within the Knights of the Golden Circle, he hadn't been in touch with his family since he'd left New Orleans just after the firing on Fort Sumter. Then, just before the fall of Vicksburg, he'd run into Traynor in Bermuda on his way back to the states. He told Brett that Suzanne had married Travis Braggette and was living with him in Virginia City, Nevada. Brett had been ecstatic.

Then a few months ago a part of his world, the world he'd left behind and hoped to rejoin when the war was over, crumbled. A faction of the KGC had attempted to rob several wagons of the ore they were hauling down to Carson from Virginia City. Normally, Brett wouldn't have given the news a second thought; it was out of his area of operation. But it was the location that caught his attention: Virginia City, where Suzanne and Travis lived. That's when he'd learned that several families had been accompanying the wagons down to Carson City. Innocent men, women, and children had been killed in the crossfire, and one of those women had been Suzanne Forteaux Braggette.

Months later he'd learned that Jay Proschaud and his radical unit of the KGC had been behind the scheme to steal the ore from the miners. Brett's rage threatened to engulf him as his hands clenched into fists. If he did nothing else in his life he would make certain that Jay Proschaud paid for taking Suzanne's life. Brett was out of the KGC now and working directly for the Confederate government; they wanted Jay Proschaud captured almost as much as he did. That afforded Brett both the opportunity and the means to track Proschaud.

Brett fought for composure against the turmoil of his hatred of Proschaud. He still hadn't communicated with his parents, other than a short note to tell them he was alive and well and not to worry, and he had no intention of communicating with them further until he could tell them he had caught the man responsible for Suzanne's murder.

Teresa stared at Brett, wondering at his look of intense sorrow. She wanted to ask him what was wrong, what he was thinking about, but remained silent, afraid to voice her questions. He was remembering something, that much was obvious, and though she wanted to know what it was that could make him feel such obvious pain, she was afraid to ask, afraid of the answer, sensing somehow that, at least for now, she was better off not knowing. Nevertheless, she felt an insane urge to reach out and offer him comfort.

"The owner's name is Lance Gracen," Brett said abruptly, surprising her and destroying the compassion that had swelled within her.

He inhaled deeply, his breath ragged as it filled his lungs. "Actually, he's more than a friend, he's my cousin." The minute the words slipped from his lips, Brett wondered why he'd said them, then decided quickly that it didn't matter. Whether or not she knew whose plantation this was, or that Lance was Brett's cousin, was unimportant.

Her gaze moved over the gently rolling landscape. "It's beautiful," she said, forcing her tone to remain neutral, almost friendly but still wary.

"Yes." He looked at her. "Beautiful."

Teresa stiffened. Though his words had undoubtedly been in reference to the plantation, she had the unsettling impression he had meant them for her. She blushed, damning herself for being ridiculous. He was merely trying to soften her up for something, perhaps gain her trust so he could take advantage of her. But that could work two ways. She forced her lips to curve upward and looked at him coyly. "And convenient," she added.

Brett's gaze remained fixed on hers and he noted that only by looking deep into her eyes was it obvious that the warmth she'd instilled in her tone was insincere.

"Not everyone is lucky enough to have cousins sprinkled about the countryside . . ." Teresa continued. "And ones who share their own traitorous views, at that. But then . . ." she shrugged, "we all have the right to believe in what we want, I guess."

Brett smiled. "Yes, we do."

She smiled back at him. Teresa was being too nice, which Brett felt certain meant she was up to something. He could almost feel it, even hear it in her voice, but he just didn't know what it was she had up her sleeve. He didn't even know why he thought there was something . . . he just knew he did, which meant he'd have to watch her all the more closely.

A small cloud passed before the sun, momentarily stealing its bright rays. That's how he'd felt ever since learning of Suzanne's death, as if something had been stolen from him. Brett looked back at Teresa. He had every intention of letting her escape so she would lead them to Proschaud, but not tonight. Tonight he wanted to rest, to enjoy Lance and Matilda's company, their food, maybe a glass of their good wine, and most especially one of their soft featherbeds.

And Emerson needed time to contact Handel and check out the situation in town.

Teresa felt her hands tremble and tightened her fingers around the saddlehorn. She didn't know what to expect from the people in the house they were approaching—southerners who cooperated with the Yankees. For that matter she wasn't certain what else to expect from Brett Forsythe. Why was he continuing to hold her his prisoner? Did he know the truth, or was it something much simpler than that? Perhaps he merely wanted an available woman for his own pleasures.

Fear and defiance roiled within her. She glanced

at Brett through half-lowered lashes. It didn't matter, really, why he was keeping her prisoner or what his intentions were. She would find out why he'd come to Richmond and then she was going to escape and get back to the capital, and to her brothers.

She turned her attention to the house in the distance. It was not unlike many other grand plantation homes Teresa had seen. In fact it was very much the same design as Shadows Noir, the Braggette plantation in New Orleans. Her gaze moved slowly over the imposing structure. It was two-storied and painted white with tall, black-lacquered shutters adorning each window, and its front veranda was graced with eight white Doric columns.

The hardships of war only became apparent as they drew closer, dismounted, and neared the shallow brick steps that led to the entry door. Only then did it become apparent that the white paint was slowly turning gray, the mortar of the steps was chipped and wearing, cracked windows had not been replaced, and several shutters hung slightly crooked, their hinges rusted or broken.

"Remember, Miss Smithers," Brett said, taking hold of her arm, "best behavior."

She flashed him an irritated glance. She'd show him *best behavior,* all right . . . but only until she found out what she needed to know. After that he'd wish he had never met her.

Fourteen

The door swung open, its hinges squeaking slightly. "Brett, I was starting to get worried." A tall man with dark blond hair smiled and thrust his hand out. "Everything go all right?"

"A few setbacks," Brett said. "But nothing important."

He glanced at Teresa and the smile dissolved into a frown. "Oh, I see you're not alone."

Teresa's gaze moved over him quickly. He was perhaps six feet tall, his limbs long and lanky. His white shirt was open at the collar, as was the front of his brown vest, and he wore riding trousers of tan kerseymere that disappeared within the confines of leg-hugging, knee-high, black boots. He was quite handsome, but where Brett's features were rugged, his cousin's were much more refined. Teresa presumed he'd just returned from riding.

She studied him as blatantly as he did her. Upon closer scrutiny she decided he had a rather roguish appearance, accentuated by a lock of hair that spilled onto his forehead and a cleft that cut deeply into his chin.

Brett nodded. "Very astute, Lance."

Teresa started at the sarcasm that fairly dripped from his tone.

Brett pulled his hand from his cousin's and took him by the arm, hurriedly ushering him across the foyer and away from Teresa. "We have to talk."

Teresa watched them, making no effort at all to hide the fact that she was interested in their whispered conversation. She strained to hear their words but Brett's tones were too hushed, and he made certain to keep his head turned away from her, only glancing back now and then to assure himself she had not moved closer.

"That's her," Brett whispered.

"Her? Her who?"

"Teresa Braggette. Proschaud's wife."

Lance screwed his face into an expression of disbelief and rolled his eyes heavenward.

"I'm serious," Brett growled.

Lance's brows rose in surprise and he glanced past Brett's shoulder to where Teresa stood near the entry door. "You're kidding. *That's* a she?"

Teresa caught the look on Lance Gracen's face as he looked at her and blushed. They were talking about her and if the expression on the face of Brett's cousin was anything to gauge their conversation by, she wasn't receiving many compliments.

"Yes, *that* is Teresa Braggette," Brett said, "and you've . . ."

Lance did a double take. "No." He shook his head. "No, my friend, no. I've seen Teresa Braggette. I'll admit, it was several years ago when I was in New Orleans on business and had occasion to meet with her father, but no," he repeated and glanced at Teresa again, "that is definitely not the young lady I remember." Lance's face crinkled slightly in disgust. "You must have been out in the wilds too long, cuz."

Brett felt his ire rising. He was not in the mood to play games. "Take my word for it, Lance, I know what I'm doing. That *is* Teresa Braggette."

Teresa suddenly realized her hair was still tucked up under the hat she'd taken from the dead soldier. She reached up to remove it and paused. What if Brett was telling his cousin she was his aide? What if he was keeping the fact that she was a woman to himself? She lowered her hand.

Lance looked past Brett's shoulder again and shook his head. "No, I can't believe that's . . ."

Brett pushed him back. "Believe it."

"But . . ."

"No buts, just listen to me. She doesn't know who I am—she hasn't recognized me. Hopefully it will stay that way and she won't remember me until we've done what we have to do, which means you've got to refer to me as Brett Forsythe. *Lieutenant* Brett Forsythe of the Union Army, understand?" He hurried on without waiting for Lance to agree. "And make certain everyone else around here does, too. One 'Forteaux' out of anyone and she just might remember where she's seen me before, and that would ruin everything."

"She knows she's seen you before?"

"Yeah, I think so. I've caught her looking at me when she thinks I'm not watching."

"Maybe she just likes you."

Brett laughed. "No, believe me, that's not it. Anyway, I've seen her watching me, and the look in her eyes tells me she definitely thinks she knows me from somewhere, but so far she hasn't been able to remember where or when."

Lance nodded. "I'll alert the servants. Matilda isn't here, and neither is my mother."

"Good. The fewer we have to worry about the better. I plan to let her escape sometime tomorrow so we only have to keep this charade going for a few more hours."

"Let her escape?" Lance repeated. He looked at Brett in bewilderment. "Wait a minute, you've changed the plan on me." He shook his head, disbelief once again clouding his eyes. "Okay, let's say I believe you and that ragamuffin over there really is Teresa Braggette. I thought you and Emerson were supposed to follow her into Richmond, not bring her here."

"That was the plan, but I didn't have a whole hell of a lot of choice, Lance," Brett snapped. "She forced me to." He glanced over his shoulder at Teresa, his anger overtaking him for a moment. Inhaling deeply, he fought for composure and turned back to Lance. "As you can see, she did her best to disguise herself and elude us."

"You mean she knew Emerson was following her?"

"No, I don't think so, but the Yankee encampment I was in . . ."

"Yankee encampment?" Lance fairly yelled.

"Lance, please, keep your voice down."

"What the hell were you doing in a Yankee encampment?"

"Getting information. With our struggle to hold on

to Petersburg, we thought that if I could find out where their heavy munitions and cavalry were we might make a counter-move and stop them. I'd planned on intercepting Emerson farther down the road, but I got delayed in the camp and Teresa made better time than I'd anticipated."

"So what happened?" Lance urged when Brett paused for breath.

"Emerson was able to ride ahead and warn me that she was almost on top of me. By that time I'd figured out that there was no way she was going to be able to get through the Yankee encampment without a little help, and it would have taken her forever to ride around it, so I stayed put."

"And impersonated a Yankee officer?"

"Yes."

"Lucky you didn't get caught."

Brett smiled. "Well, if I had, you wouldn't have to worry about which of us was the better looking anymore, now would you?"

"I never worry about that, since I know I am. But why did you have to bring her here? She might see or overhear more than she should."

"I brought her here, dear cousin, because it was the only thing I could do. We know she's meeting Proschaud but we don't know where or when, and I couldn't take the risk of letting her run loose and losing her before she led us to him. So I played her game, and now I'm forcing her to play mine."

"She thinks you still believe she's a man?"

Brett grinned. "Well, she did until last night."

Lance's brows soared again and a gleam of sly amusement lit his blue eyes. "Oh?" The one word had more insinuation in it than if he'd actually spelled out his suspicions.

Brett's snort of disdain should have chased away the look in Lance's eyes but it didn't. "Oh nothing, you dirty-minded old man. She tried to escape while she thought I was asleep but I wasn't. Her hat fell off when I grabbed her and her shirtfront ripped opened. That's all."

Lance chuckled. "I'd say that was enough. The part about the shirtfront, I mean."

Brett gave him a look that clearly said *enough.* "And she hasn't recognized you? That's amazing. I thought one of her brothers was your best friend."

"He is, but it's been a long time since she's seen me. People change."

"Yeah." Lance grinned and looked at Brett with a twinkle in his blue eyes. "They get ugly."

"Jealousy does not become you, cousin," Brett said.

"My mother always claimed that of the two of us, I was the better looking gentleman."

"Your mother was prejudiced."

Lance shrugged. "You're probably right."

"And half blind."

Lance feigned offense. "A gentleman is not defined merely by appearance."

Brett chuckled. "You're right, cousin. He has to have manners too, which . . ." He frowned and tried to suppress a grin. "As I recall, you seem to forget whenever it suits you, especially around the ladies."

Lance looked around Brett, shook his head, and straightened. "Well, you certainly don't have to worry about me around this one."

Brett felt his temper flare in defense of Teresa and immediately suppressed it.

"So, she doesn't recognize you and you brought her here," Lance said. "Dangerous move, my friend, but what's done is done so I guess there's no help for it now. What's next?"

"We give her a room and get her a bath. And, if you don't mind, maybe one of your sister's dresses and some underthings."

"Well, since Matilda's staying in town with mother, we can't ask her, but . . ." He shrugged. "She has so many she'll probably never miss a few anyway, *Lieutenant Forsythe.* Especially for such a good cause." Lance chuckled softly.

A deep yawn overtook Brett and he shook his head. He was exhausted and sore, his body aching all over. It had been a long time since he'd ridden so hard for so many hours straight. The thought of going to bed alone and simply falling asleep had never seemed so appealing.

The two men turned and walked back to where Teresa stood. She had caught a word or two here and there, but it had been Lance's frowns, chuckles, and glances that had given her a hint about their conversation and piqued her temper. They'd been talking about her, and it obviously was not flattering. Lance had looked at her as if he wanted to pinch his nose, pick her up, and toss her out onto the porch.

She glared at them both as they approached. Whatever Yankee scheme they were plotting, if they thought they were going to use her in it they were sorely mistaken.

The two men paused before her.

Lance bowed. "Miss Smithers, forgive my lack of manners. Brett has explained the circumstances to me but it's not often I see a woman attired in . . ." He waved his hand at her.

Teresa batted her lashes at him coquettishly and reached down to brush her skirts. Instead, her hand met the rough material of Brett's trousers. She looked down at herself, having momentarily forgotten how she was dressed and what she must look like. When they'd left the Yankee encampment her clothes had been clean. Now they were soiled and crumpled.

Lord, no wonder he'd looked at her as if she'd just crawled out of a New Orleans sewer trench. That's exactly what she looked like. And probably smelled like, too. She wanted to crawl into a hole, except there weren't any around. Teresa looked back at the two men, lifting her chin and gathering as much dignity as she could. "Travel arrangements dictated this attire," she said stiffly. She could have added that she didn't much care what she looked like to two traitors, but she didn't.

Lance smiled apologetically and with obvious reluctance offered her his arm. "Well, uh, if you'll accompany me I'll show you to your room and then have my housekeeper send up a hot bath and a gown and some, uh, other essentials for you."

Teresa followed Lance up the stairs. A hot bath. It sounded like heaven. And a gown. It was too good to be true. At last she'd be able to get out of these trousers that rubbed at her legs with each step and clung to her rear end like a too-tight sock. She glanced back and noticed that Brett had disappeared.

Humph. If she was lucky, if the Confederacy was lucky, maybe one of the tiles of the foyer's black and white marble floor had opened up and swallowed him.

Fifteen

Brett paused outside of her door. He had absolutely no business entering her bedchamber. There was no reason to do so. What did he fear she might do, climb out a window?

He smiled at the thought. It was ludicrous. After all, no matter the outfit she'd donned in an attempt to elude Federal troops, Teresa Braggette was still a lady.

Yeah, a lady who had once been a tomboy and climbed trees as easily as a cat.

The thought popped into his mind from long-forgotten memories and provided the impetus to override his sudden reluctance to enter her bedchamber. He would just peek in and make certain she was in the room. Then maybe, once he'd reassured himself, he could catch a few hours of sleep.

He tapped on the door, then reached for the silver plated doorknob, his fingers wrapping around the cold metal and turning it slowly. The door was unlocked. Brett smiled to himself. If she was going to try to escape, the odds were he'd have found the door secured. He slowly pushed it open. Its well-oiled hinges rotated silently and the door swung back easily and without a sound. Brett hesitantly poked his head through the opening and looked into the spacious bedchamber. He moved cautiously, not because he didn't want to see her in a compromising situation—he wouldn't mind that at all—he just didn't welcome the idea of a vase or hairbrush hurtling through the air if she saw him snooping.

Not only did he not see Teresa in a compromising situation, he didn't see her at all. Brett straightened and stepped past the door. He looked around quickly, his gaze darting from one part of the room to another. Two of its walls were painted a soft ivory, while the other two were covered with silk ivory paper depicting blue ribbons and bouquets of pale yellow roses. The fading rays of the late afternoon sun shone through two floor-to-ceiling windows on the opposite wall. These were framed by pale blue damask draperies, drawn back from paned glass panels by a midnight blue silk cord. Brett's gaze moved to the elegant cherrywood poster bed that dominated the room. Its coverlet and canopy matched the curtains, pale blue silk trimmed with blue cord.

He pictured Teresa lying in the center of that blue silk and suddenly the idea of going to bed alone didn't seem as inviting as it had only moments ago. His hands ached to caress her alabaster flesh and let the ebony silk of her hair slip through his fingers.

The sound of a door closing somewhere else in the house echoed faintly through the thick walls, but it was enough to jar Brett from his fantasy. He shook his head and snarled at himself. Pushing aside thoughts he had no business thinking, Brett's gaze moved over every piece of furniture from the ornate bed to a tall, elegantly crowned armoire set against the far wall. Next to it was a white, marble-fronted fireplace and in front of that was a pair of blue ladies' chairs.

He listened as well as looked, straining to hear the slightest sound, the faintest rustle.

A tall cheval mirror stood in one corner and reflected his image back at him. A lemonwood writing desk was set between the two windows and a mirrored dressing table stood against the wall to his right.

His eyes moved over everything once, then repeated the route again. Once, twice, a third time. Looking, searching, assessing. What they didn't find was Teresa Braggette.

The only other door in the room led to a dressing room. Brett skirted the bed and abruptly paused as the scent of violets assailed him. He sniffed at the air. Definitely violets. Indecision tore at him. The fragrance was wafting into the bedchamber from the open door of the dressing room. That meant she was most likely in there bathing, which made sense. They'd been on the trail for several days. A bath wouldn't do him any harm either.

Brett turned to leave and paused again. A long sigh escaped his lips. He'd never be able to sleep until he assured himself she was actually in that room, until he saw her with his own eyes. Brett strode quietly to the dressing room door. Hopefully she wasn't holding anything that could prove lethal if she threw it. He looked about the room. A washstand, bureau, and tub. Exactly what he'd expected to find, except for one thing: the tub was empty. He glanced at the washbowl sitting on top of the bureau, at the rack of towels hanging from the washstand, and the small chair across the room, then back at the slipper tub. It was filled with water and, judging from the strong aroma of violets that filled the room, scented bath oil. A foam of white bubbles covered the water's surface. He stepped into the room and spun around, realizing that he was alone, that she was gone!

"Damn her hide all to hell."

Whirling on his heel, Brett strode from the dressing room and halfway across the bedchamber, then abruptly paused. Something niggled at the back of his mind.

Suddenly Brett jerked around and stared at the windows, realizing at last what his mind had been hinting at. The bottom portion of one of the tall windows had been raised, creating a doorway to the gallery. He stared at the soft lace panels between the damask curtains as they softly billowed upward into the room.

Panic knotted in his throat. Stalking to the window, he slapped back the panels and stared past the frame to the wide gallery. Dammit. He was a fool. A first class, idiotic fool for trusting her for even one second. But thankfully it wasn't too late.

"Tere . . ." Brett nearly bit his tongue off to stop her name from rolling from his lips. "Smithers!" His boots crashed down on the painted wooden planks of the gallery as he stepped past the window.

Teresa paused at the sound of his voice, one leg in midair, and swung halfway over the railing. A chill of fear raced through her veins and clutched at her heart as she heard his footsteps behind her. "Damn, damn, damn," she muttered. Her leg dropped and she scrambled frantically in search of a foothold in the trellis she'd intended to climb down.

"Dammit, woman . . ."

Panic seized her heart when she glanced up and saw Brett only a few feet away and stalking toward her. Fury blazed from his dark eyes like blue fire and pulled his handsome features taut. His hands were clenched at his sides and she had the immediate impression that he would love nothing better at the moment than to wrap those long fingers around her neck and squeeze.

Well, he wasn't going to strangle her today. She rammed her foot into one of the trellis slots, no longer concerned with avoiding the thick, thorny vines of the rose wrapped around it, and prepared to swing her other leg over.

"Oh, no, you don't," Brett snarled. He lunged forward and grabbed her by the shoulders, then pulled her back over the railing.

She landed on her feet, but he didn't release her, which was good since it took her several seconds to catch her balance. "Just where in the hell did you think you were going?"

She tried to jerk her arm free. "To a soirée," she snapped.

"Really? Well, I doubt they'd let you in dressed like that. Anyway, until I find out who you really are, *Miss Smithers,* and why you're masquerading as a soldier, you're not going anywhere." At least not until I'm ready to let you go, he added silently.

Holding on to her jacket by the shoulder, Brett forcibly steered Teresa back into the bedchamber. The open door that led to her dressing room caught his attention. He glanced toward it and remembered the tub full of hot, scented water he'd seen in there only seconds before. He pushed her toward the dressing room.

Teresa's composure fled as she realized what he intended to do. She dug her heels into the flowered carpet.

Brett stopped. "Look, we can do this the easy way or we can do it the hard way, I don't particularly care which. But either way, *Miss Smithers,"* he snarled, his tone heavy with derision, "it's going to be done."

Teresa's eyes narrowed as she glared up at him.

"You can cooperate like a lady and get in there and take a bath, or I can make you do it." He purposely let his gaze rake over her body suggestively. "Hell, lady, maybe I'll even join you."

"You wouldn't dare."

Brett sighed. "I was afraid you'd say that." With any other woman he would have welcomed the challenge, but there were too many reasons why, with Teresa Braggette, he should let it pass. Yet he knew that's exactly what he wasn't going to do. Emerson hadn't been in Richmond long enough to have had time to make certain everything was set up, which meant Brett couldn't take any more chances that Teresa might slip away before they were ready for her to escape. And he certainly didn't intend to sit one more minute in her company trying to treat her like a lady when she looked more like a dirty teenage boy. Anyway, she'd have less opportunity and agility to escape if she was dressed properly in a gown and crinolines.

Brett reached out and grabbed the collar of Teresa's

jacket, ripping it away from her shoulders and brutally yanking it down over her arms.

"Oh!" She spun away from him, her eyes wide with shock and fear. Her arms automatically flew up to cross tightly over her breasts. "How dare you?"

"You dared me," Brett retorted coldly.

"I did not."

"Yes, you did, and that was your first mistake. Your second will occur if you don't take off those dirty clothes right now and get in that tub."

Teresa's gray-blue eyes turned black with anger and her chin shot upward in defiance. If he thought she was about to take a bath with him he was sorely mistaken. She'd kill him first, somehow. She turned the full fury of her indignation on him. "I will not."

"Yes . . . you . . . will." Brett lunged at her. She tried to twist away but wasn't fast enough. His hands caught her arms and he jerked her up against him, his face only inches from her own. "Beneath those trousers and oversized shirt I know there's a woman, Miss Smithers, and my guess is she's a lady, not a trollop."

"You cur," Teresa snapped. Pulling one arm free of his grasp, she lashed out with her open hand.

Brett moved to avoid the slap, though not quite far enough, and her hand connected with the side of his neck.

"Ohhh!" Teresa's hand swung up again.

Brett grabbed her arm and twisted it down behind her. "You little hellcat," he swore, "I only want you to take a damned bath and clean yourself up."

"Take it yourself," Teresa shrieked, frustrated beyond reason. It was only her rotten luck that he'd walked in and caught her climbing over the gallery railing. She hadn't been trying to escape, but of course he wouldn't believe that. All she'd wanted to do was look around the place, maybe eavesdrop on him and Lance Gracen, because she'd had no doubt they would talk again once she was safely out of earshot. But most important, she had wanted to see where the horses were stabled so that when the opportunity to escape arose she wouldn't waste time looking for the barn. Now she was going to find out absolutely nothing—except how uncouth Lieutenant Brett Forsythe could be.

"Damn it, woman," Brett snarled, "stop being so blasted foolish."

"Foolish?" Teresa tried to twist away from him. "I don't usually take my bath with a man."

"No, you climb over galleries."

"Oh!" Too angry now to put reason to her actions, Teresa threw her body to one side. Unfortunately, she went one way while the collar of her shirt, still scrunched tightly within his fist, went the other. The frail fabric gave way in a horrendous rip. Threads separated instantly, buttons popped off and flew through the air, and the shirt, or what was left of it, dropped away from her.

Brett stared, dumbfounded, at the shirt collar he still held in his hand.

"Oh!" Teresa gasped again. She lunged at him, too outraged to think.

Startled by what had just happened, Brett was not prepared for her assault. The weight of her body slammed into him and her fists pummeled at his chest. He stumbled back, felt his right ankle twist beneath the added weight, and fell.

Teresa tumbled after him and a soft scream escaped her lips as she realized what was happening.

Brett grabbed her arms and pulled her close in order to break her fall by making certain she landed on top of him. He tried to roll his body into the fall but the effort was futile.

He felt her weight smash into his chest and one knee gouge his thigh at the same time his backside crashed resoundingly and painfully onto the dressing room's wooden floor.

For a brief moment both lay still, stunned by the fall. Brett said a silent prayer of thanks that her knee hadn't been any higher. As it was, every bone in his body was probably going to ache like hell for the next few days. It was a wonder he hadn't been knocked unconscious. He twisted his head to one side in an effort to get out from under her.

Teresa lay with her head on his shoulder, not moving, her face half-buried in the fabric of his jacket. Her dark hair fanned out over his chest like a silk veil. His hands still held her arms and he felt no urge to let her go.

Slowly, as air seeped back into his lungs and his breathing steadied, Brett's body started to become all too aware of hers—of the way her breasts pushed into his chest, the feel of one of her legs tangled about one of his. But most disturbing was how her hips were settled atop his, fitting snugly, sensuously into place as if they belonged there.

Suddenly it was as if she were a flame pressed to his bare flesh. His body caught the spark and within seconds was caught in a raging firestorm, every fiber of his being smoldering with want and need. Thoughts Brett had struggled to suppress, desires he had forced himself to ignore, yearnings he had tried to deny, filled his mind, heart, and soul and threatened to overwhelm him.

Kiss her. Take her. Kiss her. Take her.

The words echoed over and over in his mind. In a desperate attempt to contest them, Brett tried to remind himself of how she looked dressed in men's clothing, her face smudged with trail dust and her hair pinned in a knot beneath a frayed slouch hat.

His body scorned his attempts to divert its growing desire. He closed his eyes, swore softly, and ordered his mind to ignore her, his body to compose itself. The attempt didn't work. Instead he remembered the ivory shoulders he'd seen when he had nearly walked into the tent while she was still bathing, the soft swell of breasts that had peeked over her camisole when he'd prevented her escape on the trail and her shirtfront had ripped open, and the way the skin of her neck had felt so soft, so inviting, when he'd pressed his lips to it.

The thought of the pleasures he would experience just by tasting her lips was too overpowering to resist. He felt the swollen length of his need push against his trousers and press into the wall of her stomach. Damn it, he wanted her more than he'd ever wanted another woman in his life. And the why of it didn't matter. They certainly hadn't fallen in love—more like fallen in hate. But he wanted her. Good Lord, it didn't make sense. It was crazy. But God help him, he wanted her.

Teresa sensed as well as felt the change in him. Seconds ago, his hold on her had been hard, tight, and unrelenting. It hadn't really loosened, yet it felt different, secure rather than tight, possessing rather than unrelenting. His breathing had changed, too. It no longer seemed edged with anger.

She felt the hard press of him between her thighs and forced herself to remain still. When she'd first experienced that swollen part of a man with Jay she'd nearly panicked. Now she knew what it meant, and though she should be angry with him, should be indignant, outraged, and maybe even scared, she wasn't. Instead of pushing away from Brett, as she knew she should, Teresa continued to lie still, curious to see what would happen next, part of her wanting him to push her away while the other part wanted desperately for him to wrap his arms around her and claim her lips with his.

A small voice of resistance murmured at the back of her mind. It ordered her to denounce anything and everything he might try to do. Instead, she lay still, waiting.

"Are you all right?"

Teresa raised her head, pushing upon his chest with the palms of her hands. Her face was barely an inch from his as she looked down into his eyes. "What do you care?" she asked softly, edging her words with a chill.

He stared up at her, blue boring into gray, as if searching beyond the words for what dwelt within, beyond his reach.

Finally, he shook his head slightly, as if in denial. "I don't really want this," Brett said. Emotion, husky and dark, clung to every word, as it did to his eyes, his lips, the smooth skin that stretched taut against his high, sharply cut cheekbones.

She had no idea what he meant . . . and at the same time, she knew exactly what he meant . . . because the same thought was racing through her own mind. Teresa stared down at him. She felt herself being drawn deeper and deeper into the blue of his eyes, yet she had no desire to resist. "I know," she said finally, her own voice little more than a whisper, "I don't want it either."

His head rose slightly from the floor. Hers lowered toward him. Their lips met, barely a brush of flesh against flesh, a featherlight touch that seared the soul and teased the senses. But the diffidence between them lasted only a moment, a flashing millisecond of time, and then slid away as if it had never existed at all.

Emotion, hot and stirring, surged through Brett's body in a volcanic wave, feelings and hungers he had not experienced in such a long time, and which now threatened to overwhelm him and rob him of the very faculties that secured him to reality.

Her hands touched the side of his face as if to draw him closer, the tips of her fingers brushing lightly against his skin like silken threads of fire, their touch heightening his excitement, intensifying his desire.

Brett wrapped his arms around her, fitting her body to his, curve to line, plane to valley. His mouth covered hers and she surprised and delighted him by surrendering immediately. Her lips parted instantly at the hot, probing touch of his tongue and a soft moan slipped from deep within her as it slid into the honey-sweet cavern beyond her lips, a flicking snake of fire that probed and teased mercilessly.

He had tasted the wine of kings and the pleasures of princesses. He had dined on caviar and enjoyed the beds and passions of more beautiful women than he could remember. But he had never felt such a deep, gnawing hunger as Teresa Braggette aroused within him by merely lying upon his body and looking into his eyes.

He knew without a doubt that he would take her this night. Nothing short of a bullet through his heart could stop that now. But he also knew without a doubt that with the coming of the morning's light he would regret it. That, however, was a thought for tomorrow, and he would worry about it tomorrow . . . not tonight.

Sixteen

Teresa knew she should fight him. But she couldn't because though she knew it was what she should do, it wasn't what she wanted to do.

His eyes, as she'd stared into them, had allowed her a glimpse of the passion that dwelt deep within him. It was dark and intense, an inferno of need that frightened her to the very core of her being. But it also called to her, beckoning her to enter a world she had never known.

But there had been something else in his eyes, something he normally kept well hidden, guarded against the world. Teresa wasn't certain what it was, she just knew that it called to her and she was powerless to deny it.

For days she had resisted the longing that burned within her to be held by him again. But no more. His arms were her wall against the world, his embrace her home, his lips her haven.

It was like the time he'd held her tight and pressed his lips to her neck. His touch set off a maelstrom of need within her, sparking desire, igniting passions.

His mouth was a smoldering brand upon her lips, demanding more. It was a sweet torture she prayed would never stop, kisses that ravished her and left her breathless. She felt his arms crushing her against him and reveled in the feeling, knowing no shame at giving herself to her enemy and wishing fervently that it would never end, that he could hold her, kiss her forever. Forgotten for the moment were all the reasons they should not be together, the differences in their lives, their beliefs, their loyalties. There was only this moment, a moment both had known was inevitable, a moment they had both fought against, feared, and knew would come nevertheless.

His lips moved hungrily over hers, ravaging the delicate flesh as a low growl of need emanated from deep within him. Her tongue sought his and danced a duel of fire, tasting and teasing as he had done only seconds before.

Her hands slipped to the back of his neck and buried themselves in his hair, her fingers tangling in the blond strands.

His hands moved over the bare flesh of her back, then one slipped beneath her arm. She felt the hot touch of his fingers on her breast, searing through her thin camisole, cupping the swollen mound of flesh and caressing it slightly. His thumb moved over her nipple and she shivered as a ripple of pleasure coursed through her body.

Teresa moaned and writhed on top of him. Hunger invaded her veins like a sweeping tide, a relentless spread of longing she could neither deny nor ignore.

He was the devil incarnate, and he was everything she wanted. Her soul would be damned forever, but her heart would soar, if only for a short while.

Holding her to him, Brett rolled Teresa onto her back and moved over her. His lips brushed hers, then traveled downward to the hand that was still kneading her breast. He slid his hand slowly down the curve of her ribcage as his mouth closed hotly over her nipple.

Teresa's body responded on its own, arching upward, silently begging for his touch to continue. Coherent thought fled her mind as swiftly as smoke on the wind, leaving her with only one thought and desire: to be his.

His fingers played with the pale blue ribbon that tied her camisole closed until it fell loose and he brushed the thin fabric aside.

Teresa slipped her hand inside of his shirt.

Brett smiled and pushed away from her.

She opened her mouth to protest, but paused as she saw him shrug the shirt over his shoulders and throw it aside. Then he pressed his broad chest to her aching breasts and wrapped her once more in his arms. For what seemed an eternity his mouth moved over hers, his tongue a rapier of seductiveness, his roaming hands velvet gloves of sensuality.

When he stripped her of the trousers and the thin pantalettes beneath them, she didn't know. Nor did she care. His hand sliding into the dark patch of hair between her legs was torment and rapture, invoking pleasure while holding its crest at bay.

She writhed beneath him, calling his name softly when his lips left hers to move over her breasts. Her hands traveled the wide range of his shoulders, sliding over muscle as hard as steel.

"Oh, Brett, yes," Teresa moaned. She raised her hips to meet him as his hand once again roamed that dark terrain.

It was almost more than he could bear. A shudder wracked his body as he fought for control.

Pushing to his feet, Brett hastily ripped off his remaining clothes and kicked his boots aside. For one brief second he stood still and looked down at her. Desire tightened his throat and fueled the savage hunger that had been raging within him since the night she'd walked into his tent. She was more beautiful than he had imagined, her body lithe and lovely. Her skin was like gold-touched ivory, her pebbled nipples the color of *café au lait,* and the hair between her thighs a thatch of downy-soft sable.

The burning ache in his groin intensified as his eyes continued their tour of her body, the mere sight of her fuel to the already raging fire.

Teresa stared up at him, her eyes blurred with desire, her lips aching to know the feel of his ravishment again. He stood naked before her, and she had never seen a more magnificent sight in all of her life. Teresa felt the breath catch in her throat as she forced her eyes to move over him. Her gaze traveled over the broad expanse of his shoulders, the chest sprinkled with blond hair, the long legs that allowed him to tower over her, and the arousal that so blatantly told her more than anything else how much he wanted her.

Her body ached for his touch, burned for the caresses he had given so freely only moments ago. She raised her arms toward him, beseeching him to return to her. "Brett," she whispered softly.

Sinking to his knees, Brett reached for her, pulling her into his arms and, as a groan filled his throat, covered her mouth with his in a kiss that was savage in its need of her, feral in its hunger. His tongue filled her mouth as his hands moved over her body, feeling every inch of her. He tore his lips from hers to trail along the curve of her neck, leaving behind burning flesh and moving on to lavish hot, hungry kisses upon each breast.

"This is mad," Brett whispered against her, as much a curse as a declaration. He rose and claimed her lips again, exulting in the ardent intensity of her response. Her hands caressed his shoulders and moved down his arms as her legs entwined with his. Her hips pushed upward and ground their lower bodies together, need against need.

Brett felt as if his self-control was about to shatter. The need to take her was almost overwhelming. He slid a hand down her body, through the thatch of dark hair, and in between her legs.

A small shriek of surprise escaped Teresa's lips and he hastily covered them with his own, his tongue plunging into her mouth as his finger plunged into the soft flesh between her thighs.

She twisted mindlessly beneath him, her body burning with the fever of his touch. When his finger plunged deeper, her senses spiraled out of control and she clung to him, needing more, wanting more. His thumb moved over the sensitive nub of flesh as his finger sunk farther, deeper into her.

Teresa's body pressed wildly against his and her fingers dug into the hard muscles of his arms. "Brett, Brett," she rasped. "Please, I can't . . . what are you doing . . . what . . . ?"

"What we were meant to do together," he said

thickly. His mouth covered hers and his tongue once more danced around hers.

Teresa thrashed wantonly beneath him, needing more, wanting more from him. Jay had taken her in the dark, kissing her into excitement and then taking his pleasure as he left her behind. He had never taken her into this world of passion, into this wanton, wonderful world of desire, but then she'd never really expected to go. Hadn't her mother always told her it was merely a woman's duty to endure?

She felt his hand move away from her. Teresa looked up at the lean, dark face that hovered above hers. At that moment he pushed into her, the hardness of his need invading the heat that smoldered between her thighs. She didn't pull away from him. This was what she wanted, what she had wanted from the first moment she'd seen him.

With each thrust he plunged deeper, moving slowly yet steadily, coaxing her body to accept him, savoring the silken heat that enveloped his swollen shaft. Brett kept his eyes closed as he hovered above her, relishing each movement. He felt her hips rise to meet his thrusts, then her arms slipped around his neck.

He looked down. Her eyes mirrored the passion that filled his body while her lips were slightly swollen from the fierceness of his kisses.

Teresa felt her body fill with his as he pushed into her. She had thought she knew what it was like to be with a man, but she had known nothing. These delicious, heady, wild feelings were all new to her. Her senses, just like her body, seemed suddenly acutely aware of everything about him, from the erotic scent of their lovemaking to the faint hint of horseflesh and tobacco that clung to his smooth, hot skin. His chest was like a wall of fire against her breasts, while his long body was a vine of sensuality entwined about her own.

His thrusts quickened and became deeper and she matched the movement of her hips to his until they moved as one, the urgency burning between them a living, breathing need that bound them together.

Suddenly the world began to spin madly out of control as a wash of pleasure swept over her. Teresa writhed and twisted beneath him, erotic abandonment seizing her in its grip and stripping her of all inhibition. In return it allowed wave after wave of the most achingly intense rapture to wash over her.

The hungry coil of need that had erupted to life deep within her when Brett had entered her exploded in a burst of physical sensations like nothing she had ever dreamed of. Lightning bolts of throbbing pleasure sped through her body, crashing into one another and shattering, only to be replaced by a new onslaught, another wave.

"Brett," she cried out loudly. Teresa threw her head back and, as her arms held tight around his neck, pushed her body up to meet his. "Oh, Brett, please."

He heard his name on her lips and tightened his arms around her, clinging to her while his control vanished with a shudder of ecstasy that wracked his body as he followed her into that same abyss of pleasure.

Teresa lay still on the floor of the dressing room and listened to the sound of his ragged breathing. He was heavy atop her, and his body was hot and moist with the perspiration caused by their lovemaking, but it was a happy feeling that she would gladly welcome every night of her life if she could. She smiled. No one had ever told her it could be like that, she thought dreamily. She had never known, until now.

As if he sensed her thoughts, Brett rose slightly and rolled off of her. Lying beside Teresa, he propped himself up with one elbow and stared down at her. "So, *Miss Smithers,* are you ready to take that bath now?"

Seventeen

Her state of euphoric satiation suddenly burst, the warm cocoon of ecstasy dissipating so quickly it left Teresa momentarily disoriented. She blinked rapidly, realized with a start where she was, and jerked away from Brett to stare into those dark blue eyes. What in the name of heaven had she just done?

Her heart, having just managed to slow to a normal beat, suddenly tripped back into a frantic pace and thumped brutally against her breast. She saw his gaze drop, followed it, and realized to her horror that she was still naked. Teresa cringed, pulled up her legs and tried to cover herself with her hands. The heat of embarrassment burned her cheeks. A furtive glance at Brett fueled the fires of her humiliation and told her more than she wanted to know. He was still unclothed, too, lying prone beside her and making no effort to cover himself. Against her will, Teresa's gaze traveled down the long length of his body, over golden flesh pulled taut by rippling muscles, past that hard wall of chest that had felt so wonderful pressed against her breasts, past the narrow waist and flat stomach to a triangle of blond curls wrapped around a part of him that was beginning to swell before her eyes.

A hot coil of need knotted deep within her as she watched his body begin to harden with desire. Once again she ached for his touch, hungered for the pleasures his lovemaking had invoked within her body. Her skin burned as her blood warmed and began to simmer with anticipation. Without thinking, Teresa raised a hand toward him, needing to touch him, to run her fingers through the crisp tendrils of blond hair that curled so softly at his nape.

She suddenly snapped her eyelids closed, her hand frozen in midair. No. This was wrong. Everything she'd done since meeting him was wrong. He was her enemy. Logic and emotion warred within her, passion struggling to overcome reason, need fighting to conquer the hard, cold rationale that would keep her out of his arms.

She forced her eyes open and recoiled instantly. Icy amusement sparkled from his deep blue eyes—amusement and satisfaction. A shudder wracked her body and Teresa hastily looked about in search of something, anything, with which to cover herself. Her soiled trousers lay nearby. She grabbed them and clutched them to her, covering her nakedness.

The smile that had pulled one corner of Brett's mouth upward disappeared and his eyes grew colder.

A sense of loss swept over her, so unexpected and profound that it left her eyes stinging with tears and her hands trembling within the folds of the trousers she clutched between her breasts. She found the feeling both unexplainable and unreasonable and tried to shrug it away. The only thing she'd really lost was her dignity, and she could regain that. Teresa raised her chin in defiance. If taking his pleasure from her body was what he'd wanted, then he'd gotten it, but it would be all he'd ever get from her. "Am I free to go now?" she challenged.

A questioning frown drew Brett's brows together. "Go? Just where do you want to go, Miss Smithers?" He hated himself for what he'd just done. He hated himself for the way he was treating her. And he had the horrible suspicion that the feeling wasn't going away soon, if ever. But he couldn't drop his guard again and risk her discovering the truth, which meant he couldn't treat her any differently, not until this thing was over.

For a few brief moments he had allowed himself the luxury of forgetting about the war, about Jay Proschaud, sabotage, betrayal, and murder. He had forgotten the reason that she had ridden halfway across the country, the reason he had intercepted her, and why she was with him now. But most of all he had allowed himself to forget that she was Proschaud's wife.

The moment he had moved away from her and looked down at her face, everything he had chosen not to think about had come crashing back down on him like an avalanche. He'd been swallowed by a chasm of guilt and self-loathing so deep that it was nearly impossible to see any light at the end of the tunnel. Yet it didn't matter. None of it mattered. At least not now. Later he could apologize, but now he had to continue with the game, and do his job.

Hatred, hot and fervent, filled his heart as the memory of why this particular mission was so important, why he knew he could not fail this time, filled his mind. Proschaud had killed Suzanne. That knowledge was a constant ache in his heart; he felt it like a physical pain he would endure for the rest of his life.

Teresa scooted a few inches away from him, but it was the gesture that counted, not the space. Brett's eyes narrowed as his thoughts were drawn back to the present.

"I would like to leave your company, Lieutenant, that's all," she said, her tone full of hatred. "I told you, I was on my way to Washington when you stopped me."

"You were impersonating a Union soldier when I stopped you," Brett growled, his memories and his guilt combining to completely sour his mood.

"Yes, well, as you said earlier, a southern woman traveling alone and forced to pass through a Yankee encampment can't be too careful. Obviously, I wasn't careful enough."

He met Teresa's hard stare. "Until I know who you are, Miss Smithers, and what you're up to, I'm afraid you'll have to remain my *aide.*"

"Prisoner," Teresa corrected.

He shrugged and pushed himself upright, then rose to his feet to tower over her.

Teresa kept her gaze pinned to the floor.

"Ready for that bath?"

Startled, she looked up. He was holding his hand out, but it wasn't his hand that caught her immediate attention. Teresa shot to her feet and took several steps away from him, retreating until she felt the wall at her back. "I . . . I've changed my mind."

As he advanced on her, Teresa swallowed, hard. If he touched her again, if he pressed his lips to hers, caressed her body with those strong, gentle hands, she would be lost forever. She knew it, longed for it, and hated it. "No. Don't," she said finally, the words slipping from her lips as a plea rather than the command she'd intended. "I changed my mind. I don't want to bathe."

"But I do," Brett drawled.

Teresa dropped one hand to touch the wall at her back, as if to make certain it wouldn't move, wouldn't give and let her pass through. "No."

He smiled, a gleam of devilment sparkling from within the cold depths of his eyes. "Yes."

Before she knew what he was about to do, Brett bent, scooped her up into his arms, and began to walk across the room toward the tub.

"Put me down!" Teresa kicked her legs and hit at him with her free hand, the other pinned between their naked bodies. Her palm smashed against the side of his face.

Brett stopped and jerked his head around to look at her. "That was not a smart move," he said, his voice a low growl.

Teresa glared at him. "It wasn't meant to be smart, it was meant to hurt. Now put me down."

"That's exactly what I intended to do."

His meaning escaped her, but only for a second. "You wouldn't dare!"

He smiled. "I warned you about saying that."

Brett bent forward slightly and his arms dropped away from her.

Teresa screamed as she fell through the air, then hit the surface of the water. It splashed up around her, sprays of white, foamy bubbles flying through the air and over the tub's rim. Her derriere smacked against the tub's tin bottom, her feet hit the narrowed foot curve and one arm banged against the side rim, the blow softened by the water. Slapping at the hot waves, she surfaced sputtering, spitting, and screaming his name. Bubbles clung to the long, wet strands of her hair, the tip of her nose, and the subtle swell of her breasts.

Brett looked down at her and felt hunger building within him again. His body was hard with desire, his blood hot. Self-control began to slip away as he struggled to recapture it.

"You blackguard," Teresa screeched finally, wiping wet hair from her face and bubbles from her nose. She glared up at him hatefully, her dark lashes spiked by the hot water and reflecting the light of a small oil lantern. "I'll kill you."

"Maybe," Brett said lazily, "but not just now, all right?" He had intended to leave after he'd seduced her. And that's exactly how he thought of it: *his seduction of her.* They hadn't made love. It took two people caring to make love. They had merely had sex. And it had been all his idea. He'd seduced her, and she didn't even know who he was. Brett cursed himself for a snake, but it didn't stop him.

He swung a leg over the tub's rim and into the water, his foot slipping down between her thigh and the side of the high-rimmed slipper tub.

Teresa jerked back, staring at his leg as if it were a cottonmouth. "What do you think you're doing?"

"Getting ready to take a bath," Brett answered easily. "If you'll move over a bit, that is."

"I will not."

"Suit yourself." He brought his other leg into the tub so that he stood behind her, then lowered himself into the water.

Teresa ended up cradled between his bent legs. With a sigh of contentment, he said, "Damn, but that feels good."

Teresa stiffened and tried to sit forward, but it didn't do any good. She could still feel him against her, his legs framing her thighs and arms, his hot breath on her neck. But that wasn't the worst of it. She closed her eyes and prayed that lightning would fill the sky, shoot through the bedchamber and into the dressing room, and strike him dead. She could feel his arousal pushing at her lower back, just slightly above her bare buttocks. The shame of the situation made her bristle. She was in a bathtub with a man who was virtually a stranger, a man who was her enemy, a man who was naked, and she wanted him to make love to her again.

She jerked forward at the feel of his hand on her back.

"Relax," Brett soothed.

Teresa felt slightly foolish when she realized he was merely rubbing soap over her back. It felt good, and she didn't want it to feel good. Her body was relaxing into his touch, even while she tried to keep it stiff. He moved the soap over her shoulders slowly, indolently, then slid it up and down her arm. She closed her eyes and let her head drop back slightly. His other hand slipped under her arm and his fingers settled around her breast.

Stop, she thought weakly. *Please, please stop.*

His thumb flicked over the tip of her nipple, back

and forth, back and forth. Teasing, taunting, until it hardened into a pebbled peak and ached for his touch, straining against the slippery movement of his fingers. Her body arched toward his hand.

Brett pulled her gently back against his chest. She settled her head upon his shoulders, snuggling into the haven of his arms, mindlessly welcoming his invasion of both her senses and her body.

Brett's other hand slipped under her arm and covered her other breast.

Teresa sighed softly, too lost in a new haze of passion to resist.

"I want you again," he whispered into her ear.

She stirred against him in answer, too choked with desire to speak.

Lifting her by the waist, Brett forced her to turn toward him. "The tub's cramped. Do you want to get out?"

She looked down at him, then shook her head.

Brett pulled her into his arms and, resting his head against the back rim of the tub, brought her lips down to cover his. Her tongue shot instantly into his mouth and Brett groaned in ecstasy. She was the embodiment of every fantasy he had ever had, the woman of his dreams. And he was doomed. She had woven her spell around his heart, to which only she now held the key.

He took her slowly this time, savoring every caress, every brush of her lips. Desire had never tasted so good.

Teresa lay cradled in his arms, her back against his chest, his bent legs framing hers. She let her head drop back to rest on his shoulder and closed her eyes. The bath water was cooling rapidly, the scented bubbles evaporating, but she didn't care. The small oil lantern on a marble-topped table in the corner filled the room with a soft glow but left the bedchamber beyond the open doorway in darkness; night had crept over the land while they'd lain in each other's arms. She wanted nothing more than to keep the real world at bay.

The sound of hoofbeats on crushed oyster shells broke the silence. Teresa did not stir, but a small sigh escaped her lips. The real world was about to intrude, and there was nothing she could do about it.

A knock on the bedchamber's outer door several minutes later confirmed her thoughts.

"Miss Smithers?"

Teresa bolted upright at the high-pitched voice.

"Miss Smithers, Mr. Gracen told me to come up and help you dress for dinner. I got some of Miss Matilda's things for you."

"It's the maid," Brett said needlessly.

Teresa nodded but didn't move. What was she supposed to do?

"Miss Smithers?"

"Are you going to answer her?" Brett asked.

"Just a minute," Teresa called out loudly. She looked across the room to the washstand where the towels hung, and on the floor beside it where her clothes lay.

Brett inhaled deeply and shifted position. Teresa felt the part of his body that had given her more pleasure than she'd ever dreamed of rub against her derriere. Her cheeks burned.

"Not that I want to move, or let you go for a second," Brett drawled easily, "but I doubt she's going to stand out there forever."

Teresa twisted around to look at him.

"If she thinks something's wrong she'll go get Lance to open the door."

The thought of their host walking in and seeing her in the tub with Brett spurred Teresa into action. What difference did it make if he saw her after what they'd just done . . . twice! She scrambled up and out of the tub, skittered across the floor, and grabbed a towel. She wrapped it hurriedly around her, but even though she'd told herself there was nothing to be embarrassed about, she could feel the heat that filled her cheeks.

Brett chuckled softly and rose. "You are one beautiful woman, Te . . . Miss Smithers."

Teresa stared at him and frowned. "What were you about to call me?"

Brett tried to look innocent and shrugged. "Miss Smithers."

Her eyes narrowed in suspicion. "No, you started to call me something else."

He smiled, a crooked grin that did little to banish her sudden suspicion.

"I don't know, maybe *Private?*"

The maid knocked on the door again. "Miss Smithers? You all right in there?"

Teresa looked toward the door. "Yes, I'll be there in a minute." She turned back to Brett. The light of the lamp turned his flesh to bronze, his hair to spun gold, his eyes to sparkling sapphires. She ached to touch him, to feel his hands on her body again. "You have to leave." Her voice was little more than a raspy whisper. "She can't see you here, like this, in my bedchamber."

"How about back in your bath?"

"No." She'd nearly screamed the word, as much as she could with a voice cracked and husky with emotion. Teresa picked up the oil lantern and walked into the bedchamber. She looked at the gallery. It was the only other way out of the room. She hurried back into the dressing room. Brett was wiping a towel over his body.

Teresa grabbed his clothes from the floor and, holding the towel tightly around herself, pushed them into his arms. "Come on." She grabbed one of his arms and pulled him into the bedchamber.

"And just where am I going?"

"Out."

"Out?" Brett stopped and looked down at her. "That is not exactly the way out."

"It's the way you're taking." Teresa tugged on his arm. "She can't see you in here."

Brett sighed. "At least let me put on my trousers."

"You can put them on out there. It's dark."

"Great." He stepped out onto the gallery and Teresa immediately shut the door behind him.

A soft chuckle emanated from the other end of the gallery and Brett whirled around to stare into the darkness. "I see you're a little bit friendlier with Teresa Braggette than you'd led me to believe. Or should I say, with Mrs. Proschaud?"

Eighteen

Brett jerked on his trousers and stalked to the other end of the gallery where Lance Gracen stood just outside of his own room. "I didn't know you were a Peeping Tom," Brett growled, nearly tripping as his foot got caught in one pant leg. He swore softly and hopped to keep his balance, then stopped in front of Lance and practically rammed the trouser buttons through their fastening holes.

"I'm not," Lance said, "but I do know which room I offered the young lady, and which I gave you, and the one you just walked out of, naked, was not yours." He raised a cheroot to his lips and drew on it deeply, causing its burning tip to glow brilliantly against the blackness of the night.

Brett graced him with a mocking smile. "It's not what you think."

"Oh?" Lance chuckled softly. "And just what *do* I think, cousin?"

Brett yanked on his shirt and shrugged it over his shoulders. "Nothing. Forget it. What's for dinner?"

"Didn't you just dine?"

"God damn it, Lance . . ."

"Tut tut, dear cousin, I would think in your type of occupation you would hold your temper better."

"I normally do, so it must just be you." Brett pulled on his boots. "I heard someone ride up. Who was it?"

"A messenger." Lance turned and walked into his bedchamber.

Brett followed. "A messenger? About what?"

"Proschaud, of course." Lance opened the door to the hallway and turned back to Brett. "Shall we go downstairs? I believe supper is almost ready."

"What the hell do you mean *Proschaud?* What was the message? Dammit Lance, you're enough to fry a man's brains."

Lance smiled. "My but your temper is sharp this evening." He sighed exaggeratedly.

"Then talk to me, you idiot."

Lance feigned insult and looked down the hall toward Teresa's door. The maid was gone, presumably into the room, and the door was shut. He lowered his voice to just above a whisper. "A few days ago I heard that Proschaud was in Manchester and thought I'd send a man to check it out."

"And was he there?"

"Who? Our man?"

"Lance, I swear, one of these days I'm going to lose my temper completely and just strangle you."

"My, but we *are* touchy tonight."

"Was Proschaud in Manchester?" Brett fairly snarled, though he made certain to keep his voice low enough so no one else could overhear.

"Yes. My man saw him in a tavern but couldn't find out where he was staying. Proschaud's smart, and slippery, as we both know. My man thinks Proschaud discovered him almost immediately."

"Great—now he might not show up in Richmond to meet Teresa."

"Time will tell," Lance said gaily.

"You really are impossible, you know?"

Lance laughed. "I try. Anyway, stop worrying. When have you ever known Proschaud to cancel his plans? Change them a bit, yes, but never cancel them."

Brett nodded. "You're right."

"Of course—I usually am."

Brett sent him a look of frustration, resignation, and fury. Lance was a valuable asset to the system, but he was also an incorrigible jokester and ladies' man. Brett looked at his cousin pointedly, suddenly remembering how they'd always vied for the same lady's attention whenever they were together. A knot formed in his gut and began to burn at the thought of Lance with Teresa.

"So, will the young lady be dining with us, or taking her leave of Gracen Plantation?"

"I'm not sure. I guess we'll just have to wait and see," Brett answered. "You do have someone posted outside to warn us in case she decides to take her leave?"

Teresa looked at herself in the mirror. Climbing down the trellis in this outfit was totally out of the question, but then she didn't intend to do that until later, and she could change back into her trousers first. Her hand moved lovingly over the silk skirt as she unconsciously compared its soft, rich texture to the coarse trousers she'd been forced to wear for the past several days.

The Gracen maid had brought Teresa several of Matilda Gracen's gowns, explaining that she was Lance's sister but away from the plantation for the time being. The maid had also brought all the accessories a proper young lady needed. Teresa had chosen a gown of midnight blue silk, its hem ruffled, hips flounced, and the puffed sleeves and low-cut decolletage trimmed with ivory Valenciennes lace. It was the perfect choice for dining with two handsome gentlemen. But, as much as she hated to admit it, there was only one gentleman she was truly dressing for. She'd thought about leaving immediately after she'd ushered him so unceremoniously from her room, but hadn't been able to bring herself to do it. She wanted to see him once more, perhaps for the last time, then leave.

Tears filled Teresa's eyes and she hurriedly blinked them back. It was silly, getting so maudlin over a man she barely knew. But then it was silly to have let a man she barely knew make love to her. She straightened her shoulders and lifted her chin. But she wasn't sorry. She should be, but she wasn't. He was her enemy, and at times the most infuriating man she'd ever met . . . but she would never forget him, or regret having made love to him.

Tucking a small wisp of hair back into the elaborate mass of curls she'd arranged to cascade down over her left shoulder, Teresa turned toward the door.

At the sound of voices drifting up from downstairs, Teresa paused at the landing and looked down into the spacious foyer. The room was aglow with light from the candles of the three-tiered chandelier hanging from the second-story ceiling, each flame burning steadily upon its wick and reflecting myriad colors within its crystal teardrop prisms. A huge grandfather clock suddenly chimed the hour, seven, and momentarily drowned out the conversation Teresa realized was coming from a room to the right.

She was halfway down the stairs when the echo of the clock's last chime died away.

"I'm surprised he allowed himself to be seen this close to Richmond."

Teresa paused at the sound of Brett's voice. She cocked her head, knowing she shouldn't eavesdrop but finding it impossible to resist.

"Why? According to him," she heard Lance respond, "he's working to further the cause."

"Yeah, him and Abraham Lincoln."

Teresa frowned. Who were they talking about? Obviously not her.

"Well, he gave our man the slip, so we have no idea if he's still in Manchester or if he's crossed over the river into Richmond."

"Then we have to make certain we don't lose her."

"You still think it's a good idea to just let her es . . ."

A knock on the front door echoed loudly through the foyer and cut off whatever Lance had been about to say.

Teresa jumped, startled by the sound and aggravated at not knowing what Lance had been about to say. He'd said *her.* Who had he meant? Her?

A maid, her body so thin she looked like little more than a handful of sticks, suddenly swept out from the back of the foyer and moved toward the front door. At the same time, the open door to the room Lance Gracen and Brett were in was suddenly closed.

Teresa stared at it. Were they talking about her? But if so, what was the idea Lance had mentioned? And if the *her* he'd referred to meant Teresa, what was it Brett was going to *let* her do that Lance was questioning?

The elderly maid opened the front door and Emerson walked in. He didn't look up to where Teresa stood on the stairs and for that she was grateful. She heard him ask the maid where Brett and Lance were and saw the woman point toward the closed door. Emerson nodded and walked to it, pausing to knock heavily on its paneled face.

A muffled response came from inside.

"Emerson," he barked loudly.

The door opened immediately, Emerson disappeared inside, and it slammed shut again.

She stared down at it. What in heaven's name was going on? Teresa began to descend the staircase again, but had taken no more than one step when she realized the maid was still standing in the foyer and looking up at her.

Teresa smiled. "Hello."

The maid's scowl deepened. "Massa Lance don't want supper served for a little bit yet."

"Oh, that's fine. I'll just . . ." She tried to think of what she'd *just* do. "I'll, umm, just get a breath of fresh air on the gallery."

"Massa Brett said I ain't to let you go outside."

Teresa felt her temper flare at the old woman's words. *"Let* me go outside?"

The maid glared and assumed a posture of defense, spreading her legs wide and crossing her arms under nearly nonexistent breasts.

Teresa glared back. It would be no problem at all to simply push the woman aside since she was nothing but a bag of bones anyway, but if she did that then she'd never find out what was going on behind that closed door. Anyway, she'd already decided she wasn't going to make her escape until she found out just what Brett Forsythe was up to.

She was just about to descend the remainder of the stairs when the door suddenly swung open and the men emerged into the foyer.

"Ah, Miss Smithers," Lance said, "you look absolutely lovely. A real vision." He hurried to the bottom of the stairs and stretched out a hand toward her.

She looked at Brett, waiting for him to say something. Instead she saw a look come into his eyes that could only be described as murderous, then he abruptly spun on his heel and stalked into the dining room.

Emerson threw her a look that was nearly as lethal, marched toward the front door, swung it open without a word of farewell, and left.

Teresa looked back down at Lance, clearly baffled.

He smiled up at her and took her hand as she neared. "A vision," he said again, and bent to press his lips to the tops of her fingers.

Teresa smiled. "Thank you, but did I interrupt something?"

Lance straightened and tucked her hand into the

crook of his arm. "Oh, them?" He laughed. "No, we were discussing business and just had a difference of opinion, that's all. Now, let's go in to supper, shall we? Obviously Brett was too hungry to mind his manners and wait for us."

"Obviously," she murmured, suspecting that was not why he'd disappeared at all, yet not quite sure what the real reason was.

Brett was standing beside an ornate sideboard with his back to them when they entered the dining room.

"Ah, I see Mary hasn't served yet," Lance said. "Good." He helped Teresa into a chair and looked up at Brett, who hadn't moved. "Brett, are you going to join us?"

Brett turned and walked toward the table.

Lance settled into the chair at the head of the table, leaving Brett to the only other one with a place setting, the chair to his right, and across the table from Teresa.

Brett threw him a look that would wither the average man but Lance merely smiled like a Cheshire cat and picked up a small silver bell and rang it loudly.

The same maid who'd confronted Teresa in the foyer entered the room carrying a large tray laden with several steaming serving dishes.

Teresa watched as she placed a bowl of creamed potatoes on the table, followed by string beans amandine, grits, roast cornish hen, bacon-wrapped ham loaves, butter biscuits, and a platter of sliced tomatoes, onions, peppers, and okra.

"You eat very well up here in Virginia," Teresa said, continuing to stare at the generous array.

"Only on special occasions," Lance said. "Everything you see here was raised or grown on the Gracen plantation, but we use it sparingly, canning and storing most of our things in case . . ." He paused and Teresa saw a shadow sweep across his eyes. "Well, in case whatever," he finished lightly.

She looked at Brett, who seemed to be purposely keeping his gaze averted from hers. "I was wondering, Mr. Gracen . . ."

"Please, call me Lance."

Teresa smiled. "Lance. I was wondering, how is it that you're not in uniform?"

She saw a quick exchange of looks cross between Lance and Brett before Lance smiled widely and reached for the bowl of potatoes, offering it to her. "Well, Miss Smithers . . ."

"Oh, please, Lance," Teresa said, purposely instilling a heavy note of flirtation to her tone, "call me Lucinda."

"Lucinda," he repeated softly. "Well, Lucinda, some men make good soldiers, out in front, fighting the battles and such, while others fight from behind the lines."

"Like politicians?" she offered.

"Yes, like politicians."

"So, are you a politician?"

Lance chuckled. "Not exactly."

Brett stared at her. *Lucinda.* That was her middle name. He'd forgotten until she'd just said it, but now he remembered the one other time he'd heard it, when she'd announced one evening at Shadows Noir that she'd decided she didn't want to be called Teresa anymore and wanted everyone to call her Lucinda.

Thomas Braggette had erupted into a rage. All of his children, he'd bellowed, would go by the name he'd chosen for them, whether they liked it or not. He'd then proceeded to whip Teresa in front of everyone, including Brett, who had been their houseguest that week, and sent her to bed in tears with no supper.

He practically shuddered at the memory. Thomas had been a tyrant, even forcing all of his children to have names that would give them the same initials as his. But that had been only one small example of the man's tyranny and abuse toward his family. Brett's eyes narrowed as he continued to stare at Teresa. What else had her father done to her, he wondered.

"Lieutenant Forsythe, do I perchance have food on my nose?" Teresa quipped, staring back at him.

Brett forced the unpleasant thoughts away and turned his gaze to his plate. "Oh, sorry, I didn't mean to stare."

"Well, normally I wouldn't apologize for my cousin's lack of manners," Lance said, "but in this case I will." He turned to Teresa and took her hand in his. "I mean, you must forgive us, Lucinda, but you have graced us with a very striking contrast to the one you presented upon your arrival earlier. And one which, I might add, is quite beautiful."

Brett saw red. Hot, burning, fiery red. He stared at Lance's hand as his fingers wrapped around Teresa's and thought about how he might cut it off.

Teresa slipped her hand from Lance's and smiled at him. "Thank you, Lance." She poked a fork at her food. She'd been starving, and the food looked delicious, better than anything she'd had in days, but her stomach had done several flip-flops in the last few seconds and she was afraid she was too nervous now to eat a thing. Glancing at Brett, she felt her stomach turn over again. Why had he been staring at her like that? And why did he suddenly look so angry?

A thought struck her that nearly made her laugh aloud. He was jealous. Her eyes darted between Lance and Brett, and then she discarded the notion. Brett Forsythe didn't care about her, at least not that way. He'd made love to her, yes, but that hadn't been love. Not the emotional kind anyway. And she didn't love him. She was attracted to him. Even cared about him, much to her chagrin. But she didn't love him. The mere thought was ridiculous.

She sipped at her wine, felt it warm her insides as it slid smoothly down her throat, and set the glass back down on the table. "So, Lance, you're not a soldier and you're not a politician." She tried to look innocent. "How are you aiding in the war effort?"

"I'm afraid that's something I just can't divulge, my dear."

"Oh. Spying perhaps?" She saw the look of alarm that flared in his eyes, but gave him credit for composure. The rest of his face showed no signs of his uneasiness.

"Spying? Me?" He laughed. "Oh, heavens no."

"Do you have many relatives come to stay here with you like this?" Teresa persisted. "I mean, stopping by while they're on assignment?"

"No, not really, just my pesky cousin here."

Teresa turned her gaze on Brett. "So, Lieutenant, you grew up around here?"

He met her gaze directly. "Yes," he lied. "Just a short distance away."

"And your family is still here?"

"My family is dead."

Teresa felt a sudden rush of guilt, followed immediately by compassion. "Oh, I'm sorry."

"No need."

Though his words were meant as a lie, they'd brought the memory of Suzanne back into his mind, and with that, the painful hurt. It hadn't been a total lie—part of his family *was* gone. Hurt turned instantly to hate, as it always did whenever he thought of Suzanne's death and Teresa's husband. Brett abruptly pushed back his chair and threw his lap cloth onto the table. "If you'll excuse me." He rose. "I find I'm in need of some fresh air."

Teresa watched him leave and wanted desperately to go after him, to ask him what she'd said that had upset him so terribly.

Lance reached over and patted her hand. "Don't mind him. He's one of the most temperamental people I know. Always has been." He reached for his wineglass and took several sips. "So, tell me, Lucinda," he signed contentedly, "why were you dressed in those horrible soldier's clothes when you arrived here?"

"Brett didn't tell you?" she asked, thoroughly surprised.

"No."

She stared into Lance's eyes, trying to see past the polished persona to the real person she felt certain he kept hidden from everyone. Or at least from her. Was this some kind of trap? Had Brett and Lance thought up this scheme as a way to get her to talk? She suddenly felt like crying. Could Brett have planned his sudden departure so that Lance could flirt with her, try to gain her confidence and thus her secrets?

Teresa dropped her gaze to her lap, then turned to look at the doorway Brett had disappeared through. She saw only darkness. He had made love to her, and though she tried to tell herself it didn't matter, that she didn't care if she ever saw him again, she knew it did and it galled her to the core. She didn't want to care about him, didn't want him to care about her. They had different beliefs, different loyalties, and different goals in life.

She rose so abruptly the hoop beneath her gown swung violently and nearly toppled her chair. "I'm sorry, Lance, please excuse me. I seem to have developed a horrible headache."

He rose instantly and reached for her hand. "Oh, I'm sorry, my dear." He steered her toward the door to the foyer. "Let me see you to your room, and I'll have Mary bring you up a pot of her special tea. She makes one for headaches that does absolute wonders."

"Thank you," Teresa said, touching a hand to her temple and trying to sound as if she was in pain, "but please don't bother yourself. I can find my own way." She left Lance at the foot of the elegant staircase and didn't dare look back for fear he'd find a reason to rush up to her side. It was becoming painfully apparent that the man was a cornucopia of personalities with an appropriate mien for each occasion, each emotion. He was handsome, wealthy, and, obviously, a gentleman. He was also a traitor to the Confederacy, and a chameleon of sorts. Teresa shuddered.

She didn't trust anything that slithered, crawled, or changed color.

The thought no sooner formed in her mind than she admonished herself for her cruelty. Whatever Lance Gracen was doing, whether asking subtle questions or attempting to seduce her with flattery and feigned concern, he was most likely doing it because Brett had instructed him to. The mere thought turned her temper to a raging inferno. Lieutenant Brett Forsythe was a scoundrel through and through. That had been her first opinion of him and she'd have been better off if she'd have remembered it instead of turning into a swooning ninny.

She hurried down the hallway and entered her room, turning the key in her door. If Brett wanted to come in now, he would have to break the door down. Teresa crossed the room to the fireplace and began to pace back and forth. What should she do now? Stay or go? There seemed little hope of finding out what Brett was planning to do in Richmond, especially if he continued to avoid her as he'd done over dinner. He'd made it quite obvious he wanted nothing to do with her. Was that how he treated all the women he came into personal contact with—bed them, then ignore them?

She stamped a foot, the sound muted by the thick multicolored Aubusson carpet. "If that's the way you want it, Lieutenant Forsythe, then that's the way it will be," she said, fairly brimming with furious indignation and forgetting the fact that she'd already decided a relationship between them was utterly impossible. "You may ignore me, but damn your hide, I'll make certain you end up sorry you ever met me."

Images of Brett's face close to hers, his hands moving over her flesh, his body pressed tightly to hers, filled Teresa's mind in spite of her anger.

Teresa felt as if her entire body were suddenly on fire, burning from the thought of the passion they'd shared, and the fury simmering her blood. She grabbed a fan from a table next to the settee and flapped it furiously in front of her face. It created a breeze that caused small wisps of hair to fly about her face, but did nothing to cool her down. Spinning around, she marched to one of the tall windows and threw up its sash, then stepped past it into the night-shrouded gallery. But she hadn't taken more than two steps when the sound of hushed voices met her ears. She realized whoever was speaking was standing in the garden just below. Pushing aside her guilt, Teresa stealthily tiptoed to the railing and, remaining partially hidden behind one of the thick columns, peered down onto the moonlit grounds.

Suddenly all thought of not caring for Brett and making him sorry he'd ever met her flew out of her mind. Teresa's heart nearly thudded to a halt as a soft gasp of shock slipped from her lips. She clutched at the pillar and closed her eyes tight, hoping against hope that when she opened them again the scene before her would have changed.

Nineteen

Teresa opened her eyes, blinked rapidly to accustom her vision to the darkness again, and looked back at the garden that she hoped would now be empty. Moonlight shone down on the landscape and blended with the pale light that filtered onto the scene from one of the downstairs windows. It turned the leaves of the giant oak trees to shimmering fragments of silver.

But it wasn't the serene beauty of the garden that drew Teresa's gaze, nor the heady fragrance of the night-blooming jasmine that wound its way around one of the pillars of the house. It was the two people standing in the center of the garden, surrounded by a profusion of rose bushes whose blooms had closed against the night.

Brett's arms were securely wrapped around the waist of the woman, while hers had intimately encircled his shoulders.

"You know, you look even lovelier than the last time I saw you," Brett said.

Teresa felt her heart constrict and tears fill her eyes as his words drifted up to her. She took a step back into the shadows, as if trying to get away from something that hurt her more than she cared to admit.

The woman laughed softly, the sound delicate and light. Teresa cringed, but found it impossible to turn away. She didn't want to see or hear any more, yet her feet would not move, her eyes would not close, and her ears would not tune out the sound. It was as if her body had turned to stone, refusing to heed her commands, yet leaving her senses and feelings totally intact.

"Oh, Brett, you really are a devil, and I've missed you dreadfully."

Teresa's heart plummeted to her toes. She forced herself to look down at the woman. Her hair, tied back with a ribbon, cascaded down her back in a luscious fall of curls that shone like strands of gold silk by the moon's light. She wore a gown of pale yellow silk, its skirt front a pretty apron flounce of white taffeta that ended at the back of her waist in a large bow. White lace fluttered at the wrists of the snug-fitting sleeves.

If Teresa had been a man she knew she would have described the woman as not only beautiful, but delicate. She sniffed unconsciously, feeling a swift flash of resentment that she'd rather not acknowledge. No one had ever described *her* as delicate, and she had never been able to wear yellow.

"Right," Brett drawled, his tone teasing, "you missed me. That's why you weren't here when I arrived."

The woman laughed again and rose on her tiptoes to press a kiss to his cheek. "I wasn't here, silly, because I didn't know exactly when you'd be arriving. All Lance would say whenever I asked was that you'd be here soon, very soon." Teresa saw her pretend to pout, then laugh again when Brett scowled. "And anyway, I had some shopping to do in town."

Brett joined in her laughter. "Even with a war going on you find time and places to shop. I don't believe it."

"There are some things, darling, that a woman just will not give up, even during a war."

"Especially not you, right, Goldie?"

Teresa didn't want to hear any more. Tears stung her eyes. Only a short while ago his arms had held her like that, and his body had pressed tight to hers like it was now doing with this Goldie. But obviously there had been no emotion behind those things, no sincerity behind the sweet words he'd whispered to her . . . merely physical need. He'd made love to her merely because he could, not because he felt anything. Teresa's hands curled into fists at her sides. How could he? She looked back down at them, then damned herself for doing it. Brett didn't care about her, he never had. He was in love with someone else, someone he called Goldie.

Teresa didn't feel the stab of her own fingernails as they pressed into her palms, nor hear the faint sob that slipped past her lips.

But Brett heard it, and as if a second sense told him exactly what it was he jerked around to stare directly at the second-story gallery where Teresa stood in the shadows. For a moment he forgot all about the woman in his arms, and a frown drew his brows together as he squinted to see into the darkness to confirm his suspicions. A slight movement on the gallery brought a stiffening of his shoulders—he watched intently as a shadow darted quickly away from the railing near one of the pillars and disappeared through the open window that led to Teresa's bedchamber.

Brett cursed silently. Dammit, Teresa cared about him and she had seen him with Matilda, seen them in an embrace and took it for what it looked like rather than what it was. How was Teresa to know that the woman in his arms was Matilda Gracen? And that Matilda was more like a sister to him than a cousin—an even more cherished sister now that Suzanne was gone.

He had to explain to Teresa. Brett looked back down at Matilda. "Goldie, I have something I have to take care of."

She pressed against him and tightened the circle of her arms. "Oh, no, you don't. I just got here and I'm not going to let you run off back to that horrid ol' war of yours before you visit awhile with me."

He glanced up at Teresa's window. "I'm not going back to that horrid ol' war, as you call it, at least not right now. I just have to . . ." He didn't finish the sentence. What was he thinking? He'd just have to *what?* Run upstairs and explain to Teresa that he was really Brett Forteaux, her brother's best friend, the one who used to tease her mercilessly when she was younger? That Matilda was his cousin? That he'd purposely had Teresa followed, then intercepted and brought her here because he wanted her to lead him to her husband, who was a murdering devil? Oh, yes, why didn't he tell her all of that—and watch Jay Proschaud disappear into thin air just like he'd always done.

And while he was at it, why not tell her he'd made

love to her because he'd lost control of his senses and fallen in . . . Brett's entire body shuddered in denial of the thought that had nearly formed in his mind. Oh, no, not that. He wasn't falling in love with anyone. Not now, maybe not ever. He merely cared about Teresa, that was all. Cared about her. Maybe a little too much, but it sure as hell wasn't love. No. He was certain of that.

"You just have to do *what?"* Matilda prodded, and poked a finger against his shoulder. "Brett?"

He looked back down at her, but even though his gaze met hers, Brett didn't see her—not the blue of her eyes, the full, pouting pink lips, or even her short, upturned nose. His mind and thoughts were elsewhere.

"Brett?"

He shook himself and smiled down at his cousin. "Nothing, Goldie," he said finally. "I was wrong, I don't have to do anything." He took her arm and steered her toward the house. "Let's go in and have a nice visit, shall we?"

Matilda laughed and clapped her hands together. "Good. And I'll have Mary make up some *café au lait* and bring us some homemade *beignets."*

"Sounds delicious," Brett murmured. He threw one last glance up at Teresa's window before he stepped onto the ground-floor gallery. Thoughts of her, of how she'd responded to his lovemaking, of how it had felt to make love to her, had been plaguing him ever since she'd shoved him, naked, out of her room. Guilt mingled with desire, need rebelled against honor. He'd made love to a lot of women in his life, but he'd never felt the fulfillment, the ecstasy and the peace, that he'd experienced with Teresa. It was as if something had been missing all those other times and finally he knew what it was but he couldn't have it.

Brett sighed, then cleared his throat hastily to hide the sound from Matilda. It was better this way. He had to let Teresa escape so that his plan would work. That meant he couldn't tell her the truth. None of it. At least not now. And anyway, once she learned the truth he had no doubt she'd hate him, if she didn't already.

At the door to the parlor he paused and glanced back over his shoulder toward the stables. He couldn't see Emerson, but he knew the man was out there, standing in the shadows with two saddled horses, waiting for Teresa to make her escape. When that happened he would come for Brett immediately and they'd follow her to Proschaud—just like they'd planned.

"Brett, whatever is the matter with you?" Matilda said, pulling on his arm to draw him into the parlor. "Land sakes, the way you keep staring into the darkness one would think you expect a horde of those filthy Yankees to come charging in from the garden any minute."

Brett whirled around and grabbed her by the upper arms. "Matilda!"

Her eyes grew wide with surprise and her mouth dropped open. "Brett," she whined, and tried to shake him off, but his grip remained firm. She slapped at his chest. "For pity's sake, Brett, you're crushing my arms."

He released her immediately. "Sorry."

She looked hurt. "Well, you should be. I swear," she said and snapped open the feather-tipped fan that hung from her wrist by a silk cord and began to flutter it back and forth in front of her face. "This war has turned all you men into beasts." She laughed. "Except for Lance, of course. He's still the most incorrigible rake."

"He didn't tell you about our guest?" Brett walked to the door leading to the gallery and closed it.

"Guest? We have a guest?" Matilda said excitedly. "Who? I mean, besides you."

Brett crossed the room and closed the door that led to the foyer. He turned back to Lance's sister. "I doubt I have time to explain the whole story, Goldie, and it would take too long anyway. In short, it's a woman from New Orleans I've been following, and she thinks I'm a Union officer so you can't go around . . ."

"Union officer?" Matilda laughed. "You? Oh, don't be silly, Brett."

"I'm serious. She also thinks Lance is a spy for the Union so don't . . ."

"A spy for the Union? My brother?" She slapped a hand to her breast as she burst into laughter again. "Oh, this is really just too much."

"Matilda." Brett's voice was stern, and he made certain the expression on his face was, too.

She stopped laughing and stared at him, the fluttering of her fan momentarily halted. "You're serious?"

"Yes."

"But why? I mean, whyever are you pretending to be a Yankee?" She shuddered and began to flutter the fan furiously. "Oh, I dare say, the mere thought of those horrid creatures, and you pretending to be one, just wrinkles my skin."

"I'm after her husband," Brett said. "I have been for quite a while now but this is the closest I've ever gotten."

"She's married to a Yankee?"

"Not exactly."

"I don't understand. If he's not a Yankee, then why are you after him?"

"He murdered Suzanne."

Matilda gasped. "Her husband is one of those . . . those KGC people?"

"He's given me the slip more times than I care to admit, Goldie, but he won't this time. He sent for her and I figure if I play my cards right, she'll lead me to him."

Matilda smiled. "You always were the sly one."

"Yeah," Brett growled, thinking of the woman upstairs who had made him feel more in a few short hours than he had in years—and experiencing a rush of guilt so intense it nearly caused him to double over in pain. "That's me. Sly."

A few minutes later Lance entered the room and the three visited. But not all of Brett's attention was on the conversation. He laughed, joked, and sympathized whenever appropriate, but all the while Brett kept one ear cocked toward any sounds outside of the room that would alert him to the fact that Teresa was making her escape.

Just before midnight Matilda yawned and excused herself, kissing his cheek and telling him they'd visit more in the morning, over breakfast.

He hadn't planned to be at Gracen Plantation for breakfast, but now Brett was beginning to wonder.

Half an hour later, after a late-night brandy with Lance, his cousin also called it a night and excused himself. Brett set his brandy snifter down and stood before one of the parlor's tall windows. He looked out at the night, seeing little through the glass pane that glistened brilliantly and reflected the room behind him like a mirror. The war had not touched the Gracen plantation, for which Brett was grateful, but it made him wonder all the more what he would find when he finally went home to New Orleans. The Yankees occupied his home city, and had for over two years now, making it a certainty there would be evidence everywhere of their ruthless hands. He only hoped his parents were all right, as well as Eugenia Braggette. The four Braggette brothers had made it this far through the war without one of them getting killed. Traxton had nearly gotten himself hung, Travis had gotten married and . . . Brett's eyes filled with tears. Travis had gotten married and then lost his wife, Suzanne, and Traynor had nearly gotten himself killed trying to save Traxton, but as far as Brett knew, they were all still alive, and he was thankful. Damned thankful. They were his best friends, and there had already been too much tragedy. Eugenia didn't need any more.

Brett sighed. *He* didn't need any more. Turning away from the window, Brett walked to a lamp on a nearby table. Teresa had probably fallen asleep, which was what he might as well do. Bending over the lamp, Brett cupped his hand about its fluted chimney and blew out the flame that danced on its oil soaked wick. The room plunged into darkness.

A soft thud sounded from just outside.

He spun around and stared at the window. No further sound met his ears. Had he actually heard something or not? Moving as quietly as he could, Brett hurried to the window and, concealing himself behind its burgundy curtain, peeked around it and through the glass. With the light in the room extinguished, the moonlit landscape beyond the gallery was now clearly visible. He stood still for several minutes. It seemed like an eternity as he stared out into that stillness, watching each shadow, each blur of blackness.

Suddenly Emerson's face loomed before him.

Brett jerked back, momentarily startled. Then he quickly composed himself and reaching for the window's sash, he threw it up. "She's gone?"

Emerson nodded. "Saddling a horse as we speak."

Brett hurried to a wall of shelves that framed the room's fireplace and, pulling out a false front of books, grabbed the gun and holster that lay coiled there. He'd placed them in the secret niche earlier so they'd be at hand if Teresa made her escape before he retired upstairs. Strapping it on, Brett grabbed the hat he'd also stowed in the niche and stepped out onto the gallery to join Emerson. "She didn't see you?"

"Nope."

"Good. We'll have to stay off the road when we follow her so she doesn't pick up the sound of our horses, and if she senses she's being followed she won't see us that way either."

"Yep."

They rounded a corner of the house. Two horses stood quietly tethered to a tree where Emerson had left them. Brett mounted, as did Emerson, and urged the animals into the shadows beneath the large oaks that grew beside the main drive. A few minutes later Teresa galloped past them, making no effort either to stay out of view or move slowly so that the sound of her horse's hooves on the crushed oyster shells that covered the drive would not be heard. Obviously she assumed everyone in the house was asleep and felt confident that if they woke now she would have enough of a lead to get safely away.

Brett felt the slow burn of anger building within him. He'd been hoping against hope that she wouldn't go to Jay Proschaud. As much as he wanted to catch the man—kill the man—he didn't want Teresa to go to him. He wanted her to go home, to Shadows Noir, to forget about the husband who was a traitor to the Confederacy and a murderer as well.

How many innocent people had died because of Jay Proschaud?

Brett's anger smoldered hotter. Probably dozens, but he cared most about one—and because of that one, he would see that Jay Proschaud paid the price.

They rode hard, forced to stop several times when Teresa abruptly reined in and turned her horse around to look back in the direction of the plantation. Each time she did, Brett held his breath. She obviously sensed she was being followed, but seeing no one, she always turned and went on, and Brett and Emerson followed her from within the shadows that bordered the road leading to Richmond.

Twenty

Teresa jerked on her mount's reins and as the horse skidded to an abrupt halt, she forced him to wheel around. Someone was back there, behind her. She could feel it as surely as if they were in plain view, yet she saw no one, heard nothing. But the sensation of being watched, of not being alone, wouldn't go away. It raised the hairs on the back of her neck, sent shivers up and down her spine, and filled her with fear. She strained to see into the darkness, cursing the sliver of moon for providing only a hint of light.

An owl hooted. Teresa's gaze darted in the direction she thought the sound had come from. Had it been merely a natural call, or had the bird been spooked? She waited, listening for another sound. Instead, a rabbit skittered across the road, sending her horse prancing frantically sideways.

Teresa held tight to the reins and tried to calm the horse. "Easy, boy," she crooned, "easy, it's okay. It was just a rabbit. Just a little rabbit."

The large gelding snorted and threw his head about.

"Easy," Teresa repeated.

"She knows we're here," Brett whispered.

"Yep."

"You think she saw us?"

"Nope."

Brett looked at Emerson, but all he could see in the dark shadows was a lanky form silhouetted against paler, but just as indistinguishable, black shapes. He tugged at the brim of his hat, pulling it lower onto his forehead. Occasionally it would be nice to hear Emerson say more than "yep" and "nope." He was getting a little weary of the man's limited vocabulary, though he couldn't ask for a better agent. The man could track a fox through water and smell trouble a mile away.

"Go," Emerson said, and nudged his horse forward.

Brett looked up and saw that Teresa had turned and was once again moving down the road, though not at a gallop as she had been, but in an easy lope.

It took nearly an hour to reach the outskirts of town, not because of distance so much as their constant stops. Brett was grateful that it was so dark. If she'd waited until the early hours of morning, they probably would never have made it to town before dawn and then she'd have seen them for certain.

Suddenly the sound of galloping horses, a *lot* of galloping horses, filled the silence. Brett and Emerson yanked on their reins and stopped, trying to determine where the sound was coming from.

Brett saw Teresa stop her horse, evidently hearing the sound, too. She looked frightened, but there wasn't anything he could do about that at the moment.

He swore under his breath. Whether these riders

were Yankees or Confederates, they could mean serious trouble. Teresa wouldn't fare too well if they were Yankees, and if they were Confederate troops, who knew what she might do?

He held his breath, not certain which color uniform he'd rather see thunder around the curve just beyond where Teresa had stopped.

Emerson moved his horse farther into the copse they'd been traveling through. Brett did likewise, knowing the shadows deepened the farther in they went, and they definitely would need the cover, unless it became necessary to rescue Teresa.

A unit of Confederate cavalry suddenly loomed out of the darkness before Teresa, the soft gray hue of their uniforms turning ghostly in the pale moonlight.

Brett didn't know whether to breathe a sigh of relief. If she told them about him they'd head straight for Lance's place, and the only way Brett could straighten the whole mess out and keep his cousin from being hanged would be to confess the whole damned thing. But that would blow his plan all to hell and Jay Proschaud would escape again.

The officer leading the unit raised a hand upon seeing Teresa, a signal to the others to rein in. He moved up beside her, the others remaining a few yards away.

Brett's hand tightened about his horse's reins as he strained to hear their conversation.

"Ma'am," the officer said, touching a finger to the brim of his hat. "Are you all right?"

"Oh, yes," Teresa said. "I was just on my way to town and . . ." She turned to glance back over her shoulder.

The tension in Brett's shoulders intensified. He hardly dared to blink, let alone breathe.

Teresa looked back at the officer. "I'm rather nervous out here alone." She laughed lightly. "I think I've been imagining things."

The officer smiled. "Understandable. With the Yankees not that far away, it's not really safe for a lady to be out here alone, night or day."

"I know but, well, I need to get to town."

"And your business there?" the officer inquired. His expression remained friendly enough, but Brett knew that behind his placid demeanor he was wondering if Teresa was a spy.

"Oh, I, um, am supposed to meet my husband in town. I should have been there hours ago but I was delayed on the road." Teresa glanced over her shoulder again, as if afraid someone might suddenly appear on the road behind her. "I think I might have run into a couple of Yankees."

"And they let you pass unaccosted?" the officer pressed, his gaze turning slightly suspicious.

"Oh, they didn't see me. I hid alongside the road, under cover of the trees and shadows."

The officer nodded, evidently convinced. "I'll have one of my men escort you." He turned to look back at his troops. "Fredricks."

A young soldier who looked little more than sixteen urged his horse forward. "Yes, sir?"

"I want you to escort this young lady into town. See that she gets where she's going safely, then report back to our barracks."

The boy saluted. "Yes, sir."

The officer tipped his hat toward Teresa again and signaled for his troops to proceed.

"Great. Just damned great," Brett swore. Now they not only had to make certain Teresa didn't hear or see them, but they had to worry about an escort, too.

The Confederate unit rode past and, after a few minutes, Brett and Emerson urged their horses forward, making certain to keep a safe and undetectable distance behind Teresa and her escort.

Half an hour later they were at the outskirts of the city.

"It's going to be harder to follow her now without being detected," Brett said, keeping his voice low so it wouldn't carry on the still night air.

"Yep."

"We have her most probable destinations staked out?"

"Yep."

"A man at the Hilliard Hotel?"

"Yep."

"The Spotswood?"

"Yep."

"And the Juliann?"

"Yep."

Brett nodded. There were probably dozens of other hotels in Richmond that Teresa could head to, but those were the three they'd decided were the most likely. Before the war the Hilliard, Spotswood, and Juliann had been the most popular and most luxurious. In trailing Jay Proschaud, if there was one thing Brett had come to know, it was that the man liked to enjoy the best. He had an almost fanatic insistence on being comfortable.

Teresa and her escort rode in the center of the road, unconcerned should anyone see them. Brett and Emerson rode as close to the buildings as they could, staying at least two blocks behind and doing their best to remain out of sight.

They passed a soldier standing guard in front of a townhouse that was obviously occupied by Confederate officers. Brett had fully expected to be stopped and questioned, but as they drew nearer he realized the guard was asleep, leaning against the house with his rifle propped on the stair railing and his hat pulled low.

"Thank you for small favors," Brett muttered under his breath.

"The Spotswood," Emerson said.

Brett turned his attention away from the sleeping soldier and back to Teresa. She and her escort had reined in before the Spotswood Hotel and dismounted. A second later they disappeared through the entry door. Brett turned to Emerson. "I'll stay here and make sure she doesn't leave. You go and get the others at the Juliann and the Hilliard and let them know where she is, then come back here. I'll be waiting over there." He pointed to a small park opposite the hotel.

Emerson nodded and pulled a thin silver flask from his jacket and handed it to Brett. "You might need some of this to keep the chill outta your bones."

"Thanks." Brett slipped the flask into the inner pocket of his jacket and urged his horse forward. Emerson rode beside him to the corner then wheeled off to the left, heading for the Hilliard.

* * *

Brett stared across the street at the front door of the Spotswood. He could almost feel the warmth that filled the lobby on the other side of the door. Almost, but not quite. He shifted position on the marble bench where he was sitting and tried to tell himself he wasn't quite as uncomfortable as his body seemed to think.

It didn't work.

The tips of his fingers felt frozen, in spite of his deerskin gauntlets, and his toes weren't faring much better.

Behind him his horse knickered softly; a branch of the tree he'd been tethered to rustled as the animal grabbed hold of a clump of leaves and tried to tug them free.

Brett reached into his jacket for the flask Emerson had given him, then thought better of it. He needed to keep a clear head. Reaching into another pocket, he pulled out the pocket watch his father had given him on his sixteenth birthday. It had been two hours since Emerson had ridden off to inform the others.

The faint sound of hoofbeats on the cobbled street reached Brett's ears. He snapped the watch closed, dropped it back into his pocket, and moved behind a nearby tree.

The dark silhouette of a horse and rider neared, turned into the park, and entered. Brett waited, hoping it wasn't a sentry. Moonlight played on the man's face as he reined in a few yards from where Brett stood, concealed by both the tree trunk and the inky shadows created by the overhead limbs.

"I was wondering when you'd be back," Brett said, and stepped into view.

The older man slid from his saddle to the ground. "Stopped over at the Red Boar. Rooney said Simms had spotted Proschaud there and thought I'd take a look-see for myself."

"And?"

"He was there, big as life, swigging brandy and smoking a cheroot."

"You couldn't take him?"

Emerson shook his head. "Nah. There was about ten men sitting around, trying to look inconspicuous, but they was with him sure enough, and I ain't into ten against one, if you know what I mean."

"Everyone in place?"

"Yep. I left Choctaw and Reynolds just outside the Red Boar. They're going to follow Proschaud when he leaves. Hanson, Boots, and Wethers will try to waylay Proschaud's men, if any of them comes with him, and I put Randiff, Devreaux, and Cardelle on the other side of the Spotswood."

"Good. There's no way Proschaud can slip through our net this time."

"Nope. Not unless there's a hole in it we don't know about."

Brett looked at him shrewdly. "What do you mean by that."

Emerson shrugged. "Spies are everywhere."

"I trust our men."

"Me, too, but I don't trust that little lady we rode up here with."

Brett didn't respond. How could he? Emerson was no fool. He was probably well aware of what had happened between Brett and Teresa, but Brett's lack of good judgment hadn't changed a thing. Their plan was the same. She'd lead them to Proschaud and they'd capture him. And, Teresa too, if it turned out to be necessary.

The rest of the night passed without event, and without the appearance of Jay Proschaud.

"What in the hell is the man waiting for?" Brett muttered. He'd been pacing steadily for an hour, his temper rising with each step.

"Maybe he don't know she's here," Emerson offered.

"He'd have had a man at the hotel, waiting for her," Brett snapped back. "He's too thorough not to."

"Maybe his man saw us."

"No. I made sure to stay out of sight."

Emerson shrugged. "Gonna be dawn soon."

Brett paused and looked up at the sky. The blackness of night was already turning gray, lightening with the approach of the sun on the horizon.

"We'll be visible."

"You go down to the corner," Brett said, "and stay there. I'm going to check into the hotel."

"Check in?" Emerson echoed, as if Brett had just gone mad.

"Yes. That way I can sit in the damned lobby and make certain she doesn't slip away unseen."

"She'll recognize you."

"No, she won't."

Brett grabbed his horse and led the animal across the street. A few minutes later he'd checked into the hotel, scouted out its lobby, and taken a seat in a large wing chair in one corner. His view of the front door was partially obscured by a circular settee in the center of the lobby, but then it partially obscured him, too, so he was satisfied.

A clerk brought him coffee from the hotel's dining room, which Brett was thoroughly thankful for. He warmed his hands around the cup, then sipped its contents slowly, feeling his body begin to thaw as the hot liquid made its way down his throat. A few times during his wait he nodded off, pulling himself back awake with a quick jerk of his body as his head dropped forward.

"Damn it all, Proschaud, will you make your move?" Brett growled to himself.

One of the hotel's other guests, passing just as Brett muttered, turned her nose up at him, murmured something to her companion about crazies being everywhere these days, and hurried down the hall to the dining room.

Brett glared after her. If he wasn't so damned tired, uncomfortable, and on edge, he might find her reaction comical. As it was, he merely found it annoying. His hair was tousled, his clothes wrinkled, his eyes bloodshot, and he had a full two days' growth covering the lower half of his face. He probably looked like a bum—and definitely felt like one.

Shifting position again, he poured himself another cup of coffee from the pot the clerk had brought. If Proschaud didn't show up soon, Brett felt certain he'd lose the battle to keep his eyes open. They already felt as if they were filled with sand.

Teresa paced the room. What was taking Jay so long? Then again, how was she supposed to alert him that she was here? His note hadn't said anything about that. She moved to the window that overlooked the street. It was still early, but the streets were not deserted. Quite the contrary. A unit of cavalry was moving past the hotel, several people were on the banquettes, and a carriage had just pulled up across the street. She watched the coachman help an elderly lady out and escort her across the street to the hotel entrance.

The woman was dressed entirely in black, with a long veil covering her face and a thick shawl over her stooped shoulders. She leaned heavily on the coachman's arm and walked with a shuffling gait.

"Poor old thing," Teresa murmured. "Bet she lost her family in the war." She felt a rise of compassion for the woman, hating the thought of losing anyone and knowing she'd be absolutely devastated if she did.

A few minutes later there was a knock on Teresa's door. She hurried to open it, then was surprised to see the same old woman she'd just watched enter the hotel. "Yes?"

The woman pushed the door open farther and swept past Teresa and into the room.

"Close the door."

Teresa whirled around and stared at the old lady. The poor thing was obviously senile and lost, but that didn't excuse her ill manners. "Excuse me, ma'am, but . . ."

"Close the damned door."

Teresa hesitated. The last thing she wanted was to be closeted in a hotel room with an old lady who was touched in the head.

The woman suddenly lunged toward Teresa, who shrieked and jumped to one side.

A large hand shot out from beneath the black veil and slapped against the door, slamming it shut.

Teresa scurried to the opposite side of the room, her eyes wide with alarm, a scream ready in her throat.

"Are you sure you weren't followed?"

Teresa frowned at the deep voice.

"Teresa!"

She jumped back at the harsh sound of her name and watched, horrified, as the woman, who had straightened and now towered over her, reached up and yanked the veiled hat from her head.

He laughed. "So, who'd you expect?"

Teresa merely stared at her husband, too dumbfounded to speak.

Tossing the shawl aside, he moved forward and drew her into his embrace before she could respond.

"Jay," she protested weakly as his arms crushed her to his body.

He pulled her tighter. "It's been a long time, Tess." His lips came down on hers, hard, brutal, hungry.

She pushed against his shoulders.

Jay backed her against the wall, pinning her to it with his sheer weight and size. His tongue darted into her mouth as she opened it to protest his assault. It flicked madly, wildly, probing and jabbing with a ferocity of need and ruthlessness that frightened and repulsed her. She felt his hands on her body, clutching at her breasts, then pulling at her dress.

She tore her mouth from his. "Jay, no, not . . ."

"Yes," he snarled, and caught her lips with his

again, plunging his tongue into her mouth and filling it. He jerked up the skirt of her gown. She felt his hand on her derriere, his long fingers grabbing her flesh and squeezing it cruelly as he lifted her up against himself, against the hard, swollen evidence of his arousal.

Teresa hit at him with her fists and writhed against him.

Jay pulled his mouth away and glared down at her. "What's the matter, dear wife? I would think you'd be as hungry for this as I am. Or have you been getting it somewhere else?"

Teresa gasped in shock. "You swine," she hissed.

Jay threw back his head and laughed, but didn't release her. "So, you *have* been saving it for me."

"No." She pushed against him.

The laugh died instantly and a look of cold hatred filled his dark eyes. His hand whipped up from beneath her skirts and clutched at her neck. "Who, Teresa?"

She stared up at him, terrified.

"I don't share, Teresa, you know that. What's mine is mine, forever."

"We're . . . we're divorced," she said, forcing the words past the tight hold he had on her throat.

His eyes turned murderous. "Divorced?" He pressed his body against hers until she could barely breathe. "You *divorced* me?"

"You left me," Teresa choked, tears burning her eyes.

"It was my duty."

"To sneak off in the middle of the night?" she said. "Our wedding night?"

He snickered. "You were already pregnant, Tess. So what else was there to accomplish? And I had things to do. Important things."

She hated him. If she'd never known it before, she knew it now.

Twenty-one

Jay abruptly released Teresa and walked to the bureau where a bottle of wine and two glasses had been left by the clerk. Without even a glance over his shoulder to make certain she was all right, Jay poured himself a glass of wine. "Very good," he said after a sip. "I'm surprised. The hotel must have a private stock somewhere."

Teresa settled into one of the chairs near the window and rubbed at her throat. She could still feel his hand there, clutching at her.

He walked toward her and though she felt like cringing, she forced herself not to, suspecting that it would only make him angry again.

Jay smiled. "It doesn't really matter, Tess—that you divorced me, I mean. As far as I'm concerned, you're still my wife and always will be. After the war we'll just say the words in front of a preacher again to make it all legal."

She stared up at him, wondering if he was crazy. Had he always been like this and she just hadn't seen it? Or had he changed? Either way, he was not the person she'd once thought herself in love with. Or maybe he was, and she just didn't like him anymore.

"I suppose you've been wondering where I've been?"

"Yes," she said softly. Once she had wondered, but she'd stopped long ago, when she'd stopped caring. This, however, was not the time to say that.

He seemed to puff up with self-importance. "I've been working for the cause. We're going to win, you know."

"I've heard things aren't going too well," Teresa said. "Ever since Vicksburg fell."

"Ah!" He waved a hand in dismissal. "The army isn't doing very well, but that's only a small part of this war. What's happening behind the lines, so to speak, is what's really going to win this war for the Confederacy."

"And you've been working behind the lines, so to speak," Teresa said. He looked the same as she remembered—tall, slightly gaunt, his face a landscape of angles and sharp features, his hair dark and straight. Whatever had she seen in Jay Proschaud? He wasn't handsome, and if she hadn't known it before, she certainly knew now that if he was not totally insane, he was, at the very least, perverse.

Jay grinned proudly. "Yes, with the KGC. And now you're going to help me."

"The KGC," Teresa repeated. It was the same organization her father had belonged to, as did the man accused of killing him, Henri Sorbonte, Belle and Lin's father. "You're working with the Knights of the Golden Circle?"

"Yes. Once they turned their attention to fighting the Yankees rather than worrying about annexing

Mexico into the Union, I was more than willing to help."

"You could have joined the army," Teresa ventured.

"Oh, mercy no, and tramp through mud? Sleep outdoors? Go for days with little or no food?" His sardonic laugh filled the room. "You should know me better than that, my dear wife."

She nearly cringed at being called his wife. "So why did you want me here?" Teresa asked. "You said something in your note about one of my brothers being in trouble."

"Yes, and quite truthfully you were the only one I felt I could trust with the information. I mean," he began to pace the room, "I have no idea if your other brothers are loyal or not, so . . ." He shrugged, leaving the sentence unfinished.

"Not loyal?" Teresa's temper flared instantly at the veiled accusation. "What are you talking about, Jay?"

"Treason, of course."

"Treason?" Teresa nearly shouted the word and bolted from her chair.

"Yes, and calm down. I don't need some nosy busybody from the next room listening."

Teresa resumed her seat.

"As I was about to explain, in my work with the KGC I've been acting as a double agent, going back and forth in the higher echelon, so to speak, and sometimes even into the camps."

"I thought you didn't want to get dirty."

"I only go into the camps when it's absolutely necessary," Jay said. "Anyway, I was in a Yankee camp only a few weeks ago and I saw Trace there."

"Trace? Was he captured?" Teresa jumped from her chair and clutched at Jay's arms.

He brushed her off, his tone filled with disdain. "No, of course not. I wouldn't have summoned you up here for that."

He was trying her patience and although she felt like ripping his tongue out, she forced herself to remain calm.

"He was passing information about Confederate troop movements."

"No, that can't be, Jay. You're saying Trace is a . . . is a . . ."

"Traitor," he finished for her, sounding quite gleeful about it. "But that's not all."

She stared at him warily. Trace was not a traitor to the cause, she would stake her life on that, but she couldn't denounce Jay, or argue with him, before she found out what he was up to, and why he was accusing her brother of treason. "What else?"

"He was at a meeting of the Knights I attended a short time back."

"The Knights?" Teresa repeated. This was starting to sound more and more ridiculous. Trace hated the Knights and everything they stood for. He thought they were too radical and self-absorbed, spouting off about supporting Mexico's annexation because it would be good for Mexico, and then backing the Confederacy because their ideals were righteous and sound, when all the time the only thing the leaders of the KGC were interested in was self-gratification.

"Yes. He didn't see me there, however." Jay stopped at one end of the fireplace, then turned to her and, pushing back the lapels of his jacket, hooked both thumbs into the armholes of an expensively cut vest. "On this particular night the KGC was planning a sabotage attack against some Union troops who had been advancing toward Petersburg from Yorktown. We'd just gotten the information and knew we had to act fast to help the army out as their lines there were almost defenseless."

Teresa remained silent, trying to commit everything he said to memory.

"The group was small that night and I knew everyone there. They could all be trusted—except Trace, of course."

"Of course," Teresa murmured.

He looked at her strangely, then continued. "Trace insisted that several units of General Pickett's battalion accompany the Knights and assist. It wasn't necessary, of course, but he persisted."

"How is that treason?" Teresa asked. "It sounds as if he was only trying to help."

Jay smiled. "Ah, I was coming to that. You see, by pulling men from Pickett's already established position, he weakened it horribly. Sheridan attacked the weak line that was left and as a result Petersburg is now nearly lost. And all because of your dear brother."

"I don't believe it." She shot from the chair, hands on hips, and glared at him. "You're lying."

He stared at her for several seconds, neither responding nor moving, his dark eyes unreadable, his expression calm. Then suddenly his lips curved upward and he broke into raucous laughter.

Startled, Teresa merely stared.

Before she could move, Jay crossed the room and

grabbed her arms. "Are you so certain of that, dear wife?"

She tried to break free of his hold, twisting against his grasp. "Yes," she snapped. "My brother has honor, which is more than I can say for you. He'd never betray his country—or sneak off and leave his wife."

Jay's fingers dug into her arms.

"Let go of me, Jay."

"You have to help me," he growled, his grip tightening until she stopped writhing.

Her arms felt as if they were caught in a vise, but she ignored the pain. "No. I'm going home. I never should have come in the first place. You're a liar and a coward and I won't help you."

Jay's hand swung up and smashed against the side of her face, sending Teresa reeling. She fell on the bed, her cheek stinging and her eyes filled with tears. Jumping up, she glowered at him. "I don't care what you do, Jay, I'm not going to help you."

His grin was pure evil and sent a shudder of fear up her spine. "If you don't," he said calmly, all trace of his anger gone, "I'll have your brother denounced and arrested as a spy."

"You can't. He hasn't done anything."

"I can, and I will. There are some very important people in the KGC, Tess, very important, and it can be done."

"But he hasn't . . ."

"This is war, Tess, and an accusation of treason is taken very seriously. Before Trace can begin to think about putting up a defense, he'll be standing on the gallows."

Teresa gasped, feeling more hatred for Jay Proschaud than she'd ever felt in her life, and more terror. The look in his eyes, the confidence in his voice, told her loud and clear that he could do exactly as he threatened. He was leaving her no choice. She had to help him, at least until she could figure out a way to expose him for the snake that he was. "All right, Jay, what do you want me to do?"

"Ah, good, I knew I could count on you." He walked over to her and, bending down, pressed a kiss to her cheek.

Teresa pulled away, feeling as if the devil himself had just touched her flesh. "What do you want me to do?"

Jay walked to the window, looking down on the street but standing just out of sight of anyone looking up. "Well, as you know, Trace is a trusted member of the President's cabinet." He paused and turned to look at her, as if to judge her reaction to his comment.

"Yes, I know."

He turned back to the window. "Well, as such, he knows all the members of the cabinet, the President's special guards, and, of course, his enemies."

"So?"

"And he also knows most of the members of the Knights, including me."

"And you want to get past him, to the President?"

"Yes."

"To kill him?"

Jay laughed. "Well, of course not. Why would we do that? We're fighting the same war he is. No, our fear is that Trace, if he truly is a traitor, and I'm leaving room for doubt only because he is your brother . . ."

She shuddered at the ribald smile that curved his lips.

He issued an exaggerated sigh. "Well, he could jeopardize the President's life."

"He would never do that."

"War changes people," Jay said.

She stared at him, remembering another man who'd said that to her just a short time ago, a man with blond hair and blue eyes who'd made her feel like a woman again for the first time in years—a man who'd made her feel safe in his arms, and loved. That last thought jerked her back to reality swifter than Jay's slap had done. Loved her? No, Brett Forsythe didn't love her, he'd only used her. He loved Goldie, whoever she was.

Teresa fought off the feeling of self-pity. She'd have plenty of time to wallow in that later. Right now she had to concentrate on Jay and what he was saying. "Yes, I guess you're right," she agreed. "What do you want me to do?"

"I want you to take a message to President Davis."

"You think I can get through to him?"

"Oh, yes. As Trace's sister there should be no problem with that."

"But what if Trace is there? What am I supposed to say? He'll want to know what I'm doing."

"I'll give you two messages. One will be the real one that you'll give to no one but Davis. The other you'll give to Trace, if he intercepts you. It will detail Yankee troop movements around New Orleans."

"But New Orleans is occupied."

"Yes, but if Trace thought there was a way to open up its ports again then the Confederacy would be able to ship in supplies from England and France."

"And in the meantime I slip the real note to the President."

"Yes."

"Which says?"

Jay's smile disappeared and his features grew hard. "You do not need to know."

"I have a right to know."

"No, you don't."

She glared at him. "Jay, I'm putting myself in jeopardy, and Trace, too. If you want me to do this you have to tell me what's going on."

He moved back to her bureau and poured himself another glass of wine. "We suspect that there's a plot to kidnap President Lincoln and blame it on the Confederacy."

"Kidnap?" Teresa blurted.

He turned to look at her. "Yes. We believe he's not only going to be kidnapped, but killed."

Teresa stared at Jay, unable to believe she'd heard him right. What was she supposed to believe?

"That's why we have to deliver a message to President Davis. He must surround himself with men he can trust to prevent anything happening to him."

"Why do you think something's going to happen to him? I thought it was Lincoln."

"Yes, but sometimes, the best-laid plans can go awry. Or perhaps the men behind this diabolical scheme want their own person in charge of the Confederacy when it becomes the new government of the South."

He put his glass down and walked to where she stood. "So, that is why I need your help." Jay reached into his pocket and pulled out two envelopes. "Now, this one," he said, and handed her a sealed envelope of pale ivory paper, "is the real letter you must get to Davis."

Teresa nodded.

"And this one," he handed her another sealed envelope that was slightly smaller and of darker paper, "is the one you can give to Trace, if need be."

She took both envelopes and walked over to the bureau, opened one of its drawers, and slipped the letters into her reticule. Closing the drawer again, she turned and smiled at Jay. He might be the father of her child and the man she once thought she loved, but he'd changed. She didn't know Jay Proschaud any longer. Maybe she'd never really known him. But she did know her brother, and he wasn't a traitor.

Twenty-two

Jay walked beside Teresa as they descended the stairs into the lobby.

"What about your disguise?" she whispered.

He chuckled softly. "I was an old woman coming into the hotel, and I'm a husband going out. No one will be looking for me to be accompanying a young lady."

"Don't they know you're . . ." She nearly bit the tip of her tongue off to keep from saying *married.* Of course Jay wouldn't volunteer that information. After all, he'd run off. Most likely he did as he pleased, and that included bedding any woman who'd have him. Teresa felt like pulling her arm from his hand, suddenly knowing all too well what it felt like to touch a snake, but she let it remain there.

Stepping past the hotel's entry, Jay steered her toward a carriage at the curb and helped her board. "Take the lady to the Capitol Building," he said to the driver. "Here's her fare. Make certain she gets there safely."

The driver nodded and picked up his reins.

"How do I contact you later?" Teresa asked.

"You don't." Jay waved at the driver, who snapped

a whip over the horse's flanks, causing the carriage to lurch forward.

Teresa fell back against her seat and cursed softly. If Jay was trying to prove that her new opinion of him as a despicable cad was correct, he was doing a very good job.

Brett watched in astonishment as Jay Proschaud exited the hotel holding Teresa's arm. Where in the hell had he come from? A sense of uneasiness filled him. Brett looked toward the corner where another of his agents was posted. The man was lazing against the side of a building and smoking a cheroot. Brett looked in the opposite direction. Another agent, holding a journal and acting as if he was checking its figures, stood by the tailgate of a large dray filled with crates.

Emerson and two other agents were in position to cover the hotel's back entrance, so how in the hell had Proschaud gotten in? Brett couldn't come up with an answer, but he did come up with another thought. Perhaps Proschaud had already been in the hotel when Teresa arrived. That would explain his sudden appearance.

Brett reached for his holster and settled a hand around the butt of his Navy Colt. As soon as the carriage was gone they'd go after Proschaud, then he'd send a man after Teresa to find out what she was up to. A controlled sense of excitement coursed through Brett. In only a few minutes the chase would finally be over.

Holding tight to his mount's reins, Brett ran a

soothing hand over the animal's muzzle. "Easy, boy," he said to the restless horse. "Just a few minutes longer."

Brett watched Jay Proschaud hand the driver a greenback and slap a hand against the side of the carriage. It moved forward instantly. Brett tensed. This was it. He drew the Colt, ready to run across the street. But almost as quickly as Brett blinked, Jay Proschaud was gone.

"Son of a bitch," Brett said, the curse a harsh whisper on the cool morning air. His eyes scanned the area looking for a clue as to the man's disappearance. Then he noticed that the entry door to the hotel was swinging slightly.

He'd gone back inside.

Brett sprinted across the street, signaling for the other two agents to accompany him. The three barged into the hotel lobby.

"Search the dining room," Brett ordered. "Check with Emerson—I'll guard the front door."

A few minutes later, cursing himself for once again letting Jay Proschaud slip through his fingers, Brett nodded and pushed the entrance door open for a crippled old woman dressed completely in black, a widow's veil covering her face.

Brett felt a wave of sympathy as he watched her shuffle toward a carriage parked across the street. She'd probably lost her husband or son to the war. He turned back the lobby.

Emerson sauntered toward him from the hallway that led to the rear exit. "He's gotta be in here."

"Well, let's hope so," Brett said. "You've got the rear exit covered?"

"Yep."

"Good." Brett called to the agent who'd just finished searching the dining room and kitchen. "Selles, stand guard here at the door, Emerson and I are going to start checking the rooms."

They walked across the lobby and mounted the staircase to the second floor. "I don't care if we have to search every room here, we've got to . . ." Brett suddenly stopped.

Emerson turned back to look at him. "You got something stuck in your craw?" the older man asked, seeing Brett's mouth agape.

"No, in my brain," he snapped. "Proschaud's not here." Brett wheeled around and ran for the stairs.

"Huh?"

"Proschaud's not here," Brett called back over his shoulder. "He's on his way to wherever Teresa's buggy is going."

Emerson sprinted after Brett. "How do you know that?"

"He came here dressed as an old lady in black, with a veil to over her head, and that's how he left."

They ran through the lobby, pausing only long enough to tell Selles to get the others and search the streets for Teresa's carriage.

"My guess is the Capitol Building," Brett said as he mounted his horse. Proschaud's note mentioned that one of her brothers was in trouble, and Trace is stationed at the Capitol."

"I'll get my horse and meet you there."

Touching his heels to his horse's ribs, Brett urged the animal into motion. Whatever Jay Proschaud was up to, it was no damned good. And the man had involved Teresa. Brett cursed softly. At least he *hoped* the man had involved Teresa, and she hadn't volunteered herself.

As he rounded a corner, the Capitol Building came into view and Brett reined in quickly. Teresa's carriage was just heading up the drive. There was still time to intercept her.

A tall figure dressed in dark clothes and sporting a long cape suddenly jumped out from behind one of the pillars supporting the entry gates and lunged at Teresa's carriage.

Brett jerked his mount to a stop again. Jay Proschaud. "Damn it all to hell," he cursed softly, watching as Proschaud climbed into the carriage while it rumbled its way up the drive. He couldn't charge up there now and order the driver to stop, and he couldn't attempt to overtake Proschaud alone. Either move would pose too much danger to Teresa—if she wasn't an accessory to whatever Proschaud was trying to pull.

Brett shrugged that thought aside. This was no time to let his feelings get the better of him. He continued to watch as the carriage stopped before the entrance and Jay got out, then turned to help Teresa.

Damn, Brett thought frantically, he had to do something. But no sooner had the decision to act entered his head than he saw Proschaud and Teresa exit the Capitol and reboard the carriage. It moved down the drive toward him. Brett reined his horse around and urged the animal into a wide space between two buildings across the street, hoping as he moved into the alley that he was out of sight.

"Easy boy," he crooned as his horse pawed the ground.

The carriage turned right and headed toward the center of town.

Brett moved out cautiously, keeping a good distance behind them, but not so far that there was any possibility he'd lose sight of the carriage. The streets were beginning to become more crowded. People were out of their houses, shopping, going to work, or visiting, and troops were on the move. Several times he passed a company of soldiers marching down the center of the street.

The carriage continued on. Brett cursed under his breath. He was on his own now. Emerson and the others would get to the Capitol Building and not find him there, and would have no idea where he'd gone. But then, at the moment, he had no idea where he was going.

The carriage turned on Clay, then again on Twelfth and suddenly Brett knew exactly where it was going—to the President's private residence. He looked around frantically, wishing, praying, hoping to see a familiar face. But it was useless. His men were on their way to the Capitol Building. By the time they headed for Davis's house, *if* they were headed for Davis's house, whatever was going to happen would have happened. And Brett was the only one who could stop it.

Ahead of him the carriage rolled to a stop before a large, two-story white townhouse, its front portico supported by four square Doric pillars.

Brett reined in and watched as Jay and Teresa descended from the carriage and walked up the short path to the front steps. A soldier suddenly stepped forward.

"Yes," Brett said beneath his breath, feeling a moment's relief. "Stop them."

Twenty-three

Traxton Braggette walked through the rear entry of the Confederate White House and into its spacious foyer. Bright rays of morning sunlight poured into the room through a fanlight window set above the main entry and sparkled a reflection in a mirror hung on one wall. It also lent a dull shine to Traxton's black, knee-high boots, but was cruel in revealing the frayed edges of his uniform's collar and cuffs.

As he walked, the silver spurs attached to his boots tinkling softly with each step, Traxton reached up and swept a gray slouch hat, given to him by Jeb Stuart just before he died, from his head. The red ostrich plume General Stuart had stuck in the hat's collar fluttered softly. "He's on his way."

Trace Braggette nodded and moved away from a window that looked out onto the street. "Good. Your men are in place, as are mine. All we can do now is wait."

"You haven't been able to talk him out of staying?"

Trace shook his head. "He says his orders continually place other men in the line of fire, so why shouldn't he face it himself?"

"Because it's not necessary," Traxton grumbled.

"He doesn't see it that way."

"He's the damned President," Traxton said needlessly. "We can't afford for him to get shot."

Trace merely shrugged. *"You* tell him that."

"What about the message that was delivered to him in church this morning? Have we verified that it was really sent by Lee? That it's genuine?"

Trace nodded again. "Yes, it's genuine."

"He's giving up Petersburg."

"He evidently has no choice."

"Damn."

"Mrs. Davis and the children left an hour ago, along with most of the servants. I've told the other members of the cabinet to prepare to leave also."

"Where's Travis?" Traxton asked.

"In with the President. Having coffee."

"Sounds good to me. I could use a cup."

They turned toward a closed door at one end of the foyer.

"Damned good thing Travis started going to those KGC meetings again or we'd never have learned about Proschaud's latest scheme," Trace said.

Traxton nodded. The Confederacy was thankful, but he doubted if their mother was. She had two sons in the army and one running the blockade. At least with Travis out in Virginia City he'd been almost as far away from the war as a body could get, though he'd kept tabs on the KGC groups established in Nevada and California and regularly sent the Confederacy whatever information he gathered.

Knowing that at least one of her sons was not in dire danger had given Eugenia Braggette some semblance of relief during the last few years. But Travis's search for his wife's missing brother, Brett, had brought them east again only a few months before.

Traxton paused at the door and glanced at his older brother. The two were almost mirror images of each other, even though they were several years apart in age. He smiled. "Think anyone would be able to tell us apart today?"

Trace chuckled, looking at his brother's dark hair and gray-blue eyes, then letting his gaze slip to Traxton's worn uniform. His own was in much better condition, and it hadn't been quite as long since he'd seen a barber. "No, but then it has come in handy, hasn't it?" he said, referring to the past when they'd often fooled friends and family alike.

Traxton held out his hand. "I don't think I've ever said it before, Trace, but thanks."

Trace took Traxton's hand but looked at him quizzically. "Thanks? For what?"

He shrugged. "Being my older brother. Staying at Shadows Noir. Protecting the others after I left. And not holding a grudge when I came back."

"You're my brother," Trace said softly.

Traxton nodded. "Yeah."

"We'd better get inside. They should be arriving any minute."

"That bastard better not hurt Teresa," Traxton growled.

"We won't give him the chance."

Travis Braggette, standing before a window across the room from the door, turned as they entered.

Except for a few silver hairs in Trace's sideburns, and the laugh lines at the corners of Traxton's eyes and framing his mouth, neither of which Travis possessed yet, the three could have been triplets.

The President looked up from his journal.

Trace stood before his desk. "Everything's ready, sir."

Davis nodded and stood, his tall, lean form made even more severe by his black frock coat and trousers.

"Mr. President, are you certain you won't go upstairs and let us handle this alone?"

Davis smiled, bringing a measure of warmth to his narrow face and hawkish features while his eyes remained weary and almost sorrowful. "No, thank you, Trace, I'll stay."

The Confederate capital was about to fall. They all knew it, yet no one spoke the words. It was easier to deal with it that way—in silence.

A guard suddenly appeared at the door. "A carriage just pulled up out front, sir."

Trace nodded and the guard disappeared. He moved to close the door, then turned to the others. Davis resumed his seat behind his desk. "Okay, we all know what's going to happen."

Traxton and Travis nodded.

"We have two priorities," Trace said. "To keep the President safe and capture Jay Proschaud."

The others nodded again. Keeping Teresa safe was also a priority, but one that the three Braggettes felt was better, at the moment, kept to themselves. They took up their positions in the room and waited.

Teresa placed her hand in Jay's and stepped from the carriage. He immediately jerked her close and wrapped a long arm around her waist, pulling her up against him. "One wrong move, my dear wife," he whispered, viciousness suddenly edging his tone, "and your precious brother will get a bullet between the eyes."

Revulsion had been her initial reaction, but his words filled her with terror. Teresa's head snapped around and she stared up at him, her body tense. "I . . . I thought you were only here to warn the President he could be in danger."

Jay laughed softly. "Among other things."

Teresa tried to pull away from him.

Jay's hand shot out and his long fingers wrapped around her wrist like the talons of a ferocious bird, squeezing her frail bones within his steely grasp. "Careful, love," he crooned nastily and smiled. "Remember your brother."

Teresa jerked back and as she did, Jay's jacket pulled open. Her eyes fell on a small leather notebook partially tucked inside his breast pocket. She felt a start of surprise and stifled a gasp.

She swallowed hard and mounted the steps of the house. Still held tightly in Jay's grasp, they approached the front door. TNB. The initials echoed over and over in her mind. The notebook had been embossed with the initials TNB—Thomas Nathan Braggette. Jay had her father's notebook! Teresa felt her blood turn cold and her heart skip a beat then plunge into a maddening pace. Thomas Braggette had never been without that notebook, and he never would have given it to anyone. She knew, from overhearing a conversation he'd once had, that it contained the names of every member of the Knights of the

Golden Circle. That was highly secret and dangerous information, especially if it got into the wrong hands.

Suddenly the mystery surrounding her father's murder, the unanswered questions about the man accused of the murder, Henri Sorbonte, became clear. Teresa felt nausea begin to rise.

Jay had gone to her father's office the night he'd been killed, supposedly to talk to Thomas Braggette about the wedding and Jay's future. He'd wanted the elder Braggette to support him in a new business, something his own father refused to consider. But they'd taken so long that Teresa had become impatient and gone to her father's office.

Her stomach churned at the memories. She'd opened the door to her father's office that night but had gone no farther. Horror held her frozen in place as a scream began to rip from her throat. Jay had run forward and drawn her into his arms, smothering the scream in the fabric of his jacket as he held her tight. His body had blocked the view of her father lying on the floor in a pool of blood.

Teresa remembered the fear she'd felt for Jay and the sensation of revulsion she'd experienced at seeing the blood. But she also remembered something else, something that brought with it a sense of guilt. She had never felt any grief over her father's death. Never felt sorrow, or a sense of loss, and she'd never cried.

She looked at the guard standing beside the door. He was waiting for her to speak. Teresa looked up at Jay, then back at the still-exposed notebook.

His gaze followed hers and she felt his grasp tighten on her arm as he realized what she was looking at. He obviously knew what she was thinking. A smile curved his lips. "Tell the man why we're here, darling."

Teresa looked back at the guard. "I . . . I would like to see my brother, General Trace Braggette."

Jay's fingers dug cruelly into her arm at her words, but the smile remained on his face. "Dear, wasn't it Mr. Davis you wanted to see?"

Teresa ignored the pain and smiled back at him, her eyes bright with defiance. "No, dear—my brother, Trace."

The young soldier nodded and reached for the doorknob. He pushed the door open and stepped back to allow them entry.

Jay pushed Teresa forward. "Remember," he growled softly into her ear, "that you don't want your precious brother to die." He stepped before her and drew back the other side of his jacket. A gun lay snuggled just beneath his arm. "And he will, if you try to warn him. Or anyone else."

He turned and pushed her toward another guard standing beside the staircase. "My wife, General Braggette's sister, has a message for the President," he said, not allowing Teresa to speak.

The guard nodded. "I'll announce you." He walked to a door several feet away, knocked on its mahogany panel, then turned the knob and pushed the door open.

Teresa hesitated. She didn't know what Jay was going to do and that terrified her. What if he intended to kill them all? Her heart nearly stopped. She'd never see Brett again. A million other thoughts raced through her mind, but that was the one she kept coming back to, the one that filled her with fear yet gave her the determination to fight Jay. She walked beside him into the room. Several officers were huddled about a table in one corner but didn't turn at their entry.

President Davis rose from his seat behind his desk. He smiled and put his hand out toward Teresa. "Ah, Miss Braggette," he said, his drawl like fine wine, deep and rich. "I can't tell you what a pleasure it is to meet Trace Braggette's sister."

Teresa reached out to accept the President's hand.

Jay suddenly jerked her aside and drew his gun. "Then you won't mind remaining in her company for a while, will you, Mr. President?"

The three men in the corner whirled around, and Teresa's mouth dropped open as her gaze darted from one to the other.

"It won't work, Proschaud," Trace said.

Jay laughed and moved to the President's side. "No? And why not, Trace?" He grabbed Davis's arm. "Who's going to stop me? You?"

"If need be."

"Give it up," Traxton said.

A burst of laughter spewed from Jay's lips. "This is one for the records," he sneered. "Three of the illustrious Braggette brothers guarding the President and I kidnap him right under your very noses. Doesn't say much for you, does it, gentlemen?"

"Jay . . ."

He looked at Teresa. "Shut up and move toward the door."

She hesitated.

"Move, Tess, or I'll kill one of them." He pointed the gun toward her brothers.

Teresa hurried toward the door.

"Now, Mr. President," Jay said, "if you'll follow my dear wife, there won't be any need to shoot anyone. Including you."

Teresa looked at her brothers. "I'm sorry," she said softly.

Jay pushed Davis ahead of him. As he stepped up alongside Teresa, she glanced back at her brothers. If she was going to do anything, it had to be now. Raising a hand to her forehead, she sighed loudly and let her knees bend beneath her, as if she were about to faint.

Jay jerked around. "Tess," he snarled.

Curling her left hand into a fist she covered it with her right and gave it a violent shove. Her elbow flew into Jay's stomach, causing him to double over.

Teresa jumped aside, as did the President.

Suddenly another figure loomed in the doorway.

"Brett," Teresa screamed.

Brett grabbed Jay's hand and struggled to gain possession of the gun. They slammed against the wall, arms and legs entwined.

"Teresa, get back," Travis yelled, and pulled her away from the struggling men.

"Help him," she cried.

Traxton lunged forward and grabbed one of Jay's arms from behind.

"He's wanted for treason," Trace said.

Teresa trembled violently, fear holding her tight in its grip as she watched Brett try to wrest the gun from Jay. "Brett," she cried finally. "Help Brett."

Suddenly an explosion filled the air as the gun fired.

Jay screamed and released his grip on the gun as blood spurted from his shoulder, instantly soaking into the fibers of his white shirt.

Traxton released Jay's arm as he slumped forward.

"Brett," Teresa mumbled softly.

Jay twisted away from Brett and ran toward the window, plunging past the sheer lace panels. Turning sideways at the last moment, he crashed a shoulder into the window.

The sound of smashing glass filled the room.

Teresa screamed. Travis spun her around and away from the flying shards.

Traxton cursed loudly and ducked.

Brett hurled Jay's name after him like a profanity, drew his gun, and charged toward the window. He stopped at its sill. "Damn, the bastard got away again." Sheathing his weapon, he turned and hurried to Teresa.

"Teresa," he said softly.

She pulled away from Travis and threw herself in Brett's arms. "I'm sorry," she mumbled against his chest. "I'm sorry."

"Teresa."

She looked up at him and shook her head, tears streaking her face. "I'm sorry. I didn't want to go with him. I didn't want to do this, but he said . . ." A sob tore at her throat. "He said he'd label Trace a traitor and see that he was hanged."

Trace moved over beside her.

Teresa turned to look at him, but her hands firmly grasped Brett's lapels. "I'm sorry," she murmured.

Trace smiled. "For what? Trying to save my life?"

She looked back at Brett again. "You're not a Yankee." It wasn't a question.

He smiled. "No. A special agent to the Confederate government. And my name's not Forsythe, it's Forteaux."

Teresa gasped. "Brett Forteaux? That's why you seemed so familiar."

"I was afraid you'd remember too soon. Then I feared you wouldn't remember me at all."

Teresa's gaze dropped from his. "How could I ever forget my first love?"

"Your first . . . ?" Laughing softly, he pulled her into his arms.

Traxton turned to the President. "Are you all right, sir?"

Davis nodded. "I'm fine, my boy, fine, but I think it's about time to meet with my cabinet and tell them about General Lee's message."

Travis slapped Brett on the back. "Well, I'm damned glad to see you've finally surfaced in one piece."

"Any reason to think I wouldn't?" Brett asked.

Traxton turned to Travis and Trace. "I'm going to gather my men and go after Jay."

Teresa pulled away from Brett and took Traxton's hand. "Be careful, Trax," she said. "He's crazy."

He bent down and kissed her cheek. "So am I," he said, and smiled slyly. "Or so Belle always tells me."

"I'll go with you," Brett said.

"President Davis."

Everyone turned toward the door to stare at the guard who had just entered. He looked flustered.

"This just came for you, sir." He handed the President an envelope. "From one of Lee's aides."

The President tore open the envelope and read its contents quickly. His face, already drawn and gaunt, seemed suddenly to cave in on itself. He dropped into his chair.

Trace stepped forward to take the letter from his hand. He read it and quickly looked up at the others. "Petersburg has fallen. Lee's troops are retreating. We've got to get the President out of Richmond. Now."

"What about his family?" Trace asked.

"They've already been sent south." Trace turned toward the President. "Sir, we have to move as quickly as possible."

Davis nodded. "Yes. Just let me get a few things." He rose and walked from the room, his steps heavy on the foyer's bare floor.

"You go with your brothers," Brett said to Teresa. "When this war is over, I'll come to Shadows Noir."

She touched a hand gently to his face. "Be careful. I don't want to lose you."

He hugged her to him, then brushed his lips across hers. "You won't," he whispered. Releasing her, Brett straightened and turned toward the others. "I'm going after Proschaud."

"No."

He stared at Trace. "No? What the hell do you mean, *no?* The man's a menace—there's no telling what he'll do now."

"We've got more important things to do," Trace said.

Brett's jaw set in anger. "I've been after that man

for well over a year, Trace." He turned to stare at Travis. "And I would think you'd want to hunt him down, too, after what happened to Suzanne."

Travis frowned. "What the hell does Suzanne have to do with hunting down Proschaud?"

"He's responsible for Suzanne's death, Travis. You must know that."

"Death?" The word was said in unison by the three brothers and Teresa. Everyone looked at him as if he were crazy.

"Brett," Travis finally said, "Proschaud didn't kill Suzanne."

"Maybe not by his own hand, but he's responsible for what happened."

"Brett," Travis tried again, "Suzanne is not dead. She's fine."

Brett's mouth dropped open. "Not dead? Suzanne's not dead?"

"No. She's in New Orleans. I saw her there myself, just a few months ago, before coming here to Virginia."

Brett felt a wash of relief sweep over him that was so intense it nearly knocked him from his feet. "My . . . my sources said she'd been killed in an explosion, on a wagon train hauling ore down to Carson."

Travis smiled. "We were on that train," he said, "but Suzanne and I were riding our own mounts. She suffered a few bruises, but that's all."

Teresa slipped into Brett's arms again and he pulled her to him, suddenly weak with happiness.

"Brett," Trace said, stepping forward, his tone and

features deadly serious, "I need you to impersonate the President."

"What?"

"My aide was supposed to do it if it came to this, but he's not here, and you're the only one around with hair light enough to pass for Davis's gray."

Brett nodded. "What's the plan?"

"I'm going to have a few of my troops escort the President and the cabinet to a train we've had prepared and waiting. It will take them to Danville. We'll take the Mayo Bridge and go in the opposite direction through Manchester and then to the James River."

"And then?" Brett questioned.

"And then, hopefully, we disappear," Trace said.

"Let's do it," Traxton said.

Trace walked to the door and signaled to the guard standing near the staircase. "Go upstairs and tell the President it's time to leave. Carry anything down he wants to take."

The man saluted and hurried to follow his orders. Five minutes later he and the President stood in the foyer. Two carriages pulled up in front of the house and several men descended, then quickly climbed the stairs to the gallery. Trace opened the entry door before they could knock. "Gentlemen," he said, his voice somber. "I assume you're ready to leave?"

Each nodded.

"Good. Then please get back into your buggies."

Another pulled up in front of the house.

Trace turned toward the President. "Sir, your carriage." He motioned to the buggy that had just stopped.

Davis offered Trace his hand. "Be careful, my boy," he said softly. "And thank you."

Trace nodded.

"Godspeed," Traxton said softly.

"Keep your back to the wind," Travis said.

Teresa tried to wipe away her tears.

Trace reached out and took her hand. "Come on, little sister, it's goodbye for you, too."

She pulled away from his grasp. "Goodbye?" she echoed. "What are you talking about?"

"You. You're going on the train with the President while we try to draw the Yankees in another direction."

Teresa stiffened and glowered at him. "I'm going with you."

"Oh, no, you're not."

"No," Brett agreed.

"It's too dangerous," Traxton said.

"If you really want to draw the Yankees away from the President, then you've got to do it right."

"We intend to do it ri . . ."

"They don't know that Mrs. Davis has already left Richmond, do they?" she challenged.

"Well, no."

"Then they'll expect Mrs. Davis to be traveling with the President."

Trace and Brett both caught on to her intent at the same time. "No," both thundered.

Teresa smiled. "It's that, or I stay here and face them by myself."

Traxton swore under his breath. "Have you been taking stubborn lessons from Belle?"

A smug smile curved Teresa's lips.

"Oh, great," Travis moaned. "And I left Suzanne with Belle."

Traxton turned to Brett. "This is what you're up against, you know, if you marry her."

Brett took Teresa's hands in his. "It's too dangerous," he said softly, his voice barely above a whisper.

"If you're going to do it, then so am I."

He sighed and looked at the others. "Does Mrs. Davis have a veil Teresa can wear over her face?"

Twenty-four

The carriage moved past the Exchange Hotel and down Fourteenth Street, jostling for room among the pedestrians, mounted riders, and other carriages that already crowded the street. News of Lee's retreat and the advance of the Yankees had spread rapidly and caused many to look at evacuation as the only route to safety. The Shockoe Tobacco warehouse came into view on the right and Teresa knew they were nearing the James River.

She sat beside Brett in the passenger seat of the open carriage, one arm holding tightly to his. Her hands trembled slightly but it was more from anxiety than fear. At least, that's what she kept trying to tell herself. Travis had donned a dark livery coat and hat that belonged to the President's driver and sat in the front seat driving the carriage. Teresa felt Brett tense as the Richmond-Danville Railroad Depot came into view, and the bridge just beyond.

"We'll be okay," he said, and covered her hand with his. "If they're going to attack us it won't be until we're across the river and nearly into Manchester."

"But there's only seven of us," Teresa said.

"Wouldn't the President be traveling with more guards? And what about his cabinet?"

"Yes to all of that," Brett said, "but Trace didn't want to put any more lives in jeopardy than he had to, and he thought it better to assign the remaining troops to guard Davis and the cabinet on the train."

Teresa nodded and leaned forward to glance back at the city as the carriage rumbled onto the already crowded bridge. Trace had ordered his men to set fire to any factories, warehouses, or arsenals holding supplies the Yankees could commandeer.

Brett followed her gaze.

Flames shot into the air from the direction of the Tredegar Iron Works. She frowned as she looked at the other fires that had started to blaze in the distance.

"The State Armory and the Paper Mill," Brett said.

She looked to the south.

"The Gas Works."

Teresa nodded. She turned back and settled against her seat. The Confederacy was writhing in death throes. No one had surrendered and the fighting hadn't stopped, but she knew, in her heart, that the cause was lost. Too many men had died, too many homes had been destroyed, cities conquered, supplies cut off. It was merely a matter of time.

A tear slipped from her eyes and she quickly brushed it away with her fingertips. Varina Davis wouldn't cry, Teresa told herself. The President's wife would hold her head high and proud, and never lose hope. Teresa straightened her shoulders and blinked back the tears that stung her eyes.

The carriage rolled across the wooden bridge, the

creaking rumble of its wheel on the old planks drowned out by the roar of dozens of other carriages, mounted riders, and people on foot both preceding and following them. It was getting late. Twilight had settled over the land, leaving it in that eerie time that was neither day nor night.

Brett closed his fingers around Teresa's. "Stay close to me," he said. "No matter what happens, stay close."

Forever, she thought to herself.

As the carriage rolled off the bridge, Travis turned it to the left, making for the frontage road that followed the James River south. Traxton and one of his men rode in front of the carriage. Trace and one of his aides rode behind.

Brett pulled his gun from its holster and laid it across his lap. "Any time now," he said.

She fingered the derringer she'd placed in her lap earlier, obscured by a fold of her skirt, then slipped her hand comfortably around its handle, pulled its small silver hammer back with her thumb, and slid her finger onto the trigger.

Suddenly a figure loomed from behind the bridge's corner post, jumped onto the carriage's boarding step, and lunged at Brett.

Startled, he jerked back, throwing himself in front of Teresa to shield her.

The jarring shift of the carriage yanked on the horse's rigging, causing the animal to whinny loudly and rear in panic.

Travis fought to maintain his hold on the reins with one hand and, glancing over his shoulder, drew his revolver with the other.

Traxton, hearing the commotion behind him, reined

his horse around and aimed his gun toward the carriage.

Jay raised his arm high, moonlight glittering off the blade of his knife. It plunged downward toward Brett's chest.

Trace cocked his gun and jammed his heels into his horse's ribs. The animal bolted forward.

Teresa's gaze remained fixed on the knife as she raised her derringer toward Jay's chest and pulled its trigger.

Almost in unison, several shots shattered the night.

A scream ripped from Jay's throat as two of the bullets pierced his chest and another his shoulder. With his face contorted into a mask of murderous fury, he clutched at his chest and fell backward, tumbling from the carriage to the ground.

The sound of gunfire threw the carriage horse into a new frenzy of panic and he reared, then crashed back to earth and stamped at the ground.

Thrown against the back of the seat as the carriage pitched wildly, Brett grabbed Teresa and wrapped her in his arms, holding her to him as if he never intended to let go.

Several people nearby screamed and pushed frantically to get away from the area.

"Whoa, damn you," Travis yelled at the horse. "Calm down." He pulled back on the reins. "Settle down."

Traxton jumped from his horse and ran to stand over Jay, who lay sprawled awkwardly on the ground, his hands clutching at his chest.

Brett climbed from the carriage, then turned back to face Teresa. "Maybe you'd better stay here."

She held out her hand. "No."

He sighed and helped her down.

She moved to where Jay lay on the ground, forcing each footstep. Compassion for the man who was the father of her child warred with feelings of loathing, fury, and contempt. She wanted to offer him some semblance of comfort in his last minutes, and she wanted to damn him to hell for all the pain and death he'd caused.

Jay looked up at her as she neared. The color had drained out of his face, just as his blood was oozing out of his body, soaking into the white silk of his shirtfront and turning it crimson beneath the moonlight.

She knelt down beside him, then was startled back to her feet when an ugly laugh escaped his lips. "You haven't stopped anything, you know," he rasped weakly. "Not you, not your lover, and not your damned brothers." A cough gurgled up from his throat, wracking his body and sending a violent shudder through him. A thin stream of blood slipped from one corner of his mouth and snaked its way down his chin. "We can't be stopped. Ever." Another cough seized him and sent his body into a trembling spasm.

Teresa knelt beside him. "Jay . . ."

His eyes rolled back slightly and he shook his head. "You . . . can't . . ." He coughed. "You can't . . . stop . . . us."

She watched his eyes close and his chest become still. "Jay?"

"He's gone," Trace said. He knelt and touched his fingers to Jay's eyelids, drawing them closed.

Brett gripped Teresa's arms and helped her rise. "Come on, we have to keep moving."

"Wait." Not wanting to touch him, but knowing she had to, Teresa reached into Jay's jacket and drew out the notebook that had belonged to her father. She rose and held it out so the others could see the gold initials embossed on its cover. "It was Jay," she said, and looked up at her brothers. "He killed Papa."

"And would have let Henri Sorbonte hang for it," Traxton snarled.

Trace nodded. "Let's go. There's nothing more we can do for him."

"And the Yankees could be on us any minute," Travis said.

Brett helped Teresa back into the carriage. "Are you all right?" he asked, as Travis snapped the reins and the carriage moved forward.

"Yes." She slipped her hand into his and closed her eyes. "I just want this whole thing to be over."

"You're not . . ."

She opened her eyes and looked at him, instantly sensing his unspoken thoughts. "Jay left me on our wedding night, Brett. I haven't felt anything for him for a very, very long time. If I ever really did."

Moving into his arms, Teresa pressed her lips to his. With sudden certainty, as his arms held her tightly and his lips covered hers, she knew he was the only man she had ever really loved, the only one she had ever really wanted in her life. Now she needed to let him know that, too. She pressed her body to his, crushing her breasts to the solid, comfortable wall of his chest, and wrapped her arms about his shoulders, letting her hands lose themselves in the ragged locks that curled over his nape. Her tongue boldly flicked his, a slender, darting bit of flame whose actions aroused her as quickly as him.

"Hey, you two," Trace said, laughing softly as he rode up beside the carriage, "I don't think the Davises do that in public."

Teresa instantly pulled away from Brett, flushed with happiness but feeling chagrined at forgetting, even momentarily, the danger they were all in. "I'm sorry," she murmured.

Her brother smiled down at her, his eyes shadowed by the brim of his hat, his mouth lit my moonlight. "Don't be. It just makes me envious, that's all."

"Lin misses you," she said softly.

He inhaled deeply. "And I miss her. More than I ever thought I could."

For the next hour they rode in silence, each lost in thought. Teresa held tight to Brett's hand, knowing they wouldn't be out of danger until they were out of Virginia, or until the President made a public appearance in Danville. Even then, however, they would not really be safe. They were southerners, Confederates, and the Confederacy was falling. If they encountered a Yankee regiment, she had no doubt they would all be taken prisoner.

Teresa shuddered at the thought, remembering some of the stories she'd heard about the Yankee prisons.

At Watkins they crossed the river again, then this time heading east. Hours passed. They followed New Market Road south. Traxton slumped in his saddle, as did Trace and the two soldiers accompanying them. Travis slouched against the back of his seat and Teresa was unable to tell if he had dozed off or was merely resting.

Brett sat beside her, one arm around her shoulders, his other hand resting on the butt of his gun. He looked haggard and weary, but refused to close his eyes.

Teresa had fallen asleep several times, only to wake with a jerk, her heart racing a mile a minute. Each time, Brett pulled her close and whispered soothing words to calm her, brushing his lips softly across hers, enough to reassure her, but not enough to arouse the passion that smoldered between them.

They needed rest. They needed sleep, but Trace said they had to keep moving.

At Strawberry Plains they left the road and headed southwest. Teresa sat up and looked over the back of the carriage. "Trace, where are we headed?"

He pushed his hat up just above his eyes with a flick of his thumb. "To the river."

"The river? The James?"

He nodded.

"But why? I mean, we've already crossed it twice."

"We won't be crossing it this time."

"Then what are we doing?"

He smiled. "Patience, little sister. You'll see."

Teresa settled back beside Brett.

"You gave up on that pretty easily," he said.

She sniffed. "After years of experience I've come to learn that when Trace calls me *little sister,* it means he's not going to tell me any more than he already has."

Brett chuckled softly. "I'll have to remember that."

Teresa gave him a mocking glare. "Don't bother. It won't work with you."

Less than half an hour later, with midnight just having passed, Traxton called out. "This is it."

Teresa, having just dozed off despite her best efforts, suddenly bolted upright and tried to look beyond the raised seat Travis occupied. "This is *what?*" she demanded.

"It."

She glared up at Travis. "I know you think you're funny, dear brother, but don't forget, I know your wife."

Travis groaned. "Yeah, and I'll bet by the time I see her again, after leaving her with you, Belle, Lin, and mother, *I* won't even know her."

"Are you trying to intimate that we're a bad influence on Suzanne?"

Travis laughed and held up his hands as if in surrender. "Me? Did I say that?"

Teresa turned her attention to her other two brothers, who had dismounted and now stood on a small knoll nearby. Trace had a rag in his hand and was tying it around the end of a dried tree limb he'd picked up. She gasped softly when Traxton struck a lucifer against his heel and held the tiny flame to the rag. It caught fire instantly, turning the stick into a torch. Trace held it high over his head and began to wave it back and forth slowly.

"I hope the wrong people don't see that," Brett muttered.

"Yeah, me, too," Travis said.

Teresa shot them both a very impatient glower. "Would one of you please tell me what's going on? Why is Trace standing on that hill waving a flaming rag?"

"Yo, ho, ho. Someone here signal for a rescue?"

Teresa stood up in the carriage. "Traynor?" she gasped in surprise.

"The one and only," he said, and swept his hat off with an exaggerated bow. Dark hair glistened beneath the moonlight and, as he looked up, gray-blue eyes met gray-blue eyes.

"Damn," Trace's aide said softly, "in the dark you four all look alike."

"In the light, too, unfortunately," Teresa said with a laugh. "I have no doubt if I'd been born a male I would look just like them, too."

"All right," Trace said, hurrying back to the carriage, "quiet down."

"Relax," Traynor said. "The Yankees are at least a mile back that way." He jabbed a finger over his shoulder.

"A mile?" Traxton echoed. "Hell, we've got plenty of time. Why don't we just make ourselves at home. I'll shoot us a rabbit or something, and we'll have a little picnic before they get here."

"Very funny," Traynor said. He looked from one to the other. "My men are waiting down by the shore with a skiff. You ready?"

"We're ready," Trace said.

"Then let's go before one of their damn blockaders comes across *The Falcon's Wing* and discovers that nice little Union flag she's flying isn't the one she normally sails under."

Teresa hurried to hug Traynor.

"Hi, little sis," he said, and pecked her cheek. "But I guess you're not so little anymore, are you?"

"No. But you're just as much of a scoundrel as ever."

They followed Traynor down the sloping landscape toward the river. "What happened to your other ship?" Teresa asked.

"Well, she got blown up. I bought *The Falcon's Wing* in Bermuda a few months back from Tom Conareaux. He caught a piece of shrapnel in the arm last time he tried to run the blockade and lost the use of it."

Teresa remembered Tom Conareaux. His wife had died of the fever the year before Beauregard had fired on Fort Sumter and the war had started.

An hour later they were all safely aboard the *Falcon* and heading out to sea.

Teresa walked across the dark deck to where Traynor stood looking at a chart by moonlight. "Where are we going?"

"Back to the islands." He looked down at her and smiled. "St. Georges, in Bermuda."

Teresa nodded. She knew that was where blockade runners picked up the supplies they'd been bringing into the Confederacy before the Union had successfully cut off their access to all the major ports. And most smaller ones.

"How did you get past the blockade?"

Traynor laughed softly. "Just sailed on through, Tess, just sailed on through."

"Traynor."

He sighed. "Actually, the Yanks are so confident they've won the war that they haven't been guarding the mouth of the James all that well. Slacked off on a couple of other places, too. I was in Savannah last month. They've kept Wilmington pretty locked up though."

"Why he'd do it, Traynor?" she asked softly.

He looked down at her, obviously not quite certain who or what she was referring to.

"Jay," she said. "Why did he kill Papa? And how did he become such a fanatic in the KGC?"

"Maybe this will answer some of your questions," Brett said, appearing out of the darkness. He held a small notebook out toward her.

She accepted the notebook, but looked at him in confusion. It was bound in plain black leather, with no markings on it.

"It was Jay's," Brett said. "His personal notebook. You took your father's from him, but you didn't know Jay had this one. I noticed it in his jacket pocket when he fell from the carriage. I read it while you slept later and I think it will tell you what you want to know." He turned and walked to the door that led to the cabins below deck. "I'll be in my cabin when you're done . . . if you want to talk."

Teresa turned and moved toward a lantern hanging near the door. She didn't want to read whatever Jay had written, didn't want to know what he'd done, but she knew she had to. She sat down on a crate and opened the notebook. The first entry was dated the day after her father had been killed.

I didn't intend to kill him, the first words said, *but*

he became enraged. Anyway, it's better that old man Braggette is dead. He wasn't loyal.

"I'll be up at the wheel if you need me, Tess," Traynor called out.

She nodded, but didn't pull her gaze from the words Jay had written. It was a daily recording of his movements and thoughts over the past several years, starting with the day Jay had joined the Knights of the Golden Circle, only a few months before her father's death.

An hour later she closed the notebook and slipped it into the pocket of her skirt, then moved to the railing and looked out at the black sea. The crests of the softly rolling waves were touched by moonlight and turned to glittering ripples of silver.

"Beautiful, isn't it?" Brett said, moving to her side.

"Yes."

"You didn't come down, and I got worried."

She turned to him. "Why?"

He shrugged. "I don't know." He sighed and stared out at the horizon, black sea against black sky, seemingly infinite, undefinable. "One of my agents intercepted Jay's letter to you and brought it to me. We'd been trying to capture him for almost two years, but every time we got close, he slipped away. We knew you were going to meet him and figured . . ." He paused, then started again. "I thought if you were followed it was our best chance of catching him. But then I got sidetracked in that Yankee camp, and you came walking right in. I improvised after that."

"You did a good job," she said, a sly smile tugging at her lips.

He turned to her. "We knew Jay was planning

something to do with the President, but we weren't sure what. There'd been a lot of rumors."

"His notebook said they were going to kill him, then make it look like Lincoln ordered it."

Brett nodded. "Obviously they hoped that would turn a lot of northerners against the Union."

"My father was overcharging the Knights for supplies he was importing and pocketing the profits."

Brett nodded, having already read Jay's notebook. "And so Jay killed him."

"I was there that night."

"I know."

"I didn't know my father was dead."

"I know."

She wanted his arms around her, his lips on hers. She wanted to feel safe in his embrace and never face the world again. What she didn't want was to keep talking, to remember what had happened, but she couldn't stop herself. "Henri was a high-ranking member of the Knights in Natchez, Mississippi. Jay hated him for his campaign to have Jay removed as a division leader."

Brett nodded.

"And Jay would have let Henri hang for killing my father."

"Come on," Brett said, "you're tired." He took her arm and urged her toward the door to the cabins.

Suddenly, out of the corner of her eye, Teresa saw a large shape loom on the horizon. Startled, she turned just as a screeching, ear piercing whine shattered the silence.

Brett grabbed her and pushed her toward the door. "Run!" he ordered harshly.

Teresa took a step and the world exploded around her.

A loud cannon boom reverberated through the air, overriding Traynor's voice as he moved into action and yelled orders.

Teresa felt herself thrown against a wall, the breath knocked viciously from her lungs.

Another high-pitched whine filled the air.

Traynor yelled at his men to position their guns and fire when ready. "Lansted," he bellowed, "get those bales of cotton down to the boiler room, douse them with kerosene and throw them in. We need to get the hell out of here."

The high-pitched whine turned to a thunderous roar and the sea just beyond the bow of the *Falcon* erupted into a mountainous spout of water that washed across the main deck, splashing over Teresa.

She coughed at the salty water that clogged her throat and stung her tongue. Long strands of wet black hair clung to her shoulders and her sopping wet gown and petticoat weighed her down.

Another explosion echoed.

One of Traynor's guns fired back, the huge cannon jerking back violently as it spit its cannonball at the other ship.

Traxton spun toward the port rail. "What can I do to help?" he yelled at Traynor.

"Get the hell below and stay out of our way," he yelled back. "Now."

Another gun fired, and another shock shook the *Falcon*.

Traynor shouted, "Geriux, get the men to general quarters and get us out of here."

A cannonball careened over the main deck and plunged into the water only a few feet from the *Falcon's* starboard side. The ship pitched as the ball exploded. Waves of water shot upward and sprayed the deck, covering everything and then instantly sliding away.

Teresa struggled to her feet.

Traynor grabbed a ratline as another wave caught him and threatened to hurl him overboard.

The *Falcon* shuddered as one of her own parrot guns exploded to life.

The main engines roared. Thick clouds of smoke spewed from the double stacks that rose from the center of the main deck while the huge paddlewheels that framed the ship churned furiously.

The attacking ship's Dahlgrens boomed again.

"Lansted," Traynor bellowed.

More smoke belched from the smokestacks.

"Porter, hard a-starboard," Traynor yelled.

Another blast rocked the ship.

Traxton, knocked to his knees, struggled to regain his feet. He looked up and yelled as he saw Teresa take an unsteady step toward the cabin door. Behind her a huge crest of water descended on the deck. "Teresa!"

He lunged for her, but it was too late. The wave slammed into the cabin wall, rolled over the deck, and washed most of what wasn't nailed down over the starboard railing . . . including Teresa.

Untangling himself from a ratline that had snapped at the last blast and tangled about his legs, Brett ran across the deck. At the railing he stared down into the roiling water in horror. "Teresa!"

"I'll get her," Traxton said, and ripped off his jacket.

"No." Brett turned to dive over the side.

At that moment the *Falcon* jerked to the helm. A canister exploded somewhere above in the sails, and a yardarm flew through the air. It grazed Brett's head, plunging him into unconsciousness and sending him careening helplessly into the water.

Twenty-five

The bow of *The Falcon's Wing* broke easily through the gently lapping waves, the ship's sails full with the wind and its fluted smokestacks belching out spiraling plumes of white smoke as the *Falcon*'s paddlewheel sliced the water and her powerful engines rumbled steadily and faintly in the background.

Evidence of her near-destruction lay everywhere on deck: broken balustrades, collapsed rigging, snapped ratlines, and torn sails. There was even a ragged hole in the main deck where a cannonball had plunged through but failed to explode.

After their escape from Virginia and the following attack by the Union blockader, they'd turned south and made for Charleston. Making port, however, had proved impossible, the Union blockade there too formidable for an injured ship to try to pass.

Savannah and St. Augustine had proven little better.

Finally Traynor announced they would head for St. Georges, the island the Confederate blockade runners had used as their supply depot and headquarters.

Teresa stood at the port railing of *The Falcon's Wing* and stared out at the landscape before her—and saw nothing. For a while after their attack, the crew had scurried around in a hustle of activity. Men had yelled orders, hammers banged as repairs were hurriedly made, ripped sails were furled, and engines groaned. She had neither heard nor seen any of it.

That had been six days ago—six days since she'd seen Brett struck by a falling mast, six days since she'd watched in horror as he'd plunged, unconscious, into the sea and disappeared beneath its churning black waves, six days since her world had ended.

Teresa's hair hung loose down her back, catching the wind and whipping about her shoulders and into her face, but she paid no mind. Nor did she concern herself with the gaunt pallor of her skin, the shadows that had appeared beneath her eyes, or the listlessness that had come over her after Brett's death and which seemed to deepen with each passing hour. Nothing mattered anymore. The world and its reality was only a place to endure; her memories were where she chose to live now. Memories of Brett, of his arms holding her to him, his lips capturing, teasing, and caressing her own, his sinewy body hot and slick with passion as it took and loved hers.

Sleep was little more than a few hours of restless tossing and turning each night as her mind, released from the strict restraint she held over it while awake, filled with images of the moment she'd lost him, replaying the scene over and over mercilessly. Her interest in everything: food, the war, her family, even her son, seemed no longer to exist, ripped from her heart and mind as thoroughly as Brett had been ripped from her life.

In the middle of each night she would rise, climb the stairs to the main deck, and stand at the railing to stare out at the dark scene that spread before her.

She stood there like that, silent and unseeing, through all the long hours before the sun crested the horizon and turned the dark sky a brilliant china blue, and before the sea was transformed from a fathomless, rolling vista of blackness to a silver-touched panorama of topaz.

Thus it was, late on the afternoon of their eighth day at sea, when the island of Bermuda came within sight, she didn't move, but merely stared into the distance.

"Teresa," Trace said, moving up to stand beside her. He dipped an arm around her waist. "Come below deck and have some supper."

She turned to him and tried to smile, not wanting to trouble him with the sorrow that seemed to fill her. "I'm fine," she said softly, and turned back to look out at the sea.

"No, you're not," Trace said. "I'm worried about you. We all are."

"I'm fine," she said again, her voice breaking.

An hour later *The Falcon's Wing* passed the ancient wreck of *The Sea Witch* and approached the wharves of St. Georges. The tiny island was little more than a speck in the middle of the Atlantic Ocean, barely three miles long and a mile wide. Even so, it had been a bustle of activity since the war had started and the blockade runners had made it their home port and the Confederacy installed an outpost within the walls of what had once been the island's hotel.

Traynor stood next to Teresa and watched as the ship approached the island. It was a gently rolling vista of soft hills and pristine beaches, a profusion of color that stemmed not only from the profusion of wildflowers that dotted its terrain, but also from the various pastel shades of the stuccoed buildings.

The docks were crowded with the anchored ships of the blockade runners, their sails furled and engines silenced. It was an unsettling sight to him, one he had hoped never to see. Normally there was much jostling for a path, either to maneuver into a dock space or go back out to sea. This deadly calm said more than anything he'd seen so far that the war was over. Maybe not officially, but essentially it was over. Without the supplies that the blockade runners brought into the Confederate states from Europe and Asia, it could not continue.

He glanced down at his sister, then slipped an arm around her shoulders and pulled her close. She was hurting, more than a person should ever have to hurt, and there wasn't anything he could do to help her. Words weren't enough, and they didn't mean anything anyway, not in this situation. "You have to go on, Tess," he said softly. "I know it hurts like hell, but you have to go on . . . for Tyler."

Teresa didn't answer.

Traynor knew she'd heard him and understood; he just wasn't so sure she agreed.

He turned and looked up at the Quartermaster. The sails had been furled and the engines cut to half speed, the huge paddlewheels that framed each side of the *Falcon* churning the water. "Cut back to one-third speed, Porter," Traynor called out. "And take us in slow and steady."

The man nodded and turned the huge spoked

wheel that steered the ship. It moved slightly starboard.

Above Traynor, several members of his crew danced about the rigging, furling sails, tying ratlines, and securing yardarms. Trace and Traxton appeared at the doorway to the cabins below deck, followed by Travis. Traynor walked over to greet them. "She's the same," he said softly.

His brothers nodded.

"Maybe when we get her home . . ." Traxton said, then let the rest of his sentence trail off.

"Having to care for Tyler again will help," Trace said.

Travis nodded. "Yeah, I'm just not sure it's enough."

"Mama will know what to do," Trace said.

"Being around Belle, Lin, Suzanne, and Marci should help, too," Traxton offered. "She needs a woman to talk to, maybe to cry with."

The *Falcon* bumped up against the wharf. Several crew members hurried to secure her ropes to the dock while another dropped anchor and yet another lowered the boarding plank.

Traxton moved to take Teresa's arm. "Come on, Tess," he said, putting gentle pressure on her arm to urge her forward. "We're going ashore."

Minutes later they were walking across the town square, each deep in thought and speculation. The usually boisterous area was as silent as a tomb, yet when they looked through several open doorways they saw that the pubs were full.

"Stay here," Traynor said when they approached the door of the Cock 'n' Boar Tavern. He disappeared into the saloon's murky interior. A few muffled greetings echoed on the still air. Moments later, Traynor reappeared before his family. "The war's over," he said, looking from one to the other. "Lee surrendered at Appomattox."

Traxton nodded. "With Richmond gone," he said, "it was only a matter of time."

"What about the President?" Trace asked. "Did they capture him?"

"No."

"Then there's still hope," Travis interjected.

"No," Traxton said. "Without Lee and the army of the Potomac, there's no more chance. It's over."

Teresa stood on the beach and looked out at the vast expanse of ocean that stretched as far as she could see. Everything was so beautiful and clean. The water was the color of topaz, an unbelievable hue that rivaled the blue sky for brilliance, while the sands of the beach were almost pure white. Flowers of every shape and color grew on the island, blue lupis, lustrous purple periwinkle, sun-touched yellow primroses, and lush pink roses.

It was a lovers' paradise, but when one lover was missing, it was hell.

Teresa wrapped her arms around herself and continued to stare through her tears at the gently rolling waves that lapped at her feet. She knew she had to pull herself together and stop sinking deeper into depression, but it was so hard. It had been ten days now since Brett had been killed. She had a son to take care of, and Tyler needed her. But she needed Brett.

A new flood of tears filled her eyes and flowed over her dark lashes, slipping down her cheeks in streams turned golden by the reflection of the setting sun.

She heard the faint, almost imperceptible sound of footsteps in the sand behind her but didn't bother to turn. She knew it would be one of her brothers. They were so worried about her.

"Smithers?"

Teresa's heart nearly stopped. The breath caught in her lungs and her hands trembled. Her mind was playing tricks on her. Hesitantly she turned to look over her shoulder, knowing there would be no one there, that she'd see nothing but the wild, grass-covered dunes dotted with blooms against the coming night.

But instead her gaze met the deep sapphire eyes of Brett Forteaux. Teresa felt her legs go weak and threaten to buckle beneath her weight. She was seeing an apparition, an image projected by her grief-stricken mind, turned into reality by her anguished heart.

And then he smiled and took a step toward her. "I thought I'd lost you," he said softly.

"Brett," Teresa whispered, praying that this was a miracle come true and terrified that she would reach out and find herself embracing nothing but air.

He pulled her into his arms—strong, muscular arms that were very real beneath the silk threads of his jacket, and against the hard wall of his chest. "Thank God," he murmured, and covered her lips.

Teresa pressed against him, slipping her arms

around his shoulders, her hands into the thick, silky hair. Her tongue dueled with his and her body blazed with a rapture she'd thought she'd never feel again.

Rational thought and reason fled as she reveled in his kiss, savoring the heat of his body as it touched hers, the sweet, protective strength of his embrace, the scent that was so uniquely his. If this was a dream or part of her imagination, then she never wanted to wake up, never wanted to return to the world that had so cruelly taken him from her.

Brett pulled his lips from hers but didn't release her from his embrace. "I was so terrified," he said, his voice deep with emotion. It flowed over her like warm satin—soothing, comforting, tantalizing. "I thought you'd drowned."

She stared up at him, too shocked, too happy to answer or ask the questions crowding her own mind.

"I regained consciousness almost the moment I hit the water, but I couldn't find you. The waves kept knocking me back and sending me under. Finally I grabbed onto a piece of plank that had blown off the *Falcon*'s deck."

Teresa touched a hand to his cheek, needing to reassure herself that he was real. "You *are* here," she said finally. "You really are here."

He smiled. "Yes, Smithers," he said. "I'm really here. And so are you, thank the saints."

"I was so afraid." She moved her hand back to his neck, her arms clasped tightly about his shoulders as if she was afraid if she loosened her hold he would disappear. "I saw you hit, saw you fall into the water and go under. My brothers tried to get to you, but they couldn't. Afterward . . ." Her voice broke as the memories returned. "Afterward we searched for hours, but we couldn't find you."

"By the time the ships quit firing at each other and sailed off, I had been washed several miles away."

She opened her mouth to ask him how he'd gotten to the island, but he pressed a finger to her lips.

"A Yankee gunboat found me and fished me out of the water."

"A Yankee gunboat?"

He nodded. "By then I was too exhausted to care who it was, and I thought you were dead. I didn't care what happened to me. A firing squad would have been a welcome relief to the agony I felt at knowing you were lost to me."

"But I wasn't," she said.

He smiled. "I didn't know that."

"Then how . . . I mean, why did you come here?"

"The Yankee gunboat that rescued me came here."

"A Yankee gunboat? Here?"

"Yes. I didn't know I'd been picked up by the same ship that had fired on the *Falcon* until later. It sustained some critical damage and while the crew was scrambling to try and make repairs, the ship drifted farther out to sea. Finally it became a matter of finding the closest port."

"St. Georges," she said softly.

"St. Georges," he confirmed.

"But when?"

"We made dock a few hours ago. I didn't care, wasn't even going to get off the ship, but then I saw the *Falcon*. It took me a while to track down your brothers."

"And they told you where I was."

"Yes, and I'd never heard such wonderful words in my life as when Traxton said you were all right."

She laid her head against his chest. "But I wasn't."

He pulled back and, holding her by her shoulders, frowned down at her. "What do you mean? What's wrong?"

Teresa smiled. "Nothing now. I just didn't want to go on without you."

Brett pulled her back into his arms. "Well, you don't have to."

His lips found hers again, and heaven descended to earth, just for a few minutes.

Teresa moved from his arms and slipped a hand in his, entwining her fingers about his longer, stronger ones. "We'd better get back to the others," she said, then paused and looked back up at Brett. A frown pulled at her brow.

He saw the uncertainty in her eyes and his heart lurched in fear. "What?" he asked simply.

"I have a son."

"I know."

"Jay's son."

"Our son," Brett said, and pulled her into his arms again.

A week later repairs on the *Falcon* were complete and she was seaworthy again. No news had reached the island of what was happening in the States, but everyone felt certain that the war had been declared officially over. The Confederacy was dead. What they weren't certain of, however, was whether they were fugitives or refugees, and what type of reception awaited them in New Orleans when they made port.

It took five days of hard sailing, but on the afternoon of the fifth day *The Falcon's Wing* moved into the mouth of the Mississippi and began making her way upriver. Within hours the Crescent City came into view, looking every bit as graceful and elegant as ever. The war had touched the people of New Orleans, their pocketbooks and their hearts, but not their buildings.

Traynor dropped anchor just off the French Quarter and the family climbed into a skiff and rowed ashore, the crew to follow later. They walked past the docks, across Levee Street, and paused before Jackson Square. Its tall, wrought iron gates were draped in black funereal cloth, as were several shopfront doors in the nearby Pontalba Buildings and the entry to the DuMonde Café.

The banquettes were unusually vacant, as were the streets. Only an occasional person was spotted here or there.

Traxton frowned. "What the hell's going on?"

An old man shuffled around the corner of the square.

Travis approached him quickly, conversed for a minute, then hurried back to where the others waited. "Lincoln was assassinated."

"What?" They all gasped.

"You haven't stopped us," Teresa whispered. She

looked up at Brett, then at each of her brothers. "Those were Jay's last words: You haven't stopped us."

Epilogue

Teresa looked around the spacious parlor of Shadows Noir and said a silent prayer of thanks. The war was over and the Braggettes and their loved ones were home.

A rumble of laughter erupted behind her and Teresa turned to glance into the foyer. It had been much too long since that sound had been heard within the walls of Shadows Noir, and it was welcome.

Her brothers, along with Brett, Belle and Lin's father, Henri Sorbonte, Jay's father Harcourt Proschaud, and her mother's friend Edward, appeared in the doorway. The evidence of war was gone now. The gray uniforms, the knee-high boots, the swords and guns, and the worry that had dulled their eyes had all been put away, tucked into their memories, to be brought out occasionally and remembered, some with fondness, some with regret, and a few . . . just a very few, with happiness.

"We were just talking about the fact that our little sister was the first to make you a grandmother, Mama," Travis said, "so we've decided since we can't beat her to it, we'll just have to outdo her."

A chorus of gasps rose from all the brothers' wives, which caused the men to laugh again.

"I am *not* one of your Texas brood mares, Traxton Braggette," Belle snapped sassily.

He chuckled and winked at her. "Just a couple more," he said, and moved to her side. Their thirteen-month-old son, Tanner, was the spit and image of his handsome father.

Belle's twin sister Lin looked at her husband, her cheeks slightly pink with embarrassment.

Trace slipped an arm around her waist and placed his other hand on her protruding stomach. "I think we should all have one before anyone tries for more," he said. "That's only fair."

Lin laughed and slapped at his hand. "And what if we have twins?" she teased. "It does run in my family, you know."

"Then we'll be one up on everybody."

"I think we've got some serious catching up to do," Traynor said to Marci, lifting a bright red curl from her shoulder and nuzzling her neck.

She blushed and pushed him away. "Traynor Braggette, behave yourself." Indignation flared in her green eyes, but no one was fooled, especially when she couldn't suppress the giggle that slipped from her lips.

"I would have thought by now you knew that was impossible."

Everyone laughed.

Suzanne turned to Travis, her blond curls dancing from the mound that had been piled on her crown and allowed to cascade down her back, and jabbed a finger into his chest. "Don't say it," she said in mock warning.

His brows rose in an innocent expression. "Say what?"

Her eyes narrowed. "Anything about catching up. It's your fault we're seven years behind."

"I know," he growled, and pulled her to him, "and I have some wonderful ideas about how we can make up for all that lost time."

Teresa picked up a small silver bell from the table beside the settee and shook it. A delicate tinkle filled the room and drew everyone's attention. Tyler skipped over from near the window where he'd been playing with the puppy Brett had brought him that morning and stood beside her, his gray-blue eyes full of curiosity. Teresa set the bell down and joined hands with both Brett and her son. "We have an announcement to make," she said softly.

"Oh, let me guess," Traxton said. "You and Brett are getting married."

She laughed. "Yes, next week in the St. Louis Cathedral."

"Well, that certainly comes as a surprise," Travis said.

"There's more," Teresa interrupted.

"More?" The brothers spoke in unison.

Her smile widened. "More."

"Okay, so don't keep us in suspense. What's the more?" Traynor urged.

Teresa squeezed Brett's hand. "We're going to have a baby."

"Oh, gee," Travis said, "so much for us catching up."

Suzanne slapped his shoulder playfully.

Travis grinned. "Congratulations," he said. "Honestly."

Five minutes later, after everyone had kissed Teresa and shaken hands with Brett, Teresa again rang the little bell and called for everyone's attention.

"Now what?" Travis grumbled. "Twins?"

Ignoring him, Teresa handed each person a glass of champagne. "I'd like to make a toast."

Everyone moved close, until they formed a tight circle.

Teresa held up her glass. The others followed suit, crystal clinking against crystal.

"To the Confederacy," she said softly, tears filling her eyes. "We will always love her, and always miss her."

Author's Note

Writing this series was a work of love for me, and one I thoroughly enjoyed. The Civil War has long been a subject I've found fascinating, and not because I am captivated by war or fighting, but more, by the people involved in this particular war, brother fighting against brother, families torn apart by their individual beliefs, and a way of life, and almost part of our nation, disappearing forever.

As a romantic at heart I have studied, not the battles, but the people and places of this time, and hope through my writing I have been able to bring just a small part of that time to life for my readers.

The Braggettes, of course, did not truly exist, except in my imagination, but I believe that in them exists a culmination of the lives and histories of all the people I know and love today.

As far as the cities and many locations I have used in this series, most of them were, or are, real. New Orleans, the setting for the first book in this series, Hearts Deceived, is still as much a fascinating city today as it was in the 1860's, especially the French Quarter where yesterday is still very much alive, and cherished. Virginia City, Nevada, the city for the second book in the series, Travis and Suzanne's story, Hearts Denied, is today a thriving tourist town, all of the old buildings loving taken care of, the old mansions restored, and several of the mines open for tours, while Vicksburg, Mississippi, part of the setting for Traynor and Marci's story in Hearts Defiant, shows little evidence today of the battles that once raged about its borders, Richmond, Virginia, used for much of the setting for this last book of the series is a thriving modern city now, but many museums there, such as The White House of the Confederacy, give a visitor an indepth look at the city's past and the important role it played during the War Between the States.